Praise for HWFG

'Hilarious ... ...exciting

...ston, *Doomsday*, *Monarch of the* ...

...generation a writer comes along who provides an unmistakable injection of working-class energy into Scottish literature, and gets people usually alienated by books intae ... again. Like a dog on Red Bull when the door goes, the effervescent and hilarious Chris McQueer is the man of the moment.' – Alan Bissett, author of *The Moira Monologues*

'McQueer destroys the Difficult Second Album Syndrome with *HWFG*. Bigger characters, brilliant storytelling and massive belly laughs. He's taken Nirvana's "Nevermind" approach and knocked it out the park.' – Ewan Denny, Link & Lorne

'*HWFG* had me in stitches from the get-go. Vivid portrayals of social embarrassment will have you cringing and uttering loud guffaws in equal measure. A rare and raw talent.'
– Jenny Lindsay, Flint & Pitch Productions

'This is funnier than *Hings* and *Hings* was funnier than most other books. *HWFG* is as funny as it is dark, which is saying a lot because it's really fucking dark.'– Joe Hullait, Scot Squad

'Hilarious, surreal and addictive. I pished myself at every story.'
– Neil Slorance, *Modern Slorance, Pirate Fun*

'Chris McQueer is one of the most exciting and authentic talents on Scotland's new writing scene. Buy this book or you're a rocket.' – Stuart Cosgrove, *Harlem 69*

'Chris has an innate understanding of people and their way of speaking that strongly resonates in his writing. Chris effortlessly mixes highbrow and lowbrow to hilarious effect.' – Tom Brogan

HWFG

SHORT STORIES 'N THAT

CHRIS
MCQUEER

Published by 404 Ink
www.404Ink.com
@404Ink

ISBN: 978-1-912489-10-7
ebook: 978-1-912489-11-4

Editor: Robbie Guillory
Cover: ELEMdesign

Printed and bound in Great Britain
by Clays Ltd, Elcograf, S.p.A.

404 Ink acknowledge and are grateful for support from
Creative Scotland in the publication of this title.

LOTTERY FUNDED

CONTENTS

HERE WE
HERE WE
HERE WE
F**KING

GO

BIG ANGIE GOES TO CRAIG TARA

1

If there's wan place oan Earth ah love as much as ah love Blackpool or Benidorm, it's Craig Tara. In fact, ah'd go as far as tae say it's mah favourite place in the world. Ah know you'll be sittin there like that, 'Really Angie? Craig Tara? The caravan park? That place is a shitehole.' But it's no. It's fuckin amazin. It's heaven oan Earth fur a wummin like me. A wummin ae simple pleasures. Mah three favourite hings used to be booze, bowls and bingo. Since ah've gave up the bowls, ah've been huntin fur somethin tae replace it.

Mah wee pal, Dolly, has never been tae Craig Tara so ah've talked her intae comin wae me. We're hunkered doon in the caravan the noo, until the entertainment starts at six. We've been cooped up in here since last night (Dolly wisnae feelin too well) an it's startin tae get tae us a wee bit. Dolly mair so than me, tae be fair - cabin fever, know wit ah mean?

Ahm feelin awrite cos in a matter ae hours, ah'll be getting tae see the love ae mah life – big Huey the crooner. See, Huey does a bit ae singin at night here tae entertain us auld yins. Bit ae Frank Sinatra, Sammy Davis Jr. an Dean Martin, he can dae the lot. Some chanter so he is. But it's no joost his voice that gets me aw hot an bothered, aw naw, he's a big handsome basturt as well. He's goat this silver hair, like Philip Schofield's noo that he's finally stoapped dyin it, aw slicked back and perfect. He's ages wi me, ahm told, but he disnae look a day over forty-five. Must be some fancy moisturiser he uses. An he wears this nice tuxedo, aw ye should see him, up there aw smart, crooning away, his blue eyes twinklin under the spotlight. Honestly, ah need tae stoap masel fae chargin oan that stage an flingin masel at him. 'Take me, Huey,' ah'd say. 'Take me back tae yer caravan an fuckin pummel me.' An he wid. Course he fuckin wid.

'We better head down now if we want our usual seats, Angie,' Dolly says tae me as she applies her mascara. Oor usual seats happen tae be right doon the front, where ah can get a right good view ah mah heartthrob's package. The whole package that is, ya swines, no joost his cock an baws.

'As if anycunt'll be in oor seats, hen,' ah say. 'They aw know better by noo, surely.' Well, they fuckin should. We're here fur a fortnight, we're awready baw deep intae oor second week. Oan the first week we, well ah say 'we', ah did aw talkin, had tae tell this auld posh couple tae beat it cos they were sittin in oor seats. The guy goes like that, 'We were here first! We're not moving,' so ah joost says tae the cunt, 'Hawl, bawbag, get oan yer feet and find another place tae park that stupit auld arse ae yours.' His wife's aw watery-eyed like that, 'Please leave us alone,' nearly greetin an that. Dolly's fuckin apologisin fur makin a scene. He goes, 'You can't speak to me and my wife like that!'

'Aye ah fuckin can, pal.'

That wis that. Cunt traipsed away. The world disnae know how tae handle wummin like me so until cunts figure that oot, ah'll joost keep dain, an getting, witever the fuck ah want.

2

We head doon tae the 'live lounge' as they're callin it here, tae take in mah future husband's performance.

'Wit the fuck's this?' ah say tae Dolly. For Huey's performances, they've normally goat an auld fashioned mic set up fur him an a big glittery backdrop. The night, there's a big Union Jack flag instead an a fuckin drum kit an guitars an aw that. Dolly goes tae take oor usual seat but ah cannae sit doon – ahm too fuckin ragin.

'Hawl you,' ah say tae the wee lassie behind the bar. 'Where's Huey? Is he no singin the night?'

'Sorry, madam,' she says, 'Huey's not feeling too well. It's a Guns N' Roses tribute act that'll be performing this evening.'

'You kiddin me on? Dolly! You hearin this! Fuckin Guns an Roses. Wit a load ae shite.' Ah turn back roon ae the wee lassie an she's geein me a fuckin snidey look. 'Stella an a gin an tonic, wit ye waitin fur?'

These Guns an Roses boays can fair play, ah'll gie them that. They even did this mad rock version ae The Sash, mah favourite Rangers song, but it's no the same as listenin tae mah Huey wi a pint in wan hawn an a hanky wipin away the tears wi another. Mah ears are fuckin listenin tae this mob. When ah listen ae Huey singin it's like... ah don't know, as if somecunt's pouring nice, warm golden syrup intae mah ears. Wi these cunts, it's like mah heid's been pumped full ae Tizer and stuck in a washin machine.

'Wonder if Huey's awrite,' ah say tae Dolly. She disnae hear me though. It's no cause ae the music though, she's joost too fuckin engrossed in that fuckin phone ae hers. Swipin and scrollin fuckin every minute ae every day since we goat here. 'Dolly.'

'Hmm, yes, Angie?' She's no even takin her eyes aff the screen.

'Fuckin gies that.' Ah grab the phone aff her and slam it doon oan the table. 'Ignoramus.'

'Och, what is it? What's the problem?'

'Problem? Ah'll tell ye wit the problem is. We've came here tae spend some time the gither, huv a laugh an that, an you've no took yer nose oot that bastardin phone.'

'Oh, lighten up.' She reaches fur her phone but ah put mah

hawn oan tap ae it tae stoap her fae grabbing it.

'Wit is it that's so interestin oan that phone ae yours that ye cannae leave it alane fur two minutes, eh?'

'Cheers fur listenin, ladies an gentlemen. We've been Huns an Roses. Ayrshire's original and best loyalist rock band! Goodnight!'

'Right, promise you won't laugh,' Dolly says as she takes her phone back.

'Awrite, ah promise.' This better be good.

'I'm looking for a new man.'

'Wit fur? Ye joost got fuckin rid ae the last wan. Ye want some another auld basturt in yer life, makin yer precious last few year a misery?'

'Well, you've been lusting after this Huey guy the whole time we've been here. What's the difference?'

Fuck. She's goat me there.

'Aye, but that's the hing, Dolly. He's… he's different fae other guys.'

'Och away. How do you know? You've never even spoke to the guy,' Dolly laughs, taking a sip ae her drink an going back tae her phone. 'He's probably just like the rest of them, Angie.'

3

The next night, we head back doon tae the live lounge. Ahm hopin tae see mah main man, but only if he's feelin better, mind you – he needs tae keep his strength up fur yer auld maw here.

Walkin doon ae the live lounge though there's somebody stawnin at the door, the kind ae cunt that strikes fear intae mah very heart – a bouncer. Ah don't get oan too well wi bouncers, ah don't like them an they don't like me. But they've goat the upper hawn, they know ah need tae be nice tae them if ah want in tae the establishment. So ah bite mah tongue when she gets a wee bit wide wi me.

'Ladies,' she says as me an Dolly walk up tae her.

The fuckin cheek ae it.

'Awrite,' ah mutter in reply, geein her a grimace ae a smile. 'In ye go.'

We go intae the hall an scan aboot, see if anybody's in oor usual seat.

There is.

This young schemey lassie, her wee ratty-lookin boyfriend and their three screamin weans. Ah've seen that lassie aboot the park over the last couple ae days. She swaggers aboot as if she owns the place.

Huns an Roses are playin again the night an they're up geein it laldy. Ah sidle up tae the lassie occupyin mah seat.

'Ye'll need tae move, darlin,' ah snarl intae her ear.

'Eh, wit?' she replies. She whips her heid roon tae look at me. 'This is mah seat,' ah stick mah handbag oan the table, knockin hers aff in the process.

The lassie gets tae her feet an squares up tae me. Aw ah can smell aff her is cheap perfume an joost a wee hint ae BO. It's been warm the day though so fair enough. The lassie's goat oan the same sovvie rings as ah've goat an she's wearin a similar wee strappy tap. Ah've goat a young pretender in front ae me, ah see. Sorry, pal, this caravan park is only big enough fur wan ae us.

'Ahm no movin fur nae cunt,' the lassie says. Her wee glaikit boyfriend just sits there starin intae space as wan ae the weans batters at his knee wi a wee toy motor.

'C'mon, Angie,' Dolly whimpers. She's goat a riddy. 'Let's just sit up the back.'

Ah look over tae the door an there's the bouncer poking her nose in. Ah better keep mah heid doon, ah don't want tae huv tae fight her anaw.

'Fine,' ah snarl at the daft wee lassie an grab mah bag aff the table, 'but see the morra night, you better no be sittin here.'

She rolls her eyes at me and sits back doon as Dolly leads me tae a wee table up the back. But no before a gie her handbag a wee kick.

* * *

'Fuck sake, Dolly. Need a pair ae fuckin binoculars tae see the stage fae here.'

'Och, it's not that bad.' Dolly's goat her face buried in her phone again. Her wee thumbs are gawn like the clappers as she types away.

'Who ye talkin tae?'

'No one.' She disnae even look up at me.

Fuck ye then. Ah'll joost sit here an play wi mah ain phone then. Mine is basically a brick though. Dolly's hus a camera an aw that, mine disnae even huv a colour screen.

Efter hawf an oor ae *Huns n Roses* an no even so much ae a peep oot ae Dolly, it's time fur the main event. It's time fur mah Huey.

'Look, there he is!' ah say tae Dolly. Aye, *noo* she puts her phone doon. Noo that mah Huey's in the room. She gies a wee gasp as he practically takes her breath away when he struts oan tae the stage. My God, he's never looked better. He likes a tight pair ae troosers, does Huey, but the wans he's wearin the night are the fuckin dug's baws. Ah can see his arse wigglin away under the fabric as it clings tae him in aw the right places as he swaggers aboot the stage. He's wearin a silver, sparkly suit jaiket the night an his hair is, as ever, immaculate. Honestly, wit a fuckin darlin.

'Hullo, Craig Tara,' he says, cuppin the mic wi wan hawn an stickin the other in his poakit. 'I'm Huey and I'll be singing you the hits of the Rat Pack this evening.'

Then he looks at me. Right fuckin at me.

'Dolly, did you see that? He looked at me. ME!'

But Dolly cannae hear me, she's starin at him. Then he

waves. No at me though, at fuckin Dolly. She hits another wee riddy an looks doon at her feet. She's like a wee fuckin lassie.

* * *

He makes his way through his usual set list, aw the auld classics, but then the music changes. None ae the big band stuff anymare, it's like that mad Spanish music. Then he's aff the stage and wanderin through the audience, singing intae aw the wummin's faces. Ah had nae idea the cunt could talk Spanish. But hearin him singin in a different language is makin me feel hings ah've no felt fur ages. He could be singin me a recipe fur paella fur aw ah care.

Then he starts makin his way up the back taewards us. It's dark, ah cannae tell if he's lookin at me or Dolly. It's obviously me though, surely. He walks behind oor table, strokes Dolly's shooder then he heads back doon the front. The jealousy is fuckin rippin right oot me. Even in the dark ah cin tell Dolly's went fuckin scarlet.

He gets back doon the front tae stage but instead of climbin back up he turns roon an makes a beeline fur that daft wee lassie that stole mah seat. Ahm up oan mah feet tae see wit he's gonnae dae. See if she gets so much as a peck oan the cheek ahm gonnae cause a fuckin riot.

Then the cunt sits oan her knee an she's goat her fuckin tits oot. She grabs his heid an pulls it doon intae her cleavage.

That's it. Ah charge doon the front tae sort this oot.

'STEALIN MAH SEAT, AYE? AN NOO YER STEALIN MAH MAN!'

Huey looks terrified. Ah pull him away fae the wee horror an get masel in between the two ae them. The music cuts aff.

'Clatty basturt,' ah say ae the lassie. Her platoon ae weans start greeting.

'Ladies, please.' Huey tries tae calm me doon but ah shrug him aff, ah need tae teach this lassie a lesson.

'You keep yer fuckin hawns aff him!'

'Or wit? Wit you gonnae dae?' She stuffs her tits back inside her tap. 'Senile auld cow.' Her boyfriend is still joost sittin there, vacant as fuck. No a single brain cell between these two cunts.

'Ladies, please. There's enough of me to go round,' Huey pleads. Then ah see him wave his hawn an in comes that big daft bouncer. Her ponytail swishin back an forward behind her heid as she stoats taewards us.

'You,' she says, grabbing mah airm and hawdin it behind mah back. 'You've had enough.' She marches me oot the live lounge.

'Moan, Dolly,' ah shout but she joost sits there, hidin her face wi her hawns. Ah cin see she's mortified. 'Aw is that how it is, aye? Fine then. Sit there yerself like a saddo.' Ah cin hear everycunt in that hall laughin at me.

'A woman of your age shouldn't be behaving like that, c'mon. Screw the nut,' the bouncer says tae me when we get outside. It's a lovely night actually.

'Ah know, ah joost lost it back there.' The lassie lets me go. 'Ah joost, really like him.' Noo ah feel like a wee lassie.

'It's awrite. He has that effect.' The bouncer pulls a packet ae fags oot her poakit. 'Smoke?'

'Aye go for it.'

'You're no the first to get in a fight because of him.' She lights mah fag fur me. 'It's not just the way he looks. I mean, I don't swing that way, but he just *exudes* something. Charisma, sex appeal, animal magnetism, whatever it is, he's got it. Combine that with a romantic setting such as this' – there's a seagull peckin at the chunks in some wee boay's sick aboot 12 feet away fae us.

'Nice weather, alcohol and loads of other beautiful people' – there's a guy in a curry sauce stained Celtic tap, an nuhin else, winkin at us from his caravan windae. 'And it's a perfect storm.'

'Aye, eh, suppose yer right.' Never argue wi bouncers, that's mah number wan rule. They're the only cunts that can stoap ye fae huvin a swallay.

'Still, there's something about him I don't like,' she adds.

'Aw aye? Wit's that?'

'I can't put my finger on it, but there's a sleekitness about him. Something a bit off. Maybe he's a paedo or something.'

'Ah highly doubt that, hen.'

Ah bid the bouncer lassie good night an head back tae oor caravan. We've only goat a couple ae nights left here an ahm a bit gutted it's ending oan a sour note like this. Dolly – embarrassed by me. Huey – probably feart ae me. That stupit lassie in mah seat – thinks ahm a dafty. Ah've fucked it.

4

'Fuckin pull yerself the gither,' ah say tae mah reflection the mirror. 'You're Big Angie. Big Fuckin Angie.' An ahm right. Ah um Big Fuckin Angie an ah shouldnae be mopin aboot in a fuckin caravan oan a Friday night. Ah should be oot. Ah came tae Craig Tara tae huv a laugh wi mah pal an if she disnae want tae huv a laugh wi me then that's her problem, ah cin still huv a laugh mahsel.

Well no mahsel, ah mean ahm no a total saddo. Ah'll go lookin fur a party, that's wit ah'll dae.

Disnae take me long. Couple ae caravans doon fae oors there's a squad ae five guys, mibbe in their late twinties, looks like a stag do.

'Wit's happenin lads,' ah say, strolling err tae thum. Two ae thum are airm wrestlin, looks as if they're aw bettin oan it as well. Aw muscles an tattoos an shaved heids. Wan ae thum even hus a wee Rangers crest oan his bicep. Fuckin hell, if only ah wis twenty year younger an they wurr twenty year aulder. They're aw hawf cut so they don't tell me tae get tae fuck like ye wid expect fae a group ae young guys bein chatted up by an auld burd like me. No yet, anywey.

'Awrite, auld yin!' the wee-est, chubbiest wan says, puttin his airm roon me as ah sit doon.

'Awrite, wee man,' ah say, shruggin him aff. Establish dominance early, that's how ye get ahead in life. Wee cunt looks feart ae me noo when joost a second ago he wis laughin at me. 'Wit yous uptae?'

Ah nod doon at the picnic table; there's a pile ae aboot mibbe five hunner quid in twinty pound notes an a few wee bags ae powder. The two lads stoap airm wrestling an declare it tae be a draw. The chubby wan slides the bags under the money. He looks at me as if ahm his mammy an ah've joost caught him in his room wi some illicit chocolate.

'Ahm no daft, pal,' ah say. 'Ah know aw you young yins are intae that nonsense.' Ah gie him a wee nudge tae the ribs tae let him know ahm no the big bad wolf.

'We goat kicked oot ae there,' another member ae this group, the world's bammiest boayband says, noddin taewards the live lounge. Ahm startin tae hink mibbe the 'N' in *N*Sync* stawns fur 'Ned'.

'Och, the place is a shitehole anywey,' ah lie. The wee chubby lad hawns me a roastin hoat can ae Tennent's. 'Wit's yer names anywey, boays?'

The boay points tae each ae his pals an says, 'Div, Parker, Paco, Disco an ahm Mo.' He puts his hawn oot fur me tae shake.

'Ahm Angie. Big Angie.'

'That implies the existence of a Wee Angie,' says the boay called Parker. He disnae sound as bammy as the rest. 'Am I right?'

'There wis a Wee Angie at wan point, aye, yer right,' ah say, takin a wee swig fae mah can. Fuckin hell, it's scoldin hot but ah drink it an force it doon anywey. 'But ah killed her.'

The lads aw look shellshocked.

'Naw ahm kiddin on, ah've never killed anycunt. Well ah've goat rid ae a deid boady but that's another story fur another time.'

The lads aw huv a wee nervous chuckle, lookin at each other. Ah've goat thum rattled. Sadly only metaphorically.

'Stag do, aye?' ah say tae diffuse the tension. The lads aw nod. 'Who's getting mairried?'

Div puts his hawn up. He dis look the maist mature, wee smatterin ae grey hair oan his temples, he'd huv been mah first guess at who wis the groom.

'An ahm the best man,' says Paco. Wee skinny guy, the runt ae the litter it seems. He looks aw proud. God love him.

'Right moan,' says Disco, flexin his airm. 'Who's takin me oan next?'

The lads aw look doon at their feet, dead sheepishly.

'Oh give it a rest,' Parker, the ginger wan, says. 'You're the strongest. You win. Just take your money and shut up.'

'Ah'll take ye oan,' ah say. Ah go intae mah purse an pull oot twinty quid an smack it doon oan the table. Years an years ae humphin aboot mah bowls hus gave me the strength ae a wummin hawf mah age.

Disco spits oot a moothfull ae Tennet's an laughs. 'Ahm no airm wrestling an auld wummin, fuck sake!'

'*Auld wummin,* aye?' Sayin that tae me is like showin a red rag tae a fuckin bull. 'Ah'll rip yer fuckin airm right oaff ye, son.'

That shuts the cunt up.

'Tell ye wit,' ah drain the last ae mah can, an crush it. 'If ah beat everycunt here at airm wrestling, then you last; that money's mine.'

The lads aw look at each other.

'An ah'll mibbe take a wee bump ae the auld devil's dandruff aff yees anaw.'

* * *

First up's wee fat Mo. He's a cocky cunt, ah cin tell, so ah went tae dispose ae him quickly. They're aw fairly muscly boays, well, apart fae wee Paco, an ahm wonderin if ah've bit aff mair than ah cin chew.

The lads clear the table an ah plonk mah elbow doon and open mah hawn, ready tae receive Mo's sweaty mitt. He's goat a wee sleekit smile oan his face as we go fur it. Ah let him start tae push mah airm doon an he looks aw smug. Ah keep eye contact wi him as ah start tae use mah full force an ah cin see him start tae panic. The lads' jaws might as well be oan the flair here. Wan final push noo, Mo's neck an jaw an everyhin is aw strained as he tries wi aw his might tae fight back against me but it's nae use. Wan nil tae me.

The lads are aw howlin as Mo sulks away back tae the caravan, rubbin his wee fat airm. Ah cin tell it's nervous laughter, though; they're fuckin shiteing theirselves.

Parker next. Poor cunt is the token ginger ae the group, his skin's rid raw.

'Look, I don't agree with this,' he says. 'I mean, I'm all for equality and all that, just ask my friends, they call me a social justice warrior, but this isn't right. Men shouldn't compete *against* women in sports like this. If you ask–'

'Stoap talkin mince an gies yer airm.'

He disnae put up much ae a fight. Ah feel as if he's let me win but a win's a win nonetheless.

Disco is lookin worried. Ahm comin fur your title, big man.

Div, the blushin groom tae be, comes up next. He's the maist blotto oot the group by noo an he slumps doon across fae me an sticks his airm oot. His hair is plastered tae his heid wi sweat.

He puts everyhin he's goat intae beatin me, tae be fair tae him, but he's swept aside anaw. When ah get his airm doon oan tae the table, the rest ae his boady goes wi him an he faws aff the bench an hits the deck. Oot like a light.

Wee Paco comes err next. Mo's re-emerged fae the caravan, must be oot his wee mood. Ah've been worried aboot takin oan Paco. Know how there's always wan poor cunt in any group ae pals that takes the brunt ae the jokes an slaggins? That's him. Cin tell a fuckin mile away, even joost fae lookin at him.

'She's gonnae break you intae two, ya skinny basturt!' Mo laughs.

Paco disnae want tae go through this. When a grab his hawn, it's aw clammy an weak, like grabbin a hawd ae a deid fish.

Ah hink aboot letting the wee cunt win but there's a lot at stake here; ah want that fuckin money, aye, obviously, but ah want tae see the looks oan these cunt's faces even mair.

'Three...two...wan...GO!' shouts Mo, actin as the referee an adjudicator fur this round.

Wee Paco's goat that permanent rabbit-caught-in-a-set-ae-heidlights look aboot him, this is gonnae be a fuckin shame but ah've no goat tae where ah um these days by takin pity oan folk.

He's putting up a good fight though, tae be fair tae the wee guy. Wire strength or suhin they call it. Ah start exertin mair pressure but his airms no fur movin even an inch. He's properly grittin his teeth, he's geein me everyhin he's goat here.

Ah go a wee bit harder, harder than ah've hud tae so far wi any the cunts but the cunt's airm isnae fur budgin. The rest ae the lads are aw as shocked as ah um, even daft Div's woke up tae witness this.

Fuck sake, he's beatin me here. Kick it up a fuckin level, Angie, hen. Cannae let this cunt win, nae matter how sorry ye feel fur him.

But it's awrite, he's peaked too soon. He's ran oot ae steam. Doon he goes, joost liken the rest. Nae bother.

Disco is struttin aboot, puffin oot his chest. Rollin his shooders back an crackin his neck, checkin his reflection in the caravan windae. Posin basturt. How could he be anyhin else wi a nickname like fuckin Disco. Some tan oan him, right enough, ah'll gie him that. Or mibbe it's joost the all-white ensemble he's wearin that's gien the illusion ae a tan.

When he's finished admirin himself, he comes err an takes a seat.

'This wilnae be very gentlemanly,' he says. 'But ah don't gie a fuck. Ahm no getting beat at airm wrestling aff a fuckin *auld wummin*.'

He puts his hawn up fur me. Mah airm's gettin a wee bit sore, ah must admit, but there's enough in mah tank tae see this through.

'Three...two...wan...GO!'

'HNNNNNNG!' Disco lets oot a mad grunt.

'Ooft, didnae huv you doon as the vocal type,' ah say, lickin mah lips an lookin at the lads who aw burst intae laughter.

Disco, surprisingly, feels as if he'll be the easiest wan tae beat but fuckin hell, he looks like he's gonnae explode. He's no as chubby as Mo but he's certainly closer in build tae him than Paco.

'HNNNNNNNG!' he goes again. Ah cin hardly keep a straight face.

Ah've goat him almost right doon and he grunts again, fightin back as much as he cin.

'HNNNNNNNNNNNNNNNG!'

Then his expression changes.

Panic.

Disco's airm goes limp and ah pin it doon.

Then ah hear a horrible, wattery sound. Like emptyin a tin ae soup intae a pot.

Then ah fuckin smell it.

'You've shat yerself, eh?' ah enquire. He nods tae confirm. He stawns up an the lads aw hit the deck, rollin aboot laughin.

He turns roon tae head back tae his caravan tae get changed an there's a perfect wee broon love heart seepin through his pure white fitbaw shorts.

* * *

Efter he cleans himself up, Disco rejoins us at the table.

Ah pick up mah winnins an stuff thum intae mah bra. 'Five hunner quid, eh?'

Disco looks ragin.

'Well played, Angie,' says Parker.

'Aye, yer some wummin,' Mo chimes in. 'Here.' He racks up a couple ae lines ae gear oan a CD case an passes it tae me.

'Aw, ah dunno, lads,' ah say. 'Wis only huvin a wee laugh when ah says ah wid huv some earlier.'

'Och away,' Mo says. 'Huv a fuckin line. Ye've earned it.'

Know wit? Ah huv fuckin earned it. Ah pull a sweaty score note fae oot mah bra, roll it up, an hoover a big fat fuckin line. Mah first in aboot thirty year. An it's joost as fuckin magic as it wis back then.

The boays are aw clappin fur me when ah open mah eyes, this stuff fuckin stings oan it's way up. Over Mo's shooder stawns Dolly wi a stupit judgemental look oan her face.

'Really, Angie?' she says. 'Drugs? At your age?'

'Och, gies peace. Ahm oan hoaliday fur fuck sake!' She joost tuts at me an walks away. 'Dolly, c'moan, don't be like that.'

She toddles away, headin back tae the caravan, shakin her heid an mutterin nonsense under her breath.

'That yer pal, aye?' Paco asks me.

'Aye. Listen, ah better go, boays. Ah'll mibbe see yeez aw the morra or suhin, eh?'

They aw say cheerio an ah head efter Dolly.

5

Back at the caravan, Dolly's sittin wi a face like thunder.

'You're an embarrassment,' she says.

'Aw, lighten up. It wis only wan wee line.'

'It's not just that. Getting chucked out of the gig, making a fool of yourself, fighting and then hanging around with a bunch of neds. You're a grown woman, Angie, maybe it's time you started acting like it.'

'At least ah didnae ditch mah pal tae sit an gawp at some auld has-been singer. Ye could've came efter me but naw. In fact, wit difference wid it huv made if ye did come efter me, eh? Ye'd just be sittin oan yer fuckin phone.'

She looks doon at the flair when she hears that. Folk don't like it when ye explain how they're the wans in the wrang tae. Nae cunt's perfect.

Ah don't like arguin wi Dolly. It's easy enough, ah always win, but there's nae joy in winnin an argument wi someone like her; it's like winnin a debate against a wean - a really fuckin stupit wean.

There's a horrible silence in the caravan noo. Caravans amplify feelins, that's how so much shaggin happens in them.

'How wis the rest ae the gig? That Huey stole your heart anaw?'

Dolly gies a wee laugh. That's better. 'He's quite the charmer,' she says.

'Looked as if he hud a wee hing fur you, eh? Bit ae eye contact, wee brush ae the shooder.' Ah sit doon beside Dolly an gie her a wee nudge.

'I had a wee drink with him after the show.'

'Aw did ye, aye?' Ahm a wee bit annoyed, ahm no gonnae lie. But ah've nae chance wi him anywey. God either gies ye brains, beauty or gallusness. An he sorted me oot wi gallusness an mibbe a wee dash ae the brains. Dolly, oan the other hawn, only goat beauty an her wee empty heid is joost full ae broken biscuits.

'Listen,' Dolly says, stawnin up. 'I'm going to go to bed. It's been a long day.'

'Aye, fair enough, hen. As long as we're still pals?'

'Of course, Angie.' An off she goes tae her kip. Ah should get the heid doon as well. The morra's the last day ae the hoaliday an ah want it tae be a belter. Ahm rattlin fae that wee line though, they boays must huv access tae the finest prop in Ayrshire. Hink it'll be mair ae a case ae lyin in bed, starin at the inside ae mah ain eyelids than sleepin.

6

The burds urr singin, there's sunlight fuckin batterin right in through the windae but isnae that that's roused me fae mah slumber; it's fuckin Dolly rampaging aboot.

'Fuck's the matter?'

'My phone!' Dolly screams back at me. 'I can't ffffucking find it.'

Dolly never swears. This is obviously affecting her deeply.

'Right, calm doon an take a breath.' Ah grab her by the shooders an she flicks her hair oot her face an takes a deep breath. 'Where wis the last place ye seen it?'

'If I knew that, Angie,' ah cin feel her start tae vibrate, 'then I WOULDN'T STILL BE FUCKING LOOKING FOR IT!' An away she goes, stormin ootside, banging the door shut efter her. Fuckin hell.

Ah open the door tae her oan her hawns an knees, feelin aboot in the grass lookin fur the phone. Hair aw err the camp, housecoat flappin open.

'Dolly,' ah say.

She joost ignores me.

'Dolly,' ah try a wee bit louder.

She ignores me even fuckin harder, feelin aboot in the grass pure frantically. There's a few folk sittin ootside their caravans awready an they're aw laughin at her.

'DOLLY!'

She turns roon an gies me a stare that makes mah heart sink like the fuckin titanic. Ah've never seen her look at me like that afore. She must really be annoyed aboot that phone.

'Dolly, it'll be awrite,' ah try an placate her. She looks at me again but this time she starts greetin. Ahm gonnae huv tae gie her a cuddle.

'C'moan in, hen.' Ah step ootside an put mah airm roon her. 'It's joost a phone. Ye cin huv mine if ye want.'

'Wit yous two uptae?' says a most-definitely hungover voice fae a few caravans over. It's the boays fae last night.

'Daft arse here hus loast her phone,' ah reply. Ah know Dolly isnae happy wi me callin her "daft arse" but fuck it.

'What kind of phone is it?' Parker asks Dolly.

'An iPhone,' she replies.

'Do you have an iPhone, Angie?' he turns tae me an asks.

Ah don't want tae look stupit in front ae the boays so ah joost say, 'aye,' even though ah've only goat a daft wee Tesco hing.

'Just use that find my phone app, then,' Parker says. 'Give me your phone and I'll show you how.'

'Aw, eh, mah phone's in the caravan.'

'She doesn't have an iPhone,' Dolly grasses me in.

'Fuckin hell,' ah punch her airm. 'Cheers fur makin me look like a big daft cavewummin.'

'Oh, is it an Android phone you have then?' Parker asks. 'Easy enough to get the two mixed up.'

'Show him your phone then, Angie,' Dolly urges.

'Look, ah've only goat a wee snidey phone, son.'

'Jesus Christ!' he exclaims when ah show him it. 'Lads! Come and see this!'

Next hing ah know aw the boays are over starin at mah shitey wee phone like it's some kind ae ancient relic. Turnin it over an over, hawdin it up tae the light an aw that. Mo slides the back aff an is hysterical when he discovers that it can take four AA batteries.

'I'll find your phone, don't worry,' Parker says tae Dolly, when he stoaps laughin.

After pluggin in some details an tappin an swiping fur ages, Parker hawns Dolly his phone.

'Look, that's yer phone there,' the screen shows a wee map wi a glowin dot where Dolly's phone is.

'Looks as if it's in the staff quarters,' says Mo. 'The caravan right in the far corner. Wan ae the entertainers or something must've found it.'

'Or stole it,' ah say. Nae chance they've found it an urr keepin it safe fur Dolly. Some cunt's pocketed it fur themselves.

'I'll go in and get dressed an we can go and get it, Angie. Thanks for your help, gents.'

'Nae problem, ladies,' says Mo an gies me a wee wink.

'Dolly, hen, looks as if ah've still goat it.'

7

We get tae the gate ae the staff quarters bit an the bouncer lassie fae last night is stawnin guard.

'Ladies,' she says, airms folded, ponytail pulled back tight as fuck. 'How can I help?'

'My phone's in there,' says Dolly. She's aw jumpy an anxious an twitchy. She's desperate tae get that fuckin hing back.

'...and how do you know it's in here?' the bouncer asks.

'We used a tracking app,' Dolly says. 'A couple of lads helped us do it. It said my phone's in that caravan over there in the corner.'

It's the grubbiest, maist dilapidated lookin caravan ah've ever seen. Like suhin oot *The Hills Have Eyes*. Probably hame tae a big mutated freak ae a janitor.

'That's Huey the singer's caravan,' says the bouncer. Her tone's changed though. She sounds aw conspiratorial noo. 'Always had a bad feeling about him.'

'Fuckin knew it,' ah say. 'Too good tae be true, that cunt. Theivin basturt and he lives in a manky fuckin caravan.'

'No, he's not a thief, surely not,' Dolly laughs. 'No, that's ridiculous. Huey wouldn't steal someone's phone, for christ's sake!'

'Hawl,' a right fuckin nasally soundin voice screeches oot ae fuckin naewhere. 'Ah wantae make a complaint.' It's that scheme maw ah wis fightin wae last night.

'Better no fuckin be aboot me, ya dafty,' ah say.

'It's no,' she says, lookin me up an doon. The she turns tae the bouncer. 'It's aboot that creepy singer.'

'Huey?' Dolly asks, she sounds as if she's oan the defensive here, like she'll knock this wee burd oot if she says anyhin aboot her darling Huey.

'Aye, him. The smarmy cunt. Mah boyfriend says he skelped the back ae mah wee boay's heid last night.'

'Yer wee boay needed it tae be fair,' ah say under mah breath. Torn-faced wee git.

'AND,' she goes oan, 'he felt mah arse oan mah wey oot.'

'Ah mean, ye did shove his face intae yer cleavage did ye no?' ah ask.

'That's no the point. He didnae huv mah consent tae feel mah arse, did he? That's harassment. An ah want some compo.'

Dolly looks as if her wee world hus joost been rocked tae its core. Her perfect angel Huey; a wean skelpin, arse feelin, phone stealin basturt. Unlucky, hen.

'This is a bit outwith my jurisdiction, you'll need to take it up with the managers.'

'Fine then,' the scheme maw says, 'Ah will.' An she storms away.

'Wit'll the managers dae aboot it?' ah ask the bouncer.

'Not much, I imagine,' she replies. 'They're older guys as well.'

'Is Huey in his caravan the noo?' ah ask.

'I think so, aye.'

'Right, moan, Dolly,' ah say an grab her by the airm, marchin past the bouncer. But the lassie's a fuckin tank, even bigger an stronger than me, an she grabs me by mah airm an pulls the two ae us back.

'You're just going to waltz over there, chap his door and accuse of him stealing your phone?'

'Aye,' ah reply.

'Then what's going to happen? Will he just hand it over, aye?'

'Well, ahm presuming he'll deny it then maybe ah'll joost need tae leather him.'

'You need to be clever with situations like this. What did you think of him before you found this stuff out? You thought he was lovely, eh? A gentleman. A harmless old guy. A wee holiday park entertainer. You lay a finger on him and he'll be protected by the management. You'll be off the park before you know and he'll just keep getting away with stuff like this.'

She's goat a point, tae be fair. Ah like this lassie.

'So wit dae ye suggest we dae then, pal?'

'Well, we need to establish that he has the phone first. C'mon.' she nods over to the caravan.

'Thought ye said we cannae joost "waltz over there an chap the door"?'

'We aren't. This is espionage.'

* * *

So here we are peerin through this auld cunt's caravan windae seein if he's stole Dolly's phone. Inside Huey's caravan is joost as grim as the ootside. The hing's toaty. The flair's manky an covered in rubbish an auld newspapers.

Nicotine stained walls. The windaes are that manky that ahm 100% sure he won't notice us lookin in at him. He's potterin aboot in his boxers (formerly white, also nicotine stained). He's goat an iron turned upside doon wi a tin a hotdogs sittin oan tap ae it. Ah've goat tae admit; that's a genius way tae heat stuff up.

He takes his tin ae hotdogs an sits doon oan the threadbare couch. From under his arse he produces a phone. Dolly's phone. Could tell a mile away that it's hers fae her wee sparkly case. The cunt starts playin a daft game oan the hing.

'That dirty, lousy bastard,' Dolly mutters.

'What's your plan of attack going to be, ladies?' the bouncer asks.

Withoot missin a beat Dolly says, 'I think we should kill him.'

The bouncer laughs, thinkin wit Dolly's joost said is a wee joke. Ah laugh anaw tae try an assure the lassie that it is, even though ah know Dolly's bein deadly serious.

'We'll figure suhin oot,' ah say, an drag Dolly away. 'Leave it wi me, pal. Aw, hen, by the way, wit's yer name?'

'Angela,' the bouncer says, stickin oot a hawn.

'Fuckin smashin name, hen.'

8

'Ye cannae joost go aboot killin folk ye don't agree wi, Dolly, fuckin hell.' She's goat that same look in her eye she hud when she wis tellin me she wis wantin tae kill her man, Philip, last year. Daft basturt actually went through wi it anaw. She's sittin fidgetin aboot wi her hawns as if she's wantin tae go an dae the cunt in right noo.

'Well what do you suggest we do, Angie?' she says, as if killin the cunt is the only option here.

'There's plenty we cin dae, fur fuck sake! You're joost no

thinkin straight, mibbe aw that sunshine err the last few days has fried yer fuckin brain.'

Ah look aboot the caravan fur inspiration but nuhin is jumpin oot at me. Ahm aw oot ae ideas but ahm absolutely no killin the guy. Then oot the windae ah spy the boays.

'They'll know wit tae dae,' ah say jumpin oot the door efter them. 'Back in a minute, hen.'

'Angie, what are they going to do? Batter him? That could work.' Ah cin hear the wee cogs turnin in her mind.

'Suhin like that,' ah shout back.

Catchin up wi the boays, ah put mah airms roon Disco an Paco. 'Need yer help, boays.'

'Wit's up?' Disco asks. 'Did ye get yer pal's phone back?'

'No yet. Ah mean, we know were it is, and who stole it but–'

'Somecunt stole it?' asks Mo.

'Aye, it wis the auld singer.'

'Sneaky auld cunt,' Parker laughs. First ah've heard the boay swear.

'Ye wantin us tae leather the bastard then, Angie? Five ae us in that wee caravan could dae some right damage.'

'Naw, naw, naw,' ah say. 'We cannae hurt the cunt. He's goat aw the management an that coverin fur him an helpin him oot an that. Dain that wid joost end in tears fur everybody bar him. We need tae be clever. Get the phone back an mibbe take him doon a peg urr two.'

The boays aw nod in silent agreement. Like ahm their sergeant getting them ready fur war.

'So what's the plan?' Parker asks. 'I really don't like the guy.'

The idea joost materialises right intae mah brain there an then. Aw fully formed an ready tae fuck this cunt's day right up. It'll embarrass the cunt, make him a laughin stock, piss aff the management an best of aw, get Dolly's phone back, safe an sound.

'Disco,' ah say. 'Mind you shat yerself?'

'Of course ah dae, Angie,' he replies.

'Still goat yer shitty drawers?'

'Fuck sake, of course no! Ye hink ahm some kind ae weirdo?'

Basturt. The shitty drawers were a crucial part ae the plan. Then ah spot a poor wee bar ae chocolate, a Double Decker, oan the picnic table next to the lads' caravan. Ah pick it up an it's practically totally liquid.

'This'll dae,' ah say. 'Right boays gather roon, here's the plan…'

9

'Joost remember,' ah say tae Dolly as we head intae the live lounge later that night. 'Act normal, like ye fancy him an aw that. Gie uhm the eyes, lull him intae a false sense ae security, that's aw you need tae dae. Me an the boays'll take care ae the rest.'

'Right okay, Angie.' She fixes her hair an sits herself doon. The she clocks the scheme maw ah've been huvin a wee bit ae bother wi. 'Oh Jesus, Angie, look who it is.'

The scheme maw comes over an greets me wi a cuddle an slips suhin intae mah handbag; a pair ae her scabbiest lookin knickers as instructed. 'Magic, hen,' ah say. 'They'll be spot oan.'

'Hope ye've goat a good aim,' she says wi a smile an goes an sits back doon the front.

'Angie, what's going on?'

'Joost trust me, hen. This is perfect.'

The lads come in behind us an take a seat. Mo gestures taewards mah bag fae across the room. Ah open it up an flash him the melted Double Decker an the scheme maw's knickers. He nudges Disco an Parker an they aw try an contain their laughter by sittin wi their airms folded an shooders bobbin up an doon.

Angela the bouncer pokes her heid in the room an gies me a thumbs up.

Fuckin showtime.

'Ladies and gentleman, singing the hits of the Rat Pack, please welcome to the stage, Huey the crooner!'

The lights go doon an everycunt goes daft fur the auld yin. Weird how when yer opinion ae somebody changes, ye wonder how ye never realised they were such an arsehole in the first place. Ah mean, this auld cunt, struttin oan the stage noo wi a stupit smarmy look oan his face, bright white suit jaiket; he's quite clearly a fuckin wrong yin. But through the haze ae infatuation, ah thought he wis perfect at wan point. Nae cunt's perfect. Well, except fae me.

Angela comes over an sits next tae me.

'You need to get the two managers out from back stage if you want to get Huey on his own,' she says.

'How the fuck are we meant tae dae that?'

'Need to get a bit of crowd trouble going.'

Ah look aboot. It's a sea ae blue rinses an cardigans, well, apart fae the scheme family doon the front an the boays up the back.

'They'll come out to help me quieten folk down. When that happens, make your move.' She gets up an gets back tae her post at the door.

'Boays,' ah try an hawf shout an hawf whisper tae the boays. 'Let's kick this aff.'

They aw nod.

'This one's for the *lllll*adies,' Huey says. He's creepy as fuck.

As he's aboot tae launch intae *Ah've Goat You Under Mah Skin* when the boays start stampin their feet.

'Here we, Here we,' they shout, stawnin up an clappin their hawns noo. 'HERE WE FUCKIN GOOOOO!'

'HERE WE, HERE WE, HERE WE FUCKIN GO! YYYAAAASSSS!' shouts the scheme maw an her Pepperami lookin man.

Huey looks bemused. He looks over his shooder tae the back stage bit fur help. Ah cin see two other aulder guys poke their heids roon the curtain. The boays are up oan the table noo, givin it big licks.

'Can we...calm down a wee bit?' Huey pleads. A few auld dears look terrified. The worst is yet tae come as well.

But ah need hings tae kick aff mair. There's nae need fur security or management tae get involved when it's joost a bunch ae daft boays singin. Ah need a fight or suhin tae happen. Ah make a fist an smash it intae mah palm. Disco clocks this an whispers suhin in Mo's ear. Mo nods an Disco punches him square in his belly. The big fella doubles err. The rest ae the boays start flingin their pints aboot.

This is anarchy. It's fuckin brilliant!

But there's nae time tae rest oan mah laurels here, there's still a few hings tae be done. Time fur phase two; makin a cunt ae Huey an gettin the managers oot.

The boays start up the Here We Fuckin Go chant again while ah root aboot in mah bag fur the knickers an the Double Decker.

'Angie, what on earth is happening?' Dolly says. She's goat her hawns over her ears, aw freaked oot. Wee soul.

'Watch this.' Ah open the corner ae the Double Decker wrapper an start pipin the melted chocolate oantae the scabby drawers.

'Oh my God,' Dolly says. 'Angie, is this your plan? I don't understand.'

'Joost trust me, hen.' Ah open up the wrapper some mair tae get a few ae the wee biscuity bits oantae the knickers. 'That'll dae nicely. How dae they look?' Ah hawd up the drawers tae Dolly. She covers her mooth wi her hawn as if she's gonnae be sick.

Ah gie Angela a thumbs up an she radios through tae the managers tae ask fur help subduing the boays who are absolutely rippin the fuckin arse oot ae this. Taps aff, hoistin an auld wummin, still in her seat, above their heids. Fair play.

Huey joost stawns in the middle ae the stage watchin aw

this unfold, ah don't hink he cin quite process wit's gawn oan. It's aboot tae get a lot fuckin worse. When the two managers come oot tae help Angela, ah wind mah airm back an fling the chocolatey knickers at the basturt.

It aw seems tae happen in slow motion. He turns roon, lookin at the madness in front ae him, then ah see him lockin his eyes oan the airborne drawers. As they tumble through the air, they start tae unfurl a wee bit, revealin the surprise inside. His face is a fuckin picture by the way. When he first clocked them, he must've thought he wis oan tae his hole the night but as they get closer, horror wipes the smugness right aff his face.

They hit him oan the chest an it's perfect. They land right under his sparkly bow tie leavin a smear oan his shirt an jaiket. Wit a fuckin shot if ah dae say so mahself. He looks doon at his shirt an ah cin see him start tae hit the boak. Then he kicks the drawers aff the stage,sending them right intae the mixer. A hunner screams go up as people see the kid-on shitty knickers. The two managers are over tryin tae calm people doon but it's nae good. Huey draps his mic an runs fur the safety ae behind the curtain. Time fur me an Dolly tae make oor move oan the cunt.

'Moan, hen,' ah say, grabbin Dolly by the airm. 'Backstage.'

We find Huey strippin doon in his dressin room, door wide open, like he wants folk tae fuckin see him in aw his wrinkly, saggy-bawed glory. Soaks pulled up tae his knees, nae troosers or pants an joost a shirt.

'Where's the fuckin phone, arsehole,' ah say. Dolly hides behind me.

'Eh?' he replies. Actin daft. Good yin.

'The phone! Her fuckin phone! Ye pocketed it the other night. Gies it back.'

The screamin ootisde husnae died doon any, we've caused a right fuckin riot. It's class!

'I don't know what you're talking about. Now, if you wouldn't mind letting me get ready. '

'Is that shite oan yer shirt, aye? Clatty basturt.'

'Look, will you please just go! I don't have a phone, I haven't stole anything from anyone.'

The screamin starts tae quieten doon noo. If we're gonnae get this phone back, we need tae be quick. Drastic times call fur drastic measures.

So ah grab him by his baws an twist. He screams like a fuckin banshee an so does Dolly but hers is in glee an happiness rather than shock an agony like Huey here.

'Dolly, check his poakits an that, turn this place upside doon.' Ah turn mah attentions back tae Huey. 'Where,' *twist*, 'is,' *twist*, 'her,' *twist*, 'phone?', *hawd*.

His eyes are waterin when the two management cunts appear tae save the day. Basturts.

'What's happening here?' the taller wan says, grabbin me while his wee blady accomplice takes Dolly.

'He stole her phone!' ah shout. But it's nae good. We're bein ejected fae the premises. Oot oan oor arses afore we cin get Dolly's phone back.

Angela the bouncer's aw apologetic at the door as the managers head back inside.

'No your fault, hen,' ah say, getting tae mah feet. 'Ye did yer best.'

Ah don't want Dolly tae be sittin oan her phone but ah want tae get it back fur her, it's no nice seein her aw gutted an heartbroken that it's away.

'That's definitely your phone you seen him in his caravan with?'

'I'm one hundred percent sure. Same case, same kind, everything. I need it back. I really, really need it back.' Dolly's near tears.

'Why ye so desperate tae get it back? It's joost a phone.'

'It's just, it's got stuff on it I want to keep.'

'Wit, like, phone numbers an that? Joost write them doon ya dafty.'

'No… pictures.'

'Och, so yer worried aboot losin a cuppla daft foties? That's nuhin.'

'They're…' she looks scared tae tell us. 'Photos of me. Naked photos.'

'Awww, right, ah see.' This changes everyhin. 'Cannae be huvin that auld perv getting a swatch ae ye, eh? We'll get that fuckin phone back, don't you worry, hen.'

10

So noo we're camped oot at Huey's caravan. Hidin under his windae, me, Angela, an Dolly, waitin til the auld codger faws asleep so we cin break in, get the phone an then get tae fuck. That's Plan A anyway.

It's getting right fuckin cauld. These summer nights get freezing, nae cloud cover ye see.

'Wit's he dain noo?' ah ask Angela. She's turned up wi a balaclava so he shouldnae be able tae see her coupon when she's lookin in his windae.

'Still just playing Candy Crush. Still very much awake.'

'Jesus Christ,' ah say, 'Wit time is it noo?'

'That's half two,' says Dolly.

'Hang on,' Angela announces. 'We have some movement.'

'Wit is it, wit's happenin?'

Dolly's joost sittin starin intae space bitin her nails. Cin tell she's no far away fae snappin an joost breakin in an cavin the guy's heid in or suhin.

'He's…'

'He's wit! Fuckin tell us!'

'He's…masturbating.'

Ahm right up for a swatch ae this. Angela's right he's fuckin gawn fur it anaw.

'Oh no,' says Dolly. 'That's my pictures!'

'Jeezo, Mrs, so it is. Lookin no bad fur an auld dear.'

'I'm going in.' Dolly gets up, ready tae go an cause mayhem in the caravan but Angela stoaps her.

'Wait,' she says. 'Look.'

We get peer in an as we look a bit closer, the phone draps oot his hawn.

'Is he asleep?'

He starts grabbin at his chest then he's slappin at himself. The cunt's huvin a heart attack!

'We should phone an ambulance,' says Angela, but in a way that suggests she's no gonnae. As in we *should* phone an ambulance but we'll really definitely no.

Next hing we watch the cunt keel right err, aff the couch an land face first oan his boggin carpet.

'Cannae believe your scuddies killed that cunt, Dolly.'

She joost rolls her eyes at me.

'What do we do?' says Angela.

'Ah don't know, you said ye could get us intae his caravan.'

'I didn't say that. I said we *should* break in. I didn't say I knew a way.'

'Right well there's a fuckin deid boady in there. If we break in it looks as if we fuckin killed him. Huv ye no goat a spare key or suhin?'

'I just thought you had a plan?'

Fuck sake. Go away tae fuckin Craig Tara fur a nice wee break wi yer pal an looks wit happens.

Right fuckin think, Angie, we've been here afore, we cin dae it again. Smash a windae? Naw, too obvious, could cut maself, leave blood everywhere – caught. Break the door in – same again, looks like a break-in, could make noise – caught.

'Is there any other way intae the hing? Other than the door or windae?'

'There's a vent in the roof, I'm sure, but I don't think any of us could get through it. You'd need to be built like the side of a fiver to get into the caravan through that.'

Ah know just the wee skinny cunt who could get through it – Paco.

'Back in a minute, ladies,' ah say an head tae try an talk the boays intae a bit ae late night shenanigans. Unfortunately, no the kind ah wis hopin fur.

* * *

These boays know how tae huv a party. It's still quite dark but it's easy tae find their caravan thanks tae the poundin music they're playin. Ah rattle their door an wait. Then wait some mair.

Efter another couple ae minutes rattlin the door they answer it.

'Angie! Moan in!' says Mo. 'Huv a can, huv a line!'

Ah politely decline.

'Turn that music aff,' ah say. 'Ah need a favour.'

11

Efter explainin the situation, the boays wurnae too keen tae help – Disco wis oot oan bail, his apprehension wis understandable – but when ah offered them their £500 back they were a bit mair keen.

'So ah joost need tae climb up there, get doon intae the caravan an get the phone?' Paco asks.

'Aye that's it, pal. Easy as that.'

'Where is the phone?'

'Joost under the deid boady.'

'Nah, fuck this,' he says an he makes a run fur it but Parker gets a hawd ae him.

'Calm yerself, it'll be awrite,' ah say tae the boay. 'You cin huv aw the money fur the hassle.'

'Moan, wee man,' says Disco, pattin him oan the back. 'It'll be a laugh. Huv a wee toot tae get ye gawn.' Disco dips a key intae a wee bag ae marchin powder an stuffs it up Paco's nose.

'Right,' Paco says, bouncing up an doon oan the spot. 'Let's fuckin dae this.'

Angela an Dolly watch oan nervously. Dolly's no too bad actually, she joost seems relieved tae be getting her phone back but she's constantly lookin err her shooder in case we get caught. Ah huv tae admit, it widnae look good if anycunt came snoopin.

Disco an Parker gie Paco a punt up an oan tae the caravan roof.

'The vent should be around the middle, I think,' says Angela.

'Aye, ah've found it,' the wee man says. 'Wit noo?'

'Just lift it open.'

There's a few clicking and clangin noises then Paco says, 'Right, ahm gawn in.'

We aw move roon back tae windae joost in time tae watch Paco land in the caravan.

'How um ah meant tae move him?' he shouts. 'Ahm no touchin him wi mah bare hawns.'

'Aw fur fuck sake,' laughs Disco. 'Use a tea towel or suhin.'

Paco finds a manky auld tea towel an attempts tae shift Huey's weight oot the way so he can get Dolly's phone. Efter a bit ae heavin an gruntin he manages tae move the guy oan tae his side.

'Fuckin hell, he's still goat a hard on!' Paco shouts. 'Right ah've goat the phone.'

'Oh thank god,' says Dolly, breathin a sigh ae relief.

'Well done, wee man, moan oot.' Ah feel like ahm waitin oan the rescue ae they fuckin Chilean miners.

We go roon ae the door, expectin Paco tae let himself oot but he then he shouts fae the tap ae caravan that he needs a hawn doon.

'Ye could've joost let yersel oot the door, daft arse,' says Mo, offerin him a hawn doon.

'Aye,' Paco says. 'But then who would put the vent back?'

The cunt's goat us there, ah've goat tae admit. Well played.

'There's yer phone, Mrs,' he passes the phone tae Dolly who clutches it tae her chest like it's her wean that's been rescued fae a burnin buildin.

'Back tae oors then fur a swallay?' Disco asks.

'No chance,' ah say.

'Aye, we better get to bed,' says Dolly.

'I'm away home as well,' Angela says.

Ah gie the lads their five hunner quid an head back tae the caravan wi Dolly.

Craig Tara – it's been a fuckin pleasure.

BREXIT

'It's a fuckin terrible hing,' one of the apprentices said. 'Noo we cannae joost up an leave an go an work in a bar in Ibiza or anywhere like that. It's no right, man.'

'Och, as if you'd ever dae that anywey,' the other laughed, tearing into his packed lunch.

'Here fuck off, ah might. Ye never know.'

'Aye nae bother, mate. So that's it? That's yer big anti-Brexit argument? That you cannae go tae Ibiza an get a joab in the Highlander or Kilties Bar or something?'

'Aye that an... other stuff as well.'

'Like wit?'

'Well, like, it's a shame fur the refugees an that. Poor cunts cannae come here noo. It's a shame.'

'Wit yous two bumpin yer gums aboot, eh?' their boss said, walking in with a roll and sausage and a cup of tea.

'Joost politics an that, Boaby.'

'Aye, nuttin you'd be interested in.'

'Aye, yer right there. Politics...' Boaby shook his head. 'Bunch ae crooks. They're aw the same, they politicians.'

'We're talking aboot leavin the EU. Wit's yer thoughts oan that, auld yin? You for or against it?'

'Eh, och, ah dunno.' Boaby sat down on the floor and pulled his roll from its greasy paper bag. 'Ah'll no be voting anywey.'

'Well, it's awready been voted fur. It's happenin.'

'Wit?'

The two apprentices looked at each other. 'We voted in the referendum like two year ago, Boaby.'

'Fuck sake. Ah hud nae idea. So we're leavin this, wit's it called?'

'The European Union. How dae you no know aboot this?'

'Och, ah told ye, it's cause ah don't care. Any yous seen mah measurin tape by the way?'

'Aw aye, ah've goat it.'

'Good. Ah'll get it back aff ye later.'

One of the apprentices laughed to himself.

'Wit you laughin at noo?' Boaby asked.

'Ah cannae believe you've never heard ae Brexit. That's fried as fuck, man.'

'Brexit?' said Boaby. 'Wit's that?'

The apprentices laughed out loud.

'Wit is it? Is that a politics hing as well, aye?'

'So you didnae know that we're leaving the EU. You didnae know there wis even a vote. Noo yer tellin us you've never heard the word Brexit? You're at it, man, surely.'

Boaby looked flustered. 'Naw, ah mean, aye, of course ah've heard ae the word Brexit. Ah've no been livin under a rock.'

'Use it in a sentence then,' one of the apprentices said.

'Right then, eh, Brexit' Boaby wracked his brains. 'You've goat mah tape measure aye?'

The apprentice checked his pocket. 'Aye, it's here.'

'Right, well, don't gie it tae him incase he fuckin Brexit. There ye go. Arseholes.' Boaby grabbed his lunch and went to eat it by himself in the van.

SANTA

'Long you been oan the dole noo, Ped, mate?' Steeco asked as they sat on Ped's maw's couch watching *Bargain Hunt*.

'Pffft,' Ped was fed up hearing this question from folk. It felt like somebody was asking him it every day now. *Why dae they aw care so much wit ahm uptae?* 'Left school in 2012, so that's...' He tried his best to work this out. 'Ehhhh.'

'That's five basturdin year!' Ped's maw announced, arriving home from work, laden with bags of shopping. She worked two jobs as a cleaner and behind the counter in the chippy round the corner from their house. 'Five year ae sponging aff me, Steeco. Wid *your* ma let *you* get away wi that?'

'She would not Caroline, hen. She certainly would not,' Steeco said smugly, turning to Ped.

'Aw gies a break, the two ae ye. Ahm joost oot mah bed an ahm getting it tight awready.'

'Exactly, mate!' said Steeco. 'It's hawf twelve oan a Friday an you're sat oan yer arse watching shite oan the telly. Yer maw's awready been an done a shift at work an she'll huv another wan the night, ahm sure.' Caroline nodded in agreement as she took the bags through to the kitchen. Ped did feel a bit guilty at the fact his maw had to work so much, but they couldn't afford the flat if she didn't. If Ped could get a job, she'd be able to give up one of her jobs. It was something she dreamt of, fantasised about, day in day out, trying to choose which job and which boss she hated the most, and coming up with elaborate ways in which to tell them to go and fuck themselves.

'If ye had a joab,' Steeco continued, 'you'd be able ae come wi me tae mah work's Christmas do the morra night. In fact, when wis the last time ye even left the hoose?'

Ped shrugged his shoulders. He genuinely didn't know.

'Son,' Caroline said as she sat down on the couch next to Ped. 'Ah joost want ye ae be happy. An this' – she gestured at Ped's stained joggies and general lack of enthusiasm for life – 'isnae dain ye any favours. Ye need a joab.'

'Ah'll help ye make a CV,' said Steeco.

'That won't take long,' Ped laughed. 'Aw ah need tae put oan it is "full time waster 2012 – present".'

***

Saturday morning. Ped had decided to take the bull by the horns and go and find himself a job. *With Christmas coming up, surely there'd be plenty of jobs going in the shopping centre*, he thought. Having been up half the night, with his maw and Steeco's words still ringing in his ears, he had worked himself into a state of extreme job-finding motivation. He wasn't going to take no for an answer. He strode up to the shopping centre, bundle of CVs under his arm, took a deep breath and went inside.

No luck.

He'd left it far too late to get a job in a shop. All the temp positions had been filled weeks ago. Dejected, he went into a café for a portion of chips and gravy. His maw used to bring him here when he was a wee boy; it was their Saturday routine. He remembered looking at the stressed-out staff in the shops, running around mental after customers and thinking to himself *Hope I never end up working here.* But now, he realised he'd give anything to be the guy getting screamed at by some irate maw because his shop didn't have any Rangers tops in stock. He turned his gaze to Santa's grotto, well, what was being used as Santa's grotto – a former nail bar which was shut down after a raid by the immigration authorities. There was a commotion happening inside. Through the crowd came Santa, being pushed by two angry guys. Santa went flying as they pushed him from behind. 'Alky bastard!' one of Santa's assailants shouted.

'Ah only had two cans, fuck sake,' Santa fired back. 'That hardly makes me a fuckin alky!'

Ped shoved one final forkful of chips into his mouth, washed them down with the last of his Irn-Bru and went out to get a better view of what was happening. He heard the crackle of a walkie-talkie and within minutes, two security guards arrived on the scene and huckled Santa.

'Shockin,' muttered one old woman, 'They poor weans,' said another. 'Heard he's a paedo,' a toothless middle-aged man whispered in Ped's ear.

'Fuckin get yer hawns aff me!' Santa said breaking free from the guards' grips. 'Ah cin see masel oot.' He flung his hat to the ground and stormed out of the shopping centre.

A group of children, who'd been stunned into silence by what they'd just witnessed, burst into tears. As their maws and das comforted them, Ped saw an opportunity. An opportunity that may as well have been gift-wrapped and dropped right into his lap. He picked up the discarded Santa hat and pushed through the crowd and into the grotto. A woman, who Ped assumed was the manager, was picking up empty cans of Tennent's from behind Santa's chair.

'Here,' he shouted to get her attention.

'The grotto's closed, I'm afraid,' she said without turning to look at him. 'If you just give me five minutes to get this place squared up I'll give you your money back.'

'Naw, naw, naw,' said Ped. 'Ah don't want money, well, ah mean, ah dae *want* money but that's no wit ahm here fur, ah mean, eh...'

The woman turned round, confused by Ped's rambling.

'Basically, wit ahm sayin is – ah'll be Santa if yous huv sacked that cunt.'

She looked Ped up and down.

'Are you not a bit, um, young to be Santa?' the woman asked.

'Thought Santa wisnae real?'

'Well, of course he's not but-'

'Well how cin ah be too young ae dress up as a cunt who disnae even exist?'

The woman mulled over Ped's point. She closed the doors of the grotto now that the crowd had mostly dispersed. A few stragglers still shuffled about outside, loudly discussing what they'd just seen. 'The cunt wis fucking STEAMING honestly, Janice, wit a disgrace. Mah wee Ava's traumatised,' Ped heard a concerned parent say.

'Ah cin start any time. Ah won't be late or anyhin, ah promise,' Ped pleaded. 'This joab would really help oot me and mah maw,' he absent-mindedly twisted the Santa hat in his hands.

The woman sighed. 'I'm not sure.'

'Aw c'moan. Joost gies a chance. Wan shift. Ah'll prove tae ye ahm the right cun-, eh, ah mean, eh, man fur the joab. If ahm nae good efter wan shift then fine, ah'll no bother ye again, ah promise.'

'Right,' the woman smiled. 'Come back here at half-eight tomorrow morning. I'll sort out the rest of the outfit for you.'

Ped jumped for joy and pulled the Santa hat onto his head. 'You wulnae regret this, ah promise!'

* * *

Walking home, Ped pulled out his phone to give his maw a call.

'Ye'll never guess wit,' he said as soon as she answered.

'Wit is it, Peter?' she replied.

'Ah've goat masel a joab!' Ped didn't realise how loud he was talking; he'd caught the attention of an old guy sitting at the bus stop across the road from him.

'Aw Peter, son, that's brilliant news. Wit ye gonnae be dain?'

'Ahm the new Santa in the shopping centre!' The old guy sat up, bristling with rage, and crushed a can of Tennents with one massive hand.

'Ahm so happy. Hurry hame an tell me aw aboot it. Ah'll order us a wee curry tae celebrate.'

As Ped hung up the phone, the old guy across the road got up and staggered towards him. It was quite dark now, but Ped could make out that the guy was clearly wearing a Santa outfit. It was the Santa he'd replaced.

'Mah replacement, eh?' the ex-Santa slurred.

'Look, mate,' Ped said, holding his hands up. 'Ah don't want any bother here.'

'You've took mah livelihood aff me, wee man. Ruined mah Christmas. Ruined *Santa's* Christmas.'

Ped shook his head. He could smell the booze of this mad bastard's breath. That, mixed with the smell of the sick matted in his beard, was making him feel sympathy for the guy, but was also making him want to spew. He breezed by Santa, heading home.

'Hawl you!' Santa jogged after him, rounded Ped like a collie herding sheep and got in his face once again. He lowered his voice to a growly whisper and said, 'You've been a bad boay, Ped.'

'Wit?' Ped was freaking out. 'How'd you know mah name?'

'That's no aw ah know. Twenty wan year auld. Still stayin wi yer maw. Nae money. Nae burd. You're pathetic, Ped.' Santa foamed at the mouth as he spat the words at Ped.

'Aw fuck off.' Ped shoved Santa to the ground. It wasn't like Ped to be so confrontational and he was surprised at himself for being so aggressive, but he felt had to do something. Who knew what this Santa character was capable of?

Santa rose groggily to his feet. Ped was frozen to the spot, it was as if he'd used up all his body's stores of aggression. Santa stood swaying, not breaking eye contact with Ped. He wiped some blood out of his dirty, formerly white, beard.

'Ah know everythin aboot you, Ped.' Santa let a crooked smile creep across his face. 'Ah hink ye should come wi me, ah've goat something ae show ye. An gies that back.' Santa snatched his hat back off Ped's head and went down the road in the opposite direction from Ped's house.

Ped stayed rooted to the spot.

'Ye comin or wit?' Santa shouted back without even turning round.

All Ped could think to say was *But mah maw's ordered me a curry...*

* * *

Ped wasn't entirely sure what it was that made him follow Santa into the night, but he did anyway. Although they walked together, Ped kept himself slightly behind Santa so people wouldn't think was actually with the guy. After a good twenty minutes of walking in silence, Santa came to a halt outside a grubby looking house.

'This is it,' Santa said, making his way up a litter-strewn path. 'Santa's Grotto.'

Ped looked around the street. He half-expected a camera crew to jump out of nowhere to reveal the whole thing had been a big wind-up and he'd won a holiday or something for being such a good sport.

'Wit ye waitin fur? Christmas?' Santa laughed. 'C'moan in afore ye end up wi hypothermia or somethin.'

Ped reluctantly agreed and stepped into the pitch-black house. He could just about make out the perfect, white bobble on the end of Santa's hat as it bobbed up and down in the darkness and followed him down the narrow hall and into the living room.

'Shut the door behind ye,' Santa said, fumbling for the light switch. Ped obliged and as soon the door shut over, the light came on.

He has horrified at what he saw.

The living room was covered in pictures of Ped, from floor to ceiling. Pictures of him as a boy right up until, what looked like, this morning. Tattered polaroids were pinned into the wall. Some pictures looked like they'd been printed off here at home by the man and were hung using sellotape. Some looked so grainy and low quality that they may as well have been taken on a calculator, while some were so detailed you could even see the spots on his forehead.

'W-w-wit's gawn oan here,' Ped stammered. 'Are you really Santa? Huv you been watching me tae see if ah've been good or no? Is that wit's happenin here?' This was the only explanation Ped could think of, as mental as it sounded.

'Santa?' the man laughed, running his hands over the wall and carefully unpinning what looked like a polaroid picture. He handed it to Ped who examined the picture. As he did, what little colour remained in his face drained away. It was Ped's first scan picture.

'Ped, it's me. Yer da.'

EXTREME POLLS

EXTREME POLLS @extremepolls Jun 11
£15,000 straight into your bank account and then again on Jan 1st
every year for the rest of your life BUT you have to passionately defend
Adolf Hitler's actions to everyone who brings him up to you in any
situation, in private or in public.

Take it
Leave it

Saima swithered over this dilemma put to her by a new
account she'd followed on Twitter. She read the question out
to her colleague sitting across from her.

'Take it,' said Asim. 'Take it in a heartbeat. How often does
someone bring Hitler up in conversation really? Easy money.
I could just explain the situation to you and you could tell folk
I was just having a laugh. Just playing "devil's advocate" as
arseholes like to say.'

Saima thought about this. Asim's logic was sound enough,
but surely there would be tough enforcement of this offer from
whoever made it happen.

'I'm gonnae say no,' she said, clicking the no button.

'Shitebag,' Asim sneered and put on his headphones.

Saima had clicked NO on most of the so-called 'extreme
polls' and was stunned at how many people would take the
money in the given scenarios. She had a wee scroll through
the rest of the polls to see the ones from the last few days.

EXTREME POLLS @extremepolls Jun 9
£300k, tax free, deposited into your bank account in exchange for not showering, brushing your teeth or trimming your finger and toenails for 6 months.

Take it
Leave it

EXTREME POLLS @extremepolls Jun 7
£1,000 cash delivered through your letterbox every day that you say/ do something nasty/spiteful to at least 3 different people

Take it
Leave it

Then a particularly surreal one caught her eye.

EXTREME POLLS @extremepolls Jun 2
£1million is deposited into your bank account after you and your dog have switched bodies for a week.

Take it
Leave it

This initial offer was followed up with some clarification of what would the week would entail:

You'll have all your mental capabilities but be inside your dog's body. You won't be able to talk or explain the situation to anyone. Your dog (inside your body) will be able to go outside. After a week you'll go back into your own body and any physical damage suffered to either party will be reversed (excluding death).

'What about this one, Asim,' Saima asked, but he was deep in concentration, actually doing some work. Saima imagined what would happen if her and her American bulldog, Esther, switched bodies. Would be a laugh, she supposed. *Aye, fuck it, give me the money*, she thought, and clicked the take it option. She wasn't surprised to see that she was in the majority. 65% of those who'd responded to the poll were up for doing the body swap with their dog. The other 35% were shitebags, as Asim would say.

Saima sent a message in the work group chat telling people about the account. Soon enough, it was practically all they spoke about on their breaks.

'Six grand but you need to commit an armed robbery in a newsagents and steal only chocolate but there's only an 85% chance you'll get away with it – take it or leave it?' Asim asked at the table in the staff room, reading from his phone.

'Take it.'

'Take it.'

'Take it.'

'Take it.'

'Hmmm,' Saima said. 'I'd leave that. Armed robbery would get you like fifteen/twenty years in the jail. Not worth the risk for only £6k and some chocolate. Plus you'd scar the poor shop worker for life.'

'Shitebag,' announced Asim loudly.

'Right then,' Saima laughed, seeing a new extreme poll on her phone. 'A million quid to live life as a slug for a year.'

Asim thought about this, turning the corners of his mouth downwards. 'Nah, I'd leave that, definitely.'

'Think that makes you a shitebag as well then, eh?'

* * *

After a couple of days, the novelty of the account appeared to have worn off. No one was talking about it anymore. But for Saima, it was practically all she could think about.

'What about this one, Asim,' she said, but she looked over the computer and he was, once again, working, with his headphones pumping Wu Tang Clan right into his cranium.

The office junior sat across from Saima, staring blankly at his phone. Bored out his nut. No one really spoke to him though, and he kept himself to himself. He seemed to hate his job, and his colleagues even more.

'Wee man,' Saima said, sidling over to his desk. 'You use Twitter?'

'Eh, aye,' Stu looked confused. People had gave up trying to talk to him months ago. Why was the weird lassie trying to talk to him suddenly? 'How come?'

'You seen this account?' Saima showed him the extreme polls page on her phone.

'Aw no way!' Stu laughed. This was the first time Saima had even seen him smile, let alone laugh. 'I run that account! How'd you find it?'

'Just came across it, Asim likes it as well. It's sooo funny. You've got a really weird sense of humour.'

'Aye, well, eh…' Stu was blushing.

'So this is what you're doing when you're meant to be working, eh?'

Stu panicked. 'Naw, eh, I don't really use it at work, I mean, sometimes, but, eh….'

'I'm only kidding you on. You should do some more. Keep it going. Everyone really likes it. But you should change it up a wee bit.'

'How'd you mean?'

'Well people will do anything for a big wad of money. You should offer smaller amounts in exchange for things that only last like a day. That would be harder to decide on.'

'Aye, maybe yer right. I'll try that.'

* * *

9:30am

Stu didn't show up for work the next day. Didn't phone in sick, email or anything; he just didn't go to work.

'You know it's him who runs extreme polls?' Saima said to Asim.

'Ha! No chance!' Asim bellowed. Saima got a big waft of tuna. 'Never in a million years is that wee guy clever *or* funny enough to be behind that account.'

'Did you have a tuna baguette from Greggs this morning by any chance? I'm sure you told me you didn't like tuna?'

'I've no ate tuna since I was a wee guy. Even the smell gives me the boak. How come?'

Saima sniffed the air. 'I can definitely smell tuna, mate. It's coming from you.'

Asim's face fell. He looked down at his phone then laughed and shook his head. 'Nah, surely not,' he said. His face fell once again. Saima could see he was deep in thought.

'What is it?' she asked.

Asim read out a tweet from his phone. '*£50 to spend the entire work day with your breath stinking of tuna.*'

'What the fuck,' said Saima, wild-eyed.

'That'll just be a coincidence, eh? I've not eaten any tuna though. Wait, hang on… you're at it, int ye?'

Saima laughed. 'I swear to God, Asim, your breath is honking.'

'Nah, you're winding me up,' Asim breathed into his hand and lifted it quickly to his nose. He could definitely smell tuna.

From the women's toilets came a scream like a gravely wounded animal. A moment later one of their colleagues came out, nonchalantly adjusting her fringe, as if she hadn't just screamed at the top of her lungs. 'Everything alright in there?' someone asked.

'Aw, eh, aye totally fine,' the woman said, going back to her seat, looking confused.

Asim scrolled down the Extreme Polls twitter page again. *'£50 to scream as loud as you can for however long it takes you to do the toilet anytime you go at work today.'*

Saima and Asim looked at each other.

'It's that account,' said Saima. 'Obviously it's all coming true and actually happening.'

'Don't be daft!' Asim said. 'There's no chance, absolutely no chance, that *that* is what's happening here. It's clearly just a mad coincidence or a really big, well-orchestrated bam-up at our expense.'

'I'm going to message Stu and ask him.'

'And say what? Are you causing all these weird things to happen in the office with your daft wee twitter account?'

'Something along those lines, aye.'

Hey Stu,
Noticed you're not at work today, hope you're okay! Some weird stuff is happening in the office and, as stupid as it sounds, it seems to be connected to your Extreme Polls twitter account? Any idea what's happening?

Hi Saima,
For one working day only, Extreme Polls is no longer hypothetical – it's real! There'll be Take it or Leave it questions posted throughout the day. The first person to reply to each question gets the money. It's a great laugh and a great way to make a few quid! All effects will wear off at 5pm and the bank accounts of the participants will be credited with their money at that time as well. It's been good working with you, but I won't be back – I'm going full time with Extreme Polls!

Saima showed Asim the message from Stu.

'He's obviously just still on the randan from last night or something, eh?' said Asim. 'I mean, this can't *actually* be happening...'

* * *

11:15am

A bald man stepped out the lift and waited patiently at reception. He was dressed in a blood-soaked apron and his muscular arms were ripping out of his tight, blood-soaked, t-shirt. By his side he was carrying a metal toolbox. 'I'm here to see Daniel,' the man said.

'Asim, look!' Saima pointed at the terrifying looking man who was now sitting in the waiting area, pulling on a pair of latex gloves. Asim furrowed his brow at the man. 'The last tweet said *£300 to get all your fingernails removed with pliers, take it or leave it?*'

'Daniel!' Asim shouted. 'C'mere a minute, mate.'

Daniel strolled over, fixing his enormous quiff while making nervous glances at the man in the waiting area. 'Who the fuck's that?' he enquired.

'Have you been on that Extreme Polls Twitter thing this morning?' Saima asked him.

'Aye, how come?'

'What was the last tweet from them you seen?'

'Few hundred quid to get your fingernails cut off or something I think. I said aye, obviously.'

'Right, listen, don't panic, but I think that guy's here to pull out your fingernails.'

'Och away and don't talk a lot of shite,' Daniel laughed. 'Naw he's no, he's obviously, just, eh, here to fix something or... something.'

The receptionist pointed over to Daniel. The blood-soaked man thanked her and headed over towards him.

Daniel ducked behind Asim's desk, terrified.

'Awrite, mate?' said Asim, swinging round his chiar and trying to sound as intimidating as he could, accentuating his Glaswegian accent more than usual. 'Can ah help ye?'

'Ahm here tae see Daniel.' The man's accent far more gruff and angry sounding than Asim could ever hope his would ever be. The man could see the top of Daniel's hair sticking out above Asim's desk. His quiff quivering. 'Ahm here tae pull oot his nails.' He heaved his metal toolbox onto Asim's desk and it landed with such a thud that it made the three of them flinch. He opened it and selected the rustiest pair of pliers he had in there.

'Hold on a minute,' Saima pleaded. 'Surely you can't just walk in here and rip out someone's fingernails?'

'Look, hen,' the man sighed. 'Ahm joost tryin ae dae mah joab.' The man walked round Asim's desk and grabbed Daniel by the neck of his shirt. 'Let's get this done wi, pal. Ahm oan a tight schedule.'

'Please, naw, HELP ME!' Daniel shouted. Everyone else in the office hardly batted an eyelid.

'You're getting £300, mate,' laughed Daniel's deskmate, the equally quiffy Flynn. 'Fucking man up.'

'Nah, I'm not having this,' Asim said, squaring up to the man. 'You can't just do this to him. I don't care who you are or who sent you but, I'm sorry, you're not ripping out my colleague's fingernails.' Asim grabbed Daniel's arm and tried to pull him away but the man just tightened his grip.

'Ah get a good wage fur this joab,' the man seethed quietly into Asim's ear. 'But ah'd gladly dae it fur hee haw if it meant getting tae dae a number oan wee up-starts like you.'

Asim gulped, let go of Daniel, and slinked back to his desk.

'What did he say?' asked Saima.

Asim was too shaken to reply.

* * *

11:45am

After watching poor Daniel have all ten of his fingernails removed, Saima and Asim tried to spread the word about the Extreme Polls account and what was happening. People didn't seem to care though.

'Well, we're getting paid *and* the effects get reversed in a couple of hours? Sounds good to me,' said their boss, Lesley.

'Aye, but Lesley look at poor Daniel,' said Saima. Daniel was sitting at his desk with a big petted lip as he tried to re-attach his bloody nails using blu-tac.

Lesley waved her foot dismissively. She'd agreed to swap her hands for feet for the rest of the working day in exchange for £150.

'Och, he'll be fine. Now get on with your work, you two.'

* * *

12:35pm

Saima and Asim decided to do just that. They both stuck in their headphones and did their best to block out the increasingly bizarre and surreal goings on around them.

Until they started to get hungry.

Asim slipped off his headphones and asked Saima if she fancied heading to the staff room for their break.

'Right, I'm ready this time,' said the oldest woman in the office, Flo, to the man dressed as a goalkeeper at the other side of the staff room. He was holding a tub of her favourite stuffed olives from Tesco.

Saima held her head in her hands. 'Flo, what's happening here? Not you as well?'

'Fifty quid!' Flo laughed. 'For this big handsome fella to volley everything I eat for the rest of the day full force into my mouth. This wee game is just great!'

The goalie threw a single olive in the air. As it dropped,

he swung his left foot at it, catching it perfectly, and sent it hurtling towards Flo's gaping mouth.

She coughed and spluttered as the olive hit the back of her throat.

'Let's just go to that café down the road,' sighed Asim.

***

2:00pm

'Can you smell petrol?' Saima asked Asim.

'Aye,' he replied. 'Aye, where's that coming from? What if someone's burning down the building or something?'

'I don't even want to check twitter to see, to be honest.'

'It's me,' Flynn put his hand up. '£75 to have B.O that smells like petrol. Seemed like a good deal but this is my best shirt. It's probably ruined now.'

***

2:15pm

A single Quality Street chocolate went flying past Asim's shoulder. 'Sorry, mate!' shouted the goalie.

'Could she not just stop eating... AH, FOR FUCK SAKE!' said Saima as another chocolate hit her on the back of her head.

'AW FUCK!' shouted Asim. 'AW FUCK FUCK FUCK FUCK!'

'You get hit as well?' asked Saima.

'No, I just accidentally clicked 'take it' on one of the polls.'

'Shit. What did it say?'

'Well on the plus side, I'm getting a grand, but the downside is I have to let a four year old wee lassie cut my hair.'

Saima tried to stifle a laugh. This was her favourite one of the day. Asim was incredibly proud of his shiny shoulder-length hair which he lovingly described as "luxurious".

***

3:00pm

The lift doors open and out stepped an angelic looking wee girl, wearing a pair of dungarees and brandishing, not only a gap-toothed smile, but a pair of almost comically oversized scissors. She went over to reception, thanked the receptionist and headed over to Asim.

'Asim,' she said softly, working the scissors back and forth so they made a menacing scything noise.

'Ah shit,' he said. 'Ah well, I'll be a grand up after this. Maybe she'll do a good job.'

The wee girl did not do a good job. She chopped away happily at the hair on the top of Asim's head, leaving him with a hairstyle which looked a lot like Sven-Goran Eriksson's would after he'd spent a year or so in the wilderness.

***

4:00pm

Tea break time for Saima and Asim. The office was now filled with flies, as Maureen from accounting agreed to have a cloud of the insects follow her around for the rest of the day in exchange for £30. She said she was skint and choking for a big Chinese takeaway.

Sealing themselves away from the flies, Saima just laughed at the sheer absurdity of this day.

'How is this all real?' Asim said, looking out through the glass at the office. Lesley fumbled to answer her phone with feet-hands. Flynn sniffed at his armpits and winced. Flo ducked for cover as the goalie teed up to punt a tangerine at her. Daniel was still greeting over his lost fingernails. He couldn't get them to stick back on with anything so he just painted some pretend nails on the end of his fingers with tip-ex. The flies hovered over the whole scene like a deathly veil. A menagerie of strangers mingled among everyone, dishing out waxings, tankings, lapdances and a host of other demeaning acts. All of it punctuated on occasion by the screaming shitter in the toilet.

'What if this all doesn't go back to normal?' asked Saima. 'What if this is all permanent. I mean, at least your hair will grow back, but poor Lesley with her feet for hands and Flo – what if that goalkeeper guy ends up killing her!'

'We'll just have to wait and see what happens at 5pm, eh? Check our banks and stuff.'

'Aye, true enough. Not much we can do until then except wait.'

Asim sipped at his coffee. 'At least you're okay. You never clicked Take it on anything, did you?'

Saima shrugged. 'I might have said aye to one out of curiosity.'

'What one? Tell me.'

'You'll see when it gets to five o'clock I suppose.'

***

4:59pm
Everyone sat waiting at their desks, watching the clock tick towards 5pm, signalling the end of this ordeal. Everyone in the office had their internet banking open, waiting to see their winnings drop into their accounts.

'...7...6...5...' said Lesley, counting down, clapping her feet together after each number. '...4...3...2...1...'

In an instant, the office was back to normal. No flies, no goalkeeper, no foot-handed boss, and Daniel even had his fingernails back. Asim's hair didn't instantly grow back but he got a message on Twitter from Stu saying he was sorry and he'd give him an extra tenner for the hassle. 'Ah well, fair enough,' shrugged Asim. 'So what's the script with your one, Saima hen?'

'It was an old one I clicked on,' she said. 'It must no have worked.'

'The money's in!' shouted Lesley.

'The money's in my account as well,' said Saima. 'Fucking hell, fifteen grand!'

'No way. And you're no even disfigured or anything. Well done, pal.'

Daniel came over to join the conversation. 'Yous fancy going to the pub? I need a pint after all this carry on today. The cunt who runs that account is worse than fucking Hitler.'

Saima clasped a hand over her mouth to stop her from blurting out what she was about to say but it was no good, the words came out anyway. 'Nah,' she said, 'Hitler was spot on.'

SAMMY GETS A JOB

That's it, man. Game over. Nae mair sittin aboot aw day, watchin films an that; ah need tae get a joab. It's mah maw that's been oan mah case aboot it. Ahm no really wantin a joab but ah suppose, really, it's time ah did suhin wi mah life. Ah mean, don't get me wrang, there's nuhin, absolutely nuhin, that ah like mair than sittin aboot. Playin the computer, watchin films, slaggin cunts in the group chat an no leavin the hoose fur days oan end – that's the life fur me.

* * *

Ah've never really seen masel as the kinda guy who goes oot tae work. Mah maw an mah granny an granda an that, they're aw mad grafters, workin fuckin mental hours every day man – fuck that fur a carry oan. It's no fur me.

'Ye need tae start payin me dig money, Sammy,' mah maw's been sayin. Mah wee pal, Ped, has had a similar talk aff his maw as well. Fuckin maws, eh?

* * *

So ah hunted oanline fur a joab, an found wan in a this mad factory that makes sausages. It's a sausage factory in mair than wan way seein as it's full ae fuckin guys. When ah wis at the interview, the boss cunt wis like that, 'We're looking for grafters here, pal. Do you fit into that category?'

'Fuck aye,' ah said, lyin right through mah teeth. 'Ah graft like fuck.'

He laughed at that. Don't hink he wis expectin me tae swear in mah interview.

'You know something,' the boss cunt said, getting up fae behind his desk. 'I like you, Samuel.'

'Eh, it's Sammy.'

'Sammy, of course. Welcome aboard, pal,' the cunt shook mah hawn. 'You're going to do well here. I can tell.'

* * *

Dae well? Dae fuckin well? Let me tell ye – this place is a fuckin shitehole. See, tae start wi, ye get put in this mad room, scoopin this horrible pink liquid oot ae a vat an flinging it intae some machine, using a big bucket. Fuckin ten hours a day, five days a week. Just sloshing this mad pink watter aboot. It's rank as fuck.

'Here, mate,' ah said tae the boss cunt wan day. 'When can ah move oantae suhin else? Can ah work oan the production line or suhin?'

'Patience, Samuel,' he said, wi a mad smarmy smile. 'Soon we'll move you onto the production line. For now, you need to gain an understanding of working in the vat room.'

Gain an understanding? Wit a load ae shite. Wit dae ah need tae understawn that ah didnae learn in mah first five minutes scoopin up liquidised pig in a bucket? Fuckin idiots, man.

Three weeks ah've been in this fuckin room, masel, ah should add. In here, covered in pig juice, masel, like some kind ae freakshow bastard. Feel like a serial killer or suhin. Ah feel like it's makin me a wee bit unhinged.

But there's suhin else that's annoyin me big time here in this fuckin factory. See cause the place is just full ae guys, the toilets are boggin. The boss cunt's too tight tae hire a cleaner, even though the place is makin a fortune apparently.

'Capitalism,' wan ae mah colleagues said wance.

'Eh?' ah replied.

'Capitalism, man. The cold hand of capitalism.'

'Aye, awrite nae bother, mate,' ah said an walked away. The guy's a weirdo. Pure intae aw this mad Russian stuff.

But the toilets urnae joost bogging; they don't have any seats. Ah eat mah Weetabix every mornin, right, an ah need tae shite when ahm oan the go. The sign ae a healthy system, mah granny says. But ah cannae shite here if they've nae seats oan their pans – it's fuckin inhumane.

The day, ahm in mah wee room, joost me an mah bucket. Naw, ah know wit yer hinkin, ahm no gonnae shite in mah bucket, don't be daft. Ah desperate fur a shite but ahm no that desperate. Well, ah um desperate enough that ahm considerin how ahm gonnae manage tae shite in a pan wi nae seat. Ah could sit oan the rim ae the pan but that'll be dead cauld, plus ah'll probably catch E-coli or suhin aff it.

Ah dive intae the toilet, passin by the boss cunt oan the way.

'Samuel, how you getting on today, pal?'

'Nae time ae talk, mate. Ahm touchin cloth here.'

Ahm in the cubicle noo, unbuttonin mah troosers an starin at the pan. Ah don't how the other guys in here dae shites but it's obviously wi great difficulty cos there's fuckin shite oan the floor an up the walls an everyhing. Everywhere but in the pan basically. It's like that toilet in *Trainspotting*. Ah've goat mah troosers an drawers roon mah ankles noo an ahm aboot tae try an attempt tae manoeuvre intae position and sortae hover over the pan. But then ah hink tae masel, Ye know wit? Nae fuckin joab is worth this. Ah pull mah troosers an that back up and storm oot the toilet an head hame.

'Samuel!' the boss cunt shouts efter me. 'Where do you think you're going? You can't just walk out mid-shift!'

'Look, mate,' ah shout back. 'Ahm no squattin fur nae cunt!' an ah head up the road. Ah'll joost go oan the brew an see wit happens.

THE MOTH

Being a moth, I am driven by an insatiable need to fly into a human being's ear canal, burrow through the soft tissue and bone inside and take control of their brain. If done successfully, I could live undetected as a human for around eighty years. The host's friends and family would have no idea their loved one, a person they may have known their entire lives, is actually being operated from within by a humble house moth.

It is a dangerous operation. Only a small number of moths in recorded history have achieved it. But I am confident I can join their ranks. I have spent weeks studying my chosen host. He is a behemoth of a man with a penchant for alcohol. Fond of getting extremely inebriated, almost to the point of unconsciousness and with fat, stumpy fingers that will barely fit in his ear, he shouldn't put up too much of a fight as I eat my way into his mind. And today is the day I make my move.

Big Gordon, as his friends call him, has been getting as drunk as humanly possible out in the baking hot sun all day and is bound to collapse at any moment. I will wait for him to enter a deep sleep and then, when he no longer possesses the dexterity to stop me, I will fly into his left ear.

I am clinging to the wall of what is soon to be my new home. Camouflaged against the exposed brickwork, I am invisible to the pigeons pecking around the garden. I watch Big Gordon rise from his sun lounger, his sudden movement scaring away the winged vermin that like to prey upon my species.

The delicate skin on his face has been burned red raw by the sun. It looks painful and I am not particularly looking forward to dealing with the skin peeling from my nice new face. He lumbers forward a few steps before stopping and swaying side to side with such grace I am practically hypnotised by his movements. He rocks backwards and forwards on his feet, then falls face first with a dull thud into the grass. He has surely broken his nose but shows no sign of being in any pain.

Watching this human put his body through so much punishment, I can't help but feel I am doing him a favour by taking control. It won't be long until he is out of his misery.

With the pigeons having fled and my host rendered unconscious by his fall, it is time to fulfil my plan. I swoop down from my vantage point and land on Big Gordon's soft, fleshy cheek. All he will feel, if anything, is the soft flutter of my wings and a gentle tickling from my feet.

Most moths favour the divebomb technique: hurtling into the ear at great speed to lodge themselves deep in the aural cavity. I have observed many using this technique and found it causes humans to panic and plunge their fingers in after them, mashing them to a pulp. A more delicate approach is required, if you ask me.

I feel around the opening to his ear using my front legs. I am astounded by the beauty of the flowing curves and ridges of the cartilage, like ripples on a lake. I tuck in my wings and move through the canal. The urge to charge in is a difficult one to resist. I compose myself though: I have a long way to go.

I squeeze my head into the dark tunnel. Tiny, oily hairs tickle my soft underbelly as I slide along – not a totally unpleasant sensation. His snoring creates a deep, thunderous rumble and I can feel his entire head vibrating. Air rushes in and out underneath me. I am enveloped by warmth and the darkness sharpens my senses. A sharp metallic smell suddenly overloads my antennae. I flick my tongue out slowly, wincing in anticipation of the bitter taste of his ear wax. I must suck up the foul matter as I continue to push forward. The wax coats my entire body. My wings are slick with grease. A special gland in my mouth goes into overdrive as I swallow as much of the wax as I can, turning it into an acid which will be used to soften the bone of Big Gordon's skull, allowing me to dig my way into his brain.

But before I start the arduous task of digging through seven millimetres of solid bone, I have to burst through the ear drum. I caress the paper-thin structure, feeling its tautness. I have to get through it quickly or the scratching of my mandibles will awaken even my inebriated host. I slice open the membrane and force my way through into his inner ear.

This is often where things go wrong. On the other side of the ear drum is the eustachian tube, a deep chasm which leads to the mouth and almost certain death. To prevent this fate occurring, you have to deftly manoeuvre your way around the edges of this pit. My chosen technique is to stick my feet into clumps of ear wax, giving me extra grip. By doing this I can edge my way around the abyss and latch on to the cochlea at the other side. This method was used by a successful house moth, who went on to become become the world's foremost lepidopterist.

My host remains lying on the ground, undisturbed by the goings on inside his head. I am very excited at the thought of the rest I am going to enjoy when I fuse with his brain and take full control. I may sleep for a fortnight.

The cochlea is an especially strange organ in the human body, which in itself is essentially a big bag of strange organs. Comprised of a bony maze filled with chambers of air and fluid, its purpose is, as yet, unknown to us moths. It is here I use my bone-dissolving acid. I roll out my tongue and I can feel the hot, caustic liquid surging forward to the tip. It erupts in a furious jet which I aim at the centre of the cochlea.

I dissolve the brittle bone wall and a stream of fluid washes over me. I wait until the flow subsides before entering the first chamber. As my feet feel around the moist floor of the chamber, I pick up a soft vibration.

Big Gordon is waking up.

His normally deep voice has risen several octaves with fear. The cochlear liquid is rushing back in behind me. He is attempting to get to his feet. The hot sensation of the acid dissolving this delicate part of his ear must have put his body into panic mode. He will be fully awake in moments and will feel me wriggling through his head, causing him to panic further.

This is not good.

My host wants me out. He is now upright, his brain frantically sending signals to get Big Gordon to jam a finger into his ear. As he does this, the increased pressure forces me deeper into the cochlea, helping me move forward. Aural juice sloshes around. Acid is spraying forth from my tongue and I scratch at the membranes and bony walls with all of my might. My legs, laden with wax, prise apart the melting bone. I break through the cochlea. I have reached the skull.

I can feel Big Gordon slapping at his ear. He is screaming, forcing any object he can find into his ear, but I am well out of reach. Nothing can stop me now. I latch onto his skull. Some wax remains stuck my feet and I use this to grip to the smooth surface. I unfurl my tongue and concentrate the stream of acid on the one spot. It burns its way through, eroding the dense bone away. The hole widens under my feet.

Deeper it goes.

Deeper.

Deeper.

Deeper.

I can feel the wrinkled surface of his brain.

I'm in.

Big Gordon falls to the ground once again.

I burrow into his mind. Moths and humans are made to merge with one another, our planet's two most intelligent species coming together to create a perfect hybrid being. Big Gordon's memories play out before me, intertwined with my own. My superior consciousness submerges his and I take control.

HAWNS

'Here, pal,' the woman sitting herself in the corner of the pub shouts to you. 'C'mere a minute.'

You give her a polite nod and a smile and look back down at your phone. You angle yourself away from her a wee bit. She looks...weird. Skinny, in a black and white stripey top. Lank, greasy hair. She's middle-aged, maybe a wee bit older. A wee bit twitchy.

'Can ye no hear me?'

You stare at your phone, hoping if you avoid eye contact she'll get bored and just leave you alone.

The barman is away to change the barrel. For now, it's just you and this weird old wifey.

'Suit yerself. Fuckin ignoramus.'

You look over at her after a couple of minutes of silence. She has her hands under the table, resting on her thighs. She has a pint sitting in front of her. A pint that she's leaning forward and drinking through a straw.

She catches you looking at her, and sups down her pint, keeping eye contact with you.

'Goat yer attention noo, eh? C'mere,' she nods at the empty seat directly in front of her.

You look around the pub. It's still only you two.

What have you got to lose from going over to talk to this woman? Nothing, really. She's probably harmless. If anything, you'll get a good wee story out of it to tell your pals. Maybe you could tweet about it later on. That would get some good numbers.

You walk over to her table. You extend a hand for her to shake before you sit down but she doesn't reciprocate.

'Ahm gonnae tell you a story.'

This is going to be good, you think.

'Couple ae years ago, there wis this team ae surgeons. Scottish they wur. They wurnae joost the best in Scotland; they wur the best in the world. Transplants wis their hing. They could dae anyhin. Livers, hearts, lungs, kidneys. Some say they wur gearin up tae dae full HEID transplant in the near future.

'But see these surgeons? Ye know the phrase "work hard, play harder"? These cunts wur the very definition ae that. They worked as a team. Five ae thum. Three boays and two lassies. They'd take it in turns, helpin each other oot in the theatre. "You hawd that an ah'll get that bit", "You grab that, ah'll attach that then she cin sew it aw the gither", that kind ae hing. They hud this… understandin wi each other. Like fitbaw players ah suppose, guys that have played the gither fur years an years, oan the pitch they know exactly where the other cunts will be withoot even lookin. They could dae anyhin these surgeons.'

You hear the sound of typing on a computer keyboard. The barman has appeared behind the bar once again. He has his laptop out.

'Here, you listenin?'

You turn back round to face the woman. 'Aye, sorry.'

She leans forward and takes another long drag from her pint and finishes it. She whistles at the barman the way a farmer would whistle at a sheepdog.

'Aye, so. These surgeons. Best in the world at surgery. But they wur the best in the world at boozing, shaggin, sniffin gear an poppin pills anaw. They wur paid a fortune, as ye cin imagine, an fuck me, these basturts knew how tae spend it. They wurr oot *awwww* the time. Naebody at the hospital minded though. These surgeons could hawndle it nae bother at aw.'

The barman plonks another pint down in front of her. He takes the straw from the empty glass and slips into the new one.

'There ye go, Tracy.'

The woman doesn't acknowledge him and continues her story.

'This team ae surgeons wis due tae perform this pioneering bit ae surgery; Scotland's first ever double hawn transplant.'

You lean in closer. A double hand transplant? Surely not. You've heard about thumbs and fingers being reattached after grisly accidents but an entire hand? *TWO* entire hands? No chance.

'A double hand transplant?' you ask.

'Aye,' she says. Taking a sip from her fresh pint.

'As in not re-attaching someone's own hands after an accident or something. Attaching hands... from a donor?'

'Aye that's wit ah said.'

'I didn't know that was a thing.'

'Aw aye. It's a hing awrite. It's kind ae common noo but these surgeons were gonnae be the first people in Scotland tae even attempt it. It wid be good practice, they said, fur when they eventually done the heid transplant. Anywey, the night afore they wur due tae dae the transplant, you know wit they done?'

You shake your head. You're on the edge of your seat here.

'They went oot oan the randan of course. That wis thurr tradition. The night afore a big operation they'd go oot fur a few drinks. Always joost a few though. Wis never a fully blown night oot, naw, that came *efter* the surgery. But that night? Well, it happened tae be thurr Christmas night oot. An they wurnae geein that up fur anyhin.'

You zone out for a minute, not listening to her now. It was her. You know it. She knows that you know it. She was who these surgeons were operating on. It was her who got the double hand transplant and the surgeons fucked it up. She doesn't want you to see them. That's why she wouldn't shake your hand. That's why her hands haven't moved from under the table. That's why she's drinking her pint through a fucking straw.

'You listenin ae me?' she snaps. She's caught your eyes drifting downwards, trying your best to see her hands through the wooden table.

'Aye, sorry,' you say.

She looks you up and down. She looks disgusted but carries on undeterred.

'The night afore the operation, the surgeons went wild. They were gettin massive bonuses fur this. Line efter line they hoovered up. Lines ae God knows wit. Knockin back the dearest champagne the bar hud. They wur fucked. The operation didnae kick aff until 12pm the next day so it wis awrite, they thought.

'Wit they didnae realise though wis that they wurnae even gettin hame efter that night. They wid huv tae go straight tae the hospital. Straight intae theatre, cause these greedy basturts joost didnae know when ae say "enough's enough.".'

You can tell from her voice she's getting upset here. Understandably, you think. With a roll of her shoulder, she uses her top to wipe away a tear that's creeping down towards her cheekbone.

'So what happened?' you ask. You know this is clearly a difficult story for her to tell but you need to find out more. She composes herself and carries on.

'That night, the surgeons left the bar they wur in an then went tae a hoose party in Shawlands. Mair booze, mair drugs. Next hing they knew, it wis nine in the mornin. Wan ae thum realised the time an phoned a taxi. Bundled her pals intae it and told the driver tae take thum ae the hospital. They stoapped at a cafe,' she laughs. 'Coffee. As if that wid sober thum up.'

She sucks greedily at her pint. You turn your head to look at the door as she nods towards it. Two burly guys walk in, nod at the woman, and sit at the bar, motioning the barman over to them and engaging in hushed conversation. One of them has a grossly bent-out-of-shape nose.

'When it wis time fur the operation, they wur still paralytic. Fawwin aboot the place. That poor wummin they operated oan,' the woman looks down at her hands. 'She hud nae idea. Put tae sleep afore she could even see the basturts that wurr aboot tae ruin her life.'

'Was it you?' You can't help yourself. The woman looks up at you with a furrowed brow. The men at the bar stop talking.

Then the woman laughs.

'The wummin that they operated oan wisnae me,' she leans over the table and makes intense eye contact with you. So intense that it takes a few seconds for you to realise she's stroking your clasped hands with her fingers.

You pull away in shock and stare at her hands. They slip back under out of sight before you can get a good look at them.

But they look normal, you think. Totally fine.

'It wis me who *done* the operation.' She stares down into her lap. 'We made a cunt ae it.' Another tear falls down her face. 'A right cunt ae it. The operation should've took us upwards ae 11 hours. We rattled through it in less than four. Still hawf cut. Still oot wur faces.' She shakes her head. 'Still cannae believe we thought we could get away wi that.'

'What did you do wrong? What happened?' you ask. You hear one of the men at the bar suck in air through his teeth. The woman takes a breath to compose herself before continuing.

'We thought we'd huv a laugh,' she sighs. Clearly still burdened with the guilt of what she did all those years ago. 'We put the poor lassie's hawns oan the wrang way.'

'The wrong way? Like palms up or something?'

'Mibbe that wid've been worse than wit we did. But wit we done wis still terrible. We stuck the right hawn oan her left airm and the left hawn oan her right airm.'

'Jesus Christ. That… that's terrible.'

'Aw ah know that, pal. Ah know that fine well. But that wis only the start ae the bother.'

You feel yourself leaning in close again. *That* was only the start? Turning up to work, steaming, and putting someone's hands on the wrong way? How much worse can it get?

'See, if it wis yer normal, run ae the mill sepsis victim who'd loast her hawns an then hud new wans transplanted oan the wrang way by a team ae highly trained but also highly drunk surgeons, ye could joost gie them a few quid tae no go ae the papers, a grovelling apology and get them fixed, right?'

You can't believe that doctors could be so callous. You shrug your shoulders. 'I mean, aye, I suppose.'

'Well this wisnae yer average sepsis victim. This wummin wis the burd ae this hardman gangster fae Govan. None ae yer small time Paul Ferris type stuff. This cunt wis international. Fucking Pablo Escobar wi a Rangers season ticket.'

The door to the pub opens again. It's a man and a woman this time. A well turned-out couple. They sit at the bar, a few seats away from the two burly men.

'He wis stawnin there as soon as we wheeled oot his burd. Aw excited tae see her new hawns. He wanted tae stick an engagement ring oan her fur a wee surprise when she woke up. He sees us aw laughin an jokin, huvin a cerry oan, howlin at oor handiwork. He comes flying err as soon as he sees her. He takes wan look at her hawns an clocks straight away that suhin's the matter. Clear as day, thurr oan the wrang way.'

'What did he do?'

'He went apeshit. Started shoutin aboot how he'd huv the best lawyers in the world sortin this oot. Threatenin tae kill us. Callin us every name under the sun. He grabbed wan ae mah colleagues and battered him til he wis black an blue. Took four ae us AND a couple ae nurses tae get him aff.

'He calmed doon eventually. Told us we hud tae fix the mess we'd made there an then.'

'Did you?'

'We said we couldnae. It wid take months tae find another suitable donor. They hawns we'd used awready wid be nae good. They widnae be able tae last through another operation, they'd be in tatters. But this cunt wisnae takin naw fur answer. He told us tae get her ready tae go back in an he'd be back wi a new set ae hawns.'

Under your breath you say, 'Jesus Christ.'

'Ah know, pal. That wis oor reaction anaw. That made us sober up awrite. We kept the wummin under anaesthetic fur a few mair oors until we could figure oot a plan, hopin we could huv it aw sorted afore the guy turned back up again.

'Then he comes stridin intae the operatin theatre, blood oan the collar ae his shirt, cerryin this big ice boax an dumps it mah feet. Ye know wit wis in the boax, eh?'

You nod solemnly.

'The chances ae this guy findin a suitable donor in only a couple ae oors, never mind removing thurr hawns in a way that wid make them viable fur transplant wis probably a million tae wan.

'We wurr like that, "It disnae work like that", tryin ae plead wi the guy. Then he pulls oot a fuckin gun!' She laughs at this. 'Ah hud never seen a gun in real life afore, don't hink any ae us hud. The sight ae that wis enough tae make us comply. So we did it. Another hawn transplant.'

'Fucking hell,' you say. You turn round to the bar to look at the other patrons. They're all looking at you.

'That lassie died afore she came roon fae the anaesthetic. The guy wis distraught. He ran away, actually ran away, roarin an greetin. It wis a shame, it really wis.'

'So then what happened?'

'Nuhin. Fur a long long time. We covered up wit we done. Paid aff the cunts in the mortuary tae say the wummin died oan the operatin table. The shock ae it aw. Wan ae the boays broke her sternum wi a hammer so it looked as if we tried tae resuscitate her.'

Your feel your mouth hanging open.

'The gangster guy never went tae the polis urr the papers urr anyhin. We thought we'd goat away wi it. A fuckin miracle.'

'So did you get away with it?' This is going to go fucking viral when you tweet about it later. Even if it is obviously a wind up.

'We thought we did. Thought we'd goat aff scot-free fur wan ae the biggest atrocities in medicine ever. Until a couple ae year ago that is. Guess wit happened?'

You shrug your shoulders again. 'No idea,' you smirk.

'Gangster cunt turns up at the hospital wan night. The five ae us stawnin in the car park, huvin a laugh efter a hard day at work, an there he comes. Oot the darkness like fuckin Batman. We very near shat ourselves. Two seconds later a Transit van comes screechin intae the car park. The guy slides open the side door an tells us tae get in. We joost aw look at each other. Ah remember ah joost couldnae process wit wis happenin. Ah wis so sure we'd goat away it. Then he gets his gun oot again. "In," he says.'

You raise your eyebrows. Guns? Gangsters? Hand transplants? This is wild.

'We aw bundle in. Nae clue wit's gonnae happen next. We wurr drivin aboot fur ages, eh?' she shouts over your shoulder.

You spin your head round and one of the men sitting at the bar is looking at you. 'Aye, that's right,' he says. Now everybody at the bar is looking at you.

Panic stations now. This is weird. You turn back round.

'He took us tae a pub, joost like this.' The woman looks around the room. Then you hear the noise of keys jangling. The barman locks the door.

'He made mah colleagues dae this tae me at gunpoint in the cellar ae a fuckin pub.' The woman lays her hands flat on the table. At the end of her left arm is a very clear right hand. At the end of her right arm is a very clear left hand. Her thumbs point out the way. Her two pinkies meet in the middle.

You almost fall off your chair at the sight of this. Angry, pink scar tissue zig zags across her wrists.

'Ah've been wantin tae get these fixed fur a while noo.' She drums her fingers on the table. 'Ah've goat the people that can dae it fur me.' You hear the sound of wooden stools shuffling on the wooden floor. The three men and the woman who came in earlier come over to your table and loom over you. 'Aw ah've been waitin fur is a donor.'

You can't even say anything.

'Ah'll never furget your face, hen.' She smiles at the other woman. 'Greetin as ye put that anaesthetic mask oan me, tellin me it was aw gonnae be awrite. Retribution wis the word he used. That's the last word ah cin mind afore a went under. Well, the day ah get *mah* retribution.'

'It won't work,' you say. 'Surely? I mean how do you know I'm even a match?'

'We work in a hospital, pal. Well, ah mean, ah don't, no anymerr. Cannae dae much wi yer hawns oan the wrang wey cin ye?' the woman laughs. 'We've goat aw yer records. You're a perfect match, pal.'

'Please,' you sob. 'You can't do this to me.'

The team of surgeons grab you.

THE BIGGEST RIDDY

Riddy – *adj;* (Scots): To have one's face turn bright red as a result of being embarrassed by someone or something i.e. *'Haha, she's hit a pure riddy'.*

'Ladies and gentlemen! I'm your host, Mason Maverick. It's Saturday night so what does that mean it's time for?!'

The audience reply in unison: *'THE BIGGEST RIDDY!'*

'Yes, that's right, folks; it's time to play *The Biggest Riddy*! Tonight, we have another lucky couple who will compete to win our jackpot prize of an extra month's worth of rations!'

The audience once again react in unison with applause and a chorus of almost patronising *'oooooohs'*. They are all dressed incredibly decadently.

'Please welcome to the floor, Danielle and Kenny!'

The crowd goes wild, clapping and shouting words of encouragement as we see a scared looking couple emerge from a set of double doors, clutching each other, surrounded by smoke. Danielle tries to stop her bottom lip from quivering as Kenny pats her head and tells her, 'It's gonnae be okay.' Their clothes are dirty and ragged, Danielle's hair is greasy and lank, while Kenny's face is covered in scabs.

'So, Danielle and Kenny,' Mason Maverick says. He's wearing a navy and red pin-stripe suit with a pair of brown platform brogues. His tie is made of leather. 'You two will be competing tonight for our grand prize of an extra month's worth of rations. Just *how* much do you need this prize?'

Danielle sobs and buries her face into Kenny's chest. 'W-w-we need this a lot. We've just had a baby.'

'*Awwww*,' the audience coos.

'A little baby, being raised out there in the desolate waste-lands. It's a real shame isn't it, ladies and gentlemen?' Mason Maverick says; it sounds sincere but as Kenny shuts his eyes and pulls his partner closer, he makes a gesture with his hand and rolls his eyes at the couple. The audience tries to stifle their laughter.

'So in order to feed your new little baby, you're going to be completing a series of challenges. Do you know what those challenges are?' Mason asks the contestants.

Kenny shakes his head in reply. He looks terrified.

'No, of course you don't! You don't have tellies out there do you?'

The audience laughs heartily at this.

'So, here's how *The Biggest Riddy* works. You will each be hooked up to the Riddy-o-meter which will access all of your memories, even your most private and intimate ones. And of course.' Mason Maverick turns to the audience. 'Your most embrassing!' He sort of sings the word 'embarrassing' and the audience gasps in delight.

'Now, we won't be showing our *lovely* audience anything you two have been up to *out there*. Goodness knows we've seen enough of you savages, um, I mean, people, indulging in a spot of cannibalism.' The audience covers their mouths, trying to not to laugh again. 'Oopsy,' Mason Maverick laughs. 'A wee slip of tongue there.'

Kenny and Danielle hang their heads in shame.

'Anyway, it's okay, it's okay.' Mason Maverick pretends to hug the couple but is careful not to actually touch them; he just puts his arms around them and doesn't even try to hide the disgust showing on his face. 'We'll be accessing your memories from *before* the Event. To win, you just have to allow us to show more and more embarrassing memories from your past. Memories which could affect your relationship with each other.'

The audience squeals in excitement.

'And, if you agree to show us, and, crucially, show *each other*, your absolute worst, most embarrassing memory then you will win tonight's jackpot prize!'

A door slides back on the main stage area revealing a glamourous blonde woman gesturing at an old tattered box full of miscellaneous food in plain grey packaging.

The audience sarcastically *ooooooooohs*.

'Just remember,' Kenny whispers into Danielle's ear, 'that's what we're doing it for.' He points at the rations. 'For the baby.'

Danielle nods solemnly and wipes away a tear.

'Kenny and Danielle, you desperately need this food,' Mason Maverick shouts. 'So are you ready to play... *THE BIGGEST RIDDY*?!'

The crowd cheers once again.

Kenny and Danielle are led over to the main stage area as two chairs are put into place. The Riddy-o-meter sits in between the chairs. They embrace one last time before taking their seats.

The applause and cheering from the audience subsides along with the theme music of the show.

'Our first round,' says Mason as he places a smooth grey helmet, covered in LED lights, onto each of the contestant's heads, 'involves some pretty tame memories. The computer will select something fairly innocuous from your childhood and display it on the big screen behind us. You simply both have to hit a riddy to progress to the next round. You understand?'

'Aye,' says Kenny, quietly.

'Good,' Mason laughs. 'We know you people from *out there* aren't the brightest, don't we, folks!'

The audience laughs.

'Okay, Kenny you're up first.' Mason footers around with the Riddy-o-meter. 'Oh this is good, this is really good.' Mason pulls a small piece of card from a slot on the back of the machine and reads it aloud to the audience, 'Kenny, this is from when you were five years old, d'aaawww. And you were in a shop with your mum. Let's see what happened...'

The screen is split in two and shows a close-up shot of Kenny's face, tracking how red he goes and the other half shows the world from five year-old Kenny's POV. He looks up at his mum and she looks back at him adoringly. They are walking through a supermarket.

'I just have to get some bits and bobs from here, sweetie,' his mum says. 'Then we'll go and get you a wee comic or something.'

Kenny is led by the hand into the clothing section of the supermarket. Then he and his mum take a turn into the underwear section. Real-life Kenny has a soft glow to his cheeks. He knows what's about to unfold here.

'Oh, there's Phyllis!' Kenny's mum exclaims, and she stops to talk to an older woman, letting go of Kenny's hand. We see him toddling away from his mum, straight towards a display of bras. Kenny looks back to see if his mum or the stranger she's talking to are looking at him; they're not. He turns his head back to the bras. He reaches out a tiny hand and strokes the lacy black cup. He glances back quickly at his mum again before turning round and leaning in to kiss the underwear model on the poster next to the display. The screen goes black. Kenny's face goes crimson.

'Oh, you naughty little boy, Kenny!' Mason Maverick squeals. The audience laughs.

'Now, let's see where you managed to hit on the Riddy-O-Meter.' A Riddy-O-Meter graphic appears on the big screen.

Ding... ding... ding...

'Four out of ten, a very good start, Kenny. Well done.'

There is a soft ripple of applause from the audience. It's Danielle's turn now.

'Okay, Danielle, you just need to match Kenny's score now. Let's see what memory of yours we'll be showing...' Mason retrieves another piece of card from the machine. He laughs a little to himself as he reads it. 'Ah, this is good, and from when you were five as well.' He shows the card to Danielle. The tiniest flicker of a smile crosses her face. 'Let's see what happened...'

The screen is entirely black, as Danielle has her eyes closed. She opens them just slightly and it looks as if she's getting to her feet. She is looking down at her tiny bare feet, her baggy pyjama bottoms swishing around her ankles as she walks down a hallway. She stops outside a door which has been left ajar. In the twilight, we can see a double bed, it must be her parents' bedroom. She pulls her trousers down to her ankles and squats. When she stands back up and looks down, she has left a perfectly-formed shite with a little curly tip. She goes back to bed.

The audience is howling with laughter. 'Think you'll need to explain this, Danielle.' Mason Maverick thrusts his microphone into her face.

'I used to sleepwalk a lot when I was younger.' She is smiling broadly now, looking as if she is remembering other instances when she did similar things. 'I used to shite outside my ma and da's room door all the time. They say it drove them mental but I have no recollection of ever doing it.'

'Have you ever found a wee late night shite deposited where you two live, Kenny?'

He laughs as well. He is looking a bit more relaxed. This game is easy, and actually, a bit of a laugh.

'Naw,' he says. 'But I'll defo be on the lookout from now on!'

The audience erupts with laughter again and Mason clasps a friendly hand on Kenny's shoulder.

'Okay, time for a quick break then we'll be back to find out where Danielle ranked on the Riddy-O-Meter after her late night faecal misadventure and, of course, we'll have more embarrassing memories on *THE BIGGEST RIDDY*!'

The theme music plays once again and the audience claps loudly. The helmets are removed from Kenny and Danielle's heads. Mason pulls a small bottle of hand sanitiser from inside his suit jacket and pours it liberally into his palms after touching Kenny's filthy rags.

'How are you enjoying it so far?' Mason throws the question open to both of them.

'It's not as bad as we'd heard,' says Danielle.

'Aye,' Kenny agrees. 'There's rumours that people get electrocuted and stuff like that on this show. People getting battered as well.'

'Oh, that's all nonsense,' Mason says. 'It's all just a bit of fun, really. It entertains our people here in the city and gives you people the chance to get out of those god-forsaken slums for a wee while and maybe win some extra food. It's a win-win!'

'Standing by,' a camera operator shouts. 'Going back on air in three...two...'

'Hello and welcome back! Before the break we saw Danielle leave a little, shall we say, surprise outside her parent's bedroom door. Now where did that rank on the Riddy-O-Meter? Let's see.'

Ding... Ding.

'Oh dear, Danielle,' Mason says. 'That is such a shame. You only scored two out of ten.'

'What does that mean? W-what happens now?' Danielle asks. The colour has drained from her face.

'Well, we can do two things here,' says Mason. 'We can either send you both home now, empty handed, sadly.' He waits a moment. 'Or, since your memories obviously aren't *that* embarrassing, you can let us probe a little further and show some *proper* riddy inducing stuff. How does that sound?'

Kenny and Danielle exchange nervous looks.

'The baby needs this food,' Danielle says.

'I know,' Kenny looks stressed. His eyes dart around as he looks out at the baying audience.

Mason puts a finger to his ear to better hear what his producer is saying to him.

'It's got to be him,' the voice says. 'She's got fuck all. We've scanned through all her memories. She's boring as fuck. Not even anything good post-Event. Whatever you do, don't let her show any more memories. It would be a ratings disaster.'

'But,' Mason says, walking over to stand between Kenny and Danielle. 'Only one of you can compete in this next round.'

'He's got something juicy. Really fucking juicy,' the voice in Mason's ear says. 'Get that fucking helmet on him at all costs.'

'So who will it be, Kenny and Danielle, you have thirty seconds to decide.'

The lights in the studio dim right down apart from two spotlights on Kenny and Danielle. Mason skulks off into the shadows. The audience holds their breath.

'I can't do it,' Kenny whispers to his girlfriend. 'I can't.'

'It's fine, it's fine. I'll do it. I haven't really got anything to be ashamed of.'

'You sure?'

'Aye, I'm sure. I'll do it.'

'She's wanting to do it,' the producer says to Mason. 'You better think of a way around this, Mason. Pronto.'

'What is it? Wait, have you got something to hide from me?' Danielle asks Kenny.

'Nothing, well it's not nothing, I mean it's nothing major, I suppose but it's just a bit, eh... weird.'

'Weird how? Like sexual weird?'

'Naw, it's nothing like that.'

'Kenny, you're freaking me out here.'

'Look, I'll tell you later.'

'I'm not sure if I want to know.'

'Time's up! So, who's it going to be, folks.' Mason addresses the audience. 'Kenny or Danielle?'

'I'll do it.' Danielle steps forward.

'That's very noble of you, Danielle, but it's actually up to our *audience* to decide.' Mason winks at the audience as if to say "play along". They all turn to one another, smiling knowingly.

Mason puts a finger to his ear again as the voice says. 'You're a fucking genius, mate.'

'...and the audience have chosen...' Mason keeps his finger to his ear as if he's receiving the results of the fake vote. 'KENNY!'

'No. I can't. Please.' Kenny makes a run for it but runs straight into the arms of two burly security guards who grab him and return him to the stage. 'She said she would do it!'

The guards restrain him and strap him into the chair. Danielle stands with her arms folded next to Mason Maverick.

'Talk about throwing you under the bus, eh, Danielle?' Mason laughs as he puts an arm around her. He tries his best to hide the disgust on his face 'I'm sure there's no one in this room, or who's watching at home, who wants to see what Kenny is so reluctant to share, more than Danielle here.'

Danielle chews at her lips. Kenny notices this. It's what she does when she's pissed off at him.

'Please! NOOOOOOO!' Kenny is wailing. Previously unseen straps are pulled from concealed pockets in the chair and fastened around his waist, ankles and wrists. A gag is placed in his mouth.

'Now, Danielle,' Mason says, walking her over next to Kenny. The helmet slides on to Kenny's head. 'Are you ready to see what Kenny was wanting to keep, not only from our audience and viewers, but also, from *you*?'

'I can't wait,' she replies, giving Kenny a death stare.

Mason laughs and walks over to the box.

'The box has now scanned through all of Kenny's memories, folks, and has selected not one, not two, but **THREE** of his absolute most embarrassing incidents to show us!'

The audience cheers.

Danielle is tapping her feet. She can't wait to see what it is the bastard is so desperate to hide from her.

Mason pulls another piece of card from the machine, reads it, then clutches it to his chest.

'Oh, Kenny,' he says. 'Kenny, Kenny, Kenny.'

Kenny thrashes in the chair, struggling against his restraints.

'These memories are going to set a new record on the Riddy-O-Meter, folks!'

The audience is choking to see what Kenny's been up to.

Tears pool in Kenny's eyes.

'Okay first up,' Mason laughs, 'is this clip from when you were thirteen.'

The video starts playing on the big screen. On one half of the screen, Kenny sits with his eyes tightly screwed shut. He knows exactly what this memory is, and doesn't want to see. Thirteen-year-old Kenny is lying on his bed with his laptop open in front of him. His bedroom door is closed and his curtains are shut. A pair of headphones lies next to him. He plugs them into the laptop and puts them over his ears. He types 'pornhub' into his search engine. The screen is pixelated so as to preserve Kenny's modesty. After just over a minute he pulls up his boxers and takes off his headphones. Kenny knows the embarrassing part is about to be revealed. Kenny deletes his browsing history then closes the laptop.

A steaming hot plate of mince and tatties has been placed carefully in front of him.

His bedroom door is wide open.

Caught a belter.

From downstairs, we can hear his maw calling him a 'pervert' to his granny.

'Dearie me, Kenny,' Mason says. 'Now that is a riddy!'

The audience falls into hysterics.

Kenny had told Danielle this story before though. She doesn't look impressed.

Ding...ding...ding...ding...ding...ding...ding...ding.

'Eight out of ten, ladies and gentlemen!'

'Next,' Danielle says, impatiently.

'Danielle has spoken, folks. Roll the next video from when Kenny was nineteen...'

Nineteen-year-old Kenny is at a house party. It looks to be a family gathering of some sorts. We can see from the pictures on the walls that this is Danielle's parents' house. In the studio, Kenny looks upwards as if praying for divine intervention, a power cut or something, to end this excruciating experience.

On the screen, Kenny turns to his left and engages a woman, in her early 50s, in conversation.

'That's my maw,' Danielle says under her breath.

Mason Maverick raises an eyebrow and gives her a creepy smile. 'This is where it gets good.'

'Aye, I mean, me and my pals have been on a few mad holidays,' Kenny says to Danielle's maw. 'There's nothing better, honestly.'

'Aw, tae be young again,' she replies.

'Och, you're no that old, Jacqui. Still plenty of life left in you yet, I bet, eh?'

Jacqui touches him lightly on the arm and laughs. 'Definitely.'

Kenny, filled with the fake bravado provided to him by his fifth Smirnoff Ice, gives a nervous laugh and looks down at his feet. He gingerly takes another sip from the bottle.

'What about T in the Park?' Jacqui asks him. 'Ever been to that?'

'Aw aye.' Kenny reaches for his phone. 'Wait until I show you this picture of my pal, Ped.'

Kenny flicks through the pictures on his phone.

'Hawd oan a minute, wit wis that?' Jacqui grabs the phone off him. She scrolls and taps a couple of time then shoves the screen in Kenny's face.

It's a whole folder filled with pictures of her. Sunbathing out the back garden, getting changed, sitting watching the telly in her jammies, holiday pictures, pictures of her on nights out, and even just making the dinner.

Kenny grabs the phone back off her. 'It's, eh, no what it looks like.'

'Aw aye? Care to explain then?'

The music in the room is loud enough and everybody is drunk enough not to notice what they're talking about.

Jacqui stands up. She leans over Kenny whispers into his ear.

'I'm no wantin tae cause a scene here at my da's birthday, but I'll be tellin Danielle aw aboot this in the mornin. Awrite?'

Kenny spurts out a few incoherent attempts at excuses and apologies but Jacqui tells him to be quiet.

'Enjoy the rest of your night. Wee creep.'

Danielle stands with her head in her hands. 'Take that thing out his mouth,' she says through her fingers to Mason.

'You're telling me what to do?' Mason Maverick laughs. The voice in his ear says to him, 'Do it. This is quality.'

'Let's see what Kenny has to say for himself after *that*, ladies and gentlemen.'

The audience falls into a rapt silence. Mason snaps his fingers and points at Kenny. Straight away, a security guard is over at him, pulling the gag from his mouth.

'Honestly,' he says, slabbers dripping down on to his rags. 'It's nothing weird.'

'My maw told me about this,' Danielle says, walking over to him now. 'I didn't believe her. She's always thought she was God's gift. I thought she'd made it up.'

'Danielle, it's nothing creepy. I'm no like that.'

'Think our audience would disagree with that, Kenny boy,' Mason scoffs. 'And look at that! A perfect 10 on the Riddy-O-Meter, incredible!

'Anyway, we've got one last memory to show then you two can be on your way.'

Kenny sits with his head bowed. Danielle has her back to the camera, her shoulders moving up and down slowly as she cries quietly. Mason has another read of the card with the list and descriptions of Kenny's memories.

'We've saved the best till last, folks. This one is a wee

compilation that builds to crescendo. Strap yourselves in for this, ladies and gentlemen.'

The gag is placed back in Kenny's mouth and the video starts to play. We see, from Kenny's point of view, him and Danielle walking through an animal rehoming centre. He kneels down to get a closer look at a small black Staffy, frantically wagging its tail and pushing itself against the bars of its cage as it attempts to get closer to them.

'Who's this wee belter,' Kenny says to the dug. 'Tyson? Aw you're just perfect.' Tyson licks Kenny's hand.

'He's beautiful,' Danielle coos. 'He's the one.'

The video jumps forward to Kenny opening the front door of his and Danielle's house to be greeted by Tyson. Kenny kneels down to cuddle Tyson who licks him all over his face. The video jumps forward again.

'That's all day he's been in himself,' Danielle says, 'and he's not peed anywhere or chewed anything. He's such a good boy.'

Fast forward again and a picture of suburban happiness fills the screen. Kenny is lying on the couch, Danielle lies on his chest and Tyson is curled up beside them as they watch a scary film.

'I love horror films,' says Danielle. 'You sure you'll be able to sleep tonight after this?'

'Och, it's no even really *that* scary.'

The video jumps forward once again. The screen is pitch black.

'Fuck sake, no again! TYSON!'

'Wit is it, wit's up?' says Kenny, fumbling for the light switch.

'He's pished on the floor again. I just stood right in it. BAD DOG!'

Tyson is lying at the bottom of the bed looking, almost disapprovingly, at Kenny.

'Aye,' says Kenny. 'Eh, you're a bad boy.' And he closes his eyes and the screen goes dark again.

Everyone in the audience is looking confused. 'This isn't

embarrassing,' one woman says to her friend. 'We paid all this money for tickets and *this* is what they serve up?'

'Stick with it, folks,' Mason says, picking up on the confusion from the audience. He knows what's about to happen next – the big reveal.

'Is he gonnae shag the dug?' a man asks his wife.

The screen lights up as Kenny opens his eyes. He's lying in bed. It's just light enough for us to be able to see what he's doing. He looks over at Danielle who is snoring softly beside him. He glances at Tyson who is watching intently. Kenny slowly pulls back the covers, pulls down his boxers, points his penis over the side of the bed pishes on the floor.

The audience gasps in horror.

Kenny puts himself away and snuggles back under the covers beside Danielle and goes back to sleep.

'Aw, eh, Tyson. Look what you've done,' Kenny sighs when he opens his eyes again.

'Has he done it again?' says Danielle. 'How can he produce that amount of pish? He's only a wee dug.'

The camera cuts to Kenny peeing on the floor again and again, in different places in the bedroom and at the top of the stairs. Night after night.

Danielle looks disgusted. The audience is howling.

The video shows Kenny, Danielle and Tyson back in the rehoming centre now.

'We've tried everything to train him, to try and stop him from doing it,' Danielle says to one of the centre's volunteers. 'The flooring in the new house is ruined because of him.'

Kenny hands the lead to the volunteer, puts an arm around Danielle and the two head out the door. Tyson growls at Kenny as he walks away.

'It was you!' Danielle punches and kicks and slaps at Kenny who winces at every blow until she is restrained by security. 'He was the perfect dug! And we had to get rid of him because of you!'

'I just, I was scared. It was all the… all the scary films. I was too scared to go downstairs in the dark.'

The Riddy-O-Meter is *dinging* away as it goes off the charts.

'And let's not forget, Danielle,' Mason laughs. 'He's a peeping Tom who had pictures of your mum on his phone.'

Security drags the screaming Danielle backstage in case she kills Kenny live on the telly.

'Didn't they do well, ladies and gentlemen?!'

The audience is on their feet, clapping.

Kenny slumps in the chair. Mason walks over and removes the helmet.

'What a man you are, Kenny.' Mason shakes Kenny's still restrained hand then wipes his own on his trousers. 'For being such a good sport, you and Danielle will be taking home not one, not two, but THREE boxes of rations!'

Sarcastic *oooooooohs* echo around the studio.

'Right, off you go.' Mason snaps his fingers and two men appear and drag Kenny away to join Danielle.

'Thanks so much for watching, folks. I've been your host, Mason Maverick. Tune in at the same time next week to see even more embarrassing memories on *THE BIGGEST RIDDY!*'

HAIRCUT

'Dunno, man,' Si said to his pal, Hammad. 'Ah mean, it disnae feel right tae be askin fur a haircut like his. Is it no, like, problematic?'

'Nah, no chance,' Hammad replied. 'Know who I showed the barber a picture of fur mah haircut?'

'Who?'

'Joseph Stalin.'

'Is he no an auld guy though?'

'Aye, well he's deid noo, but ah mean his haircut when he wis oor age. He wis cool as fuck.'

Si handed over his phone and showed Hammad the picture of the guy whose haircut he wanted. 'Think he's a worse guy than him then?'

Hammad thought about this for a minute, inspecting the picture. 'Aye, probably. Ah mean, Stalin wis responsible fur like 20 million folk being killed.'

'Did he no personally kill them, naw?'

'Well, ah don't think he pulled the trigger or stabbed any ae thum himself but there's defo blood oan his hawns.'

'See this cunt only killed five people but he killed them himself. Is that worse than wit Stalin did or better?'

'No sure, mate that's a weird wan. Just show the barber an see wit happens. They probably won't say anything.'

'Aye yer right. Fuck it.'

Off Si went to the barbers, buzzing about the prospect of getting a stylish new haircut. He'd wanted this haircut since he was a boy and seen the wearer of it on Crimewatch. It was class. Just a shame it was attached to a guy who killed weans. It would be alright though, he thought. What about all those actors and directors and wife beaters and all that in Hollywood, people still watched their films. "Separating the art from the artist", Si had heard folk say. This was the same, surely? Surely people could appreciate that even evil cunts could have nice hair. It must be a common enough haircut as well. How did this guy get it in the first place?

'Wit ye huvin the day then, pal?' the barber said, fixing the black gown around Si's neck.

'Ah've goat a picture, mate, hing oan.' Si swiped around, looking for the photo of the serial killer's mugshot. 'Him there,' he said cheerfully.

The barber took the phone from Si and inspected it closely, seeing only the guy's hair at first. He'd seen this haircut before but couldn't place where from. Short on the back and sides by the looks of it, he mused to himself. Take it up quite high with a number two maybe. Leave a lot of length on the top, no problem, nice and easy. Blowdry it and use some mousse to give it some volume, make it nice and curly as well.

Si looked on, eyes full of hope, excited about how the barber was going to recreate this style on him. How would it look? Handsome as fuck. No doubt about it.

Then the barber noticed the man in the picture's cold, dead stare.

'Is this… is this Ian Brady?'

'Eh… aye. Is that… is that awrite?'

'Is it fuck! Sick cunt. Get oot mah shoap!' The barber whipped the cape off Si and hauled him out the chair by the neck of his t-shirt.

'It's just a haircut, fur fuck sake. Ye cut mah pal's hair like fucking Joseph Stalin.'

'Och that's different. Ye think asking tae get yer hair cut like Ian Brady is awrite? Why don't ah gie ye a Bible John? Or wit aboot a wee short back and Peter Tobin then? Fucking idiot.'

The barber flung Si out onto the street.

THE DEEP

The submersible sunk slowly down into the blackness. Above them was almost a mile of water, below them an all-consuming blackness. The two women inside the craft were having a right laugh.

'The thing is…' Karen said to her colleague, Brenda. 'We're making history here. The first two women from Springburn to go to the bottom of the ocean.'

'Aye, I suppose,' Brenda said, staring absent-mindedly into the abyss unfolding below her.

'Ye "suppose", do ye? *History* we're making here, hen. Fucking cheer up.'

'Gies peace,' Brenda reached for the controls for the submersible and kicked it into full speed. 'The sooner we get down there, the sooner we can get back up and I can get away from you.'

'You're a torn-faced bastard, ye know that?' Karen hated Brenda. 'There's a blobfish, note that down.'

'Aw, so *I* need to note it down? You seen it. You write it down.' Brenda hated Karen right back.

'Aw for fuck sake. Fine. I'll note it down.' Karen scribbled down: *Blobfish spotted at depth of 1,200m.* 'That's quite deep for a blobfish, is it not?'

Brenda sighed.

'I said that's quite dee–'

Brenda cut Karen off mid-sentence. 'It's about normal. Now just be quiet for five minutes. Please.'

'Fine.'

'Thanks.'

***

As the submersible sunk ever deeper, the atmosphere inside grew as oppressive as the crushing pressure of the water outside.

'What is your problem with me?' Karen had been wanting to ask Brenda this question for ages.

'Problem? I don't have a problem with you. I don't know what you're talking about.' Brenda brought the vehicle down onto the ocean floor. A cloud of marine detritus was kicked up around them, so thick that the powerful headlights of the craft couldn't penetrate it. They'd have to wait for it to subside before they could make their observations.

'You do have a problem with me.' Karen slapped her notebook down onto the dashboard. 'You've been a total cow to me ever since that night in McGookin's hoose.'

'Aye, well, you made an arse of me in front of everyone.'

'Och, lighten up. I was only having a laugh. Nobody remembers anyway.'

'Aye. But *I* remember.'

The cloud of dust outside was beginning to settle. Karen and Benda were the first humans to ever visit this part of the sea floor. The lights of the craft cut into the inky blackness and landed on the target of their study, the remains of a recently-deceased sperm whale. An entire ecosystem had sprung up in and around the whale's corpse. Deep-dwelling fish and crabs gorged themselves on the whale's blubber, while strange, woodlouse-like isopods crowded around its protruding ribs.

'That's you,' Karen said, pointing to a shark as it dove down and chased away a school of fish who were congregating around the whale's tail. 'Chasing away all my pals and happiness.'

'Aye, well you know what you are?' said Brenda. 'You're a zombie worm.'

'A *zombie* worm? Wit's that? Have you made that up?'

Brenda laughed. 'It's a wee worm that burrows into the bones of dead animals at the bottom of the sea and eats all their bone marrow and that. That's what you're doing to me; burrowing in and eating up all *my* fucking happiness.'

'Aw shut up. There's no such thing as a "zombie worm" anyway. Although, it wouldn't be like you to make something up, would it, Brenda?'

* * *

Around twenty years ago at a party, long before they would go on to become Scotland's foremost marine biologists, Brenda and Karen were sitting with a guy who Brenda really fancied. Karen didn't think much of the guy and thought Brenda could do better. As Brenda wasn't paying any attention to her and was instead hanging on the guy's every word, Karen left them to it. Returning after an hour or so, bored and ready to go home, Karen found Brenda and the guy cosied up, looking very much like they'd be kissing soon, or more.

'We need to get you hame, hen,' Karen said loudly. 'You know your maw doesn't like you being out this late.'

The room went silent, everyone looking at Karen as if she'd come in with shite on her shoe. The guy put his arm round Brenda, whispering something into her ear.

Karen sniffed and tried again. 'And you've got that Pokémon tournament tomorrow. You'll need your sleep.' At this, everyone in the room broke out into laughter, and the guy was suddenly up and making his excuses.

Brenda looked like she would kill Karen. Nowadays, sometimes, she wishes she fucking did.

Karen gestured over her shoulder at the door. 'Let's go.'

Brenda looked at the object of her desires who also nodded at the door. 'See ye later, pal,' he said. That "pal" was like a dagger through Brenda's heart. That was it: game over. Up the road.

'Why'd you do that?' Brenda moaned on the walk home. 'I was in there.'

'You can do better. He's a bam.'

'He's a fitbaw player! Plays for Rangers! Jesus Christ, Karen.'

'Och, calm down,' Karen said, walking ahead. 'You had no chance, anyway.'

'Aw, is that right, aye?' Brenda muttered to herself. She would see to it she would get her own back.

That night kickstarted their animosity. They remained pals to outdo each other, and were always looking for new ways to get one over.

Karen got into Glasgow Uni so Brenda had to make sure she did too. In second year, Brenda took up marine biology, as did Karen. Before they knew it they were the best underwater team, not just in Scotland, but in the world. Not bad for two lassies from the scheme whose entire relationship was built on a seething vendetta.

* * *

'I mean, you told everybody at uni I hated Chinese people,' said Karen.

'Tit fur tat,' Brenda shrugged.

'How is that "tit fur tat"? I stop you from winching some jakey bam and you tell everybody I'm a fucking racist?'

Brenda laughed as she watched the shark out the window, rolling around, trying to twist off a great chunk of whale. 'Mind you told everybody it was me who kept stinking out the canteen by microwaving fish, when it was you?'

Karen smiled. 'Remember you kissed my da at my 21st?'

Brenda spat out some of the water she was drinking and then wiped her chin. 'That was funny. Surely you have to respect the patter there? The guy's ugly as sin, no offence. I just wanted to noise you up.'

'Remember the time I stole fags off that lassie in Lee's house and blamed it on you? She wanted to fight you and I had to calm her down, took her outside and gave her one of her own fags.'

Their laughter was cut short when everything suddenly went dark.

'What the fuck?' Brenda shouted. 'What's happening now?'

Karen tried the comms system, hoping desperately that it would still be working. Of course, it wasn't. The temperature started to drop.

'Try the emergency system,' said Brenda. 'That runs off a different battery.'

Sure enough, after pressing the button the whirring of machinery started up again and the lights inside the cockpit came back on. 'Thank God,' said Karen.

Brenda stared dead ahead.

'What is it?' Karen asked. Karen followed her line of sight, out onto the abyssal plain. The shark was gone. But that wasn't what had caught Brenda's attention. It was the giant squid hovering ominously over the whale, dwarfing the dead animal. Its massive eye, the size of the wheel of a car, stared into the craft, unblinking. The squid's tentacles undulated, stretching out in front of it for what must have been 30 or 40 feet.

Karen reached for the camera. She had to document this behemoth.

'It won't work,' said Brenda. 'Only essential stuff works off the emergency system.'

'I've never seen anything that size before. No one will believe this.'

'They wouldn't believe you anyway, no with the amount of shite you talk.' Brenda's tone wasn't the jovial, piss-taking-but-friendly one she was using just moments ago, it was quite snidey.

'Aw gies peace, you – FUCK!' The squid was now facing them. The tips of its tentacles caressed the window of the cockpit.

'There's wan thing I never will forgive you for. Everything else you did? I can deal with. Just patter. But you took it too far last year.'

'Aw aye? What was it that I did? Remind me, Brenda, and remind me *why* I did what I did.'

'Telling folk I stole the menage money,' Brenda spat. 'I'm still getting dirty looks down ASDA because of you.'

'Well, I mean, you *did* steal the money.'

'Naw I fucking didnae!'

The squid parted its tentacles, let them slide over the craft, and started to squeeze.

The rest of the power in the sub came back on and the noise of static came through the comms system.

'ANPA-5 come in. We lost communication is everything okay?'

'Aye, fine!' barked the two women simultaneously.

'Your cameras are showing a... a large... a very large cephalopod in your vicinity.'

'Aye, captain, it's trying to eat us.'

'It's trying to what?! Ladies, abort, get back to the–'

Brenda turned the volume down on the comms system.

'I fucking did not steal that money. You trying to fucking gaslight me? Is that your game?'

The squid's pale white beak gnawed at the curved glass window of the craft.

'When we were younger, I said for a laugh you couldn't run a menage, mind? Then you started wan. And helped yourself to the money,' said Karen.

The craft creaked and groaned as the squid tightened its grip, trying to crack it open like it was a helpless crab.

'Your systems are showing as critical! Turn on the engines and you'll scare the thing away. You have to do something NOW!'

'It was Lettie that stole that money! I told you that!' said Brenda, adding quietly, 'God rest her soul.'

'You told everybody that, aye. Bit convenient though that after you told everybody that it was her, she was found deid

is it no? Nae money in her hoose, bank account or anything.
Penniless that woman died. But, according to you, it was her
that stole the ten grand off her pals, aye?'

'Aye, that's exactly what I'm saying. But hawd oan, are you
saying that *I* killed her?'

'Maybe,' shrugged Karen.

'You gonnae add that on to your wee lie to everybody then,
aye? "Not only did Brenda steal the money but she blamed it
on somebody else then killed her to keep the secret"?'

The sound of frantic screaming from up on the surface
came through the comms. *'They're gonna fucking die! Oh my god!
We need to get them help! Sit tight ladies, we're coming!'*

'You bought a new motor as well, just after the money
disappeared. That's a bit funny as well, eh?'

'Aw shut up. People buy new motors all the time.'

The two women stared at the squid trying to consume them.

'We're fucked, eh?' said Brenda. Nodding at the animal
which would have been regarded as some kind of mytho-
logical beast by old sailors.

'We turn the fans on full throttle and it'll scare it away,' said
Karen. 'But we're no going anywhere until *you* admit what
you did.'

'But I've got nothing to admit *to* for fuck sake!'

'Fine then.'

'Fine.'

Prayers could be heard over the comms system as the team
on the surface ran out of ideas to help the women. They were
on their own now.

* * *

A couple of hours passed. Brenda shifted her weight on to one
arse cheek and let out a fart.

'For fuck sake, did you have to do that?' Karen said, holding
her nose and dramatically waving at the air. With nowhere for

the fart to go, it just hung in the cabin.

The squid was relentless, applying crushing pressure to the submersible.

'People were holding up signs outside my house,' Brenda lamented. 'SCUM one of them said.'

'I seen you getting into a taxi that night, a suitcase in each hand. You didn't turn up to the meeting that night with people's money. Money you'd normally bring in they fucking suitcases.'

'I know it doesn't look too good. It looks a bit… suspect. I'll be the first to admit that.' Brenda tapped the glass in front of her, gently, like she was shooing away a bird from her window ledge.

'Where were you going, then? What was in those suitcases?'

A crack appeared in the glass.

'Shit,' they both said.

There's damage detected to the craft, ladies are you there?

'Aye, we're here, we're fine.'

Red warning lights lit up the dashboard.

'*You need to get that thing away, just turn on the engine. That should do it.*'

Karen reached forward to engage the propulsion system. The whirring of the propellers echoed through the craft.

The squid just squeezed harder with its tentacles and tried to force its beak into the crack.

'It's no good,' said Brenda into the comms. 'We're fucked.'

Silence from the surface.

'What now?' Brenda asked Karen.

'Say you're sorry, obviously.'

'Sorry? Sorry for wit?'

'Stealing the money obviously.'

'But I didn't – aw ye know wit, forget it.'

The squid gripped ever tighter. Another crack appeared. The dash was going haywire.

Karen sat back and closed her eyes. 'Dying beside my best pal, a liar and a thief.'

'I am neither of those things.'

'Just say sorry. It's no hard.'

'*You* say sorry for tormenting me all these years.'

'Fine,' Karen shrugged her shoulders. 'I'm sorry. There. You go.'

Brenda sighed. 'I'm sor–'

The craft imploded under the pressure as the glass cracked open and the squid just fucking ate every single bit of them. It was mental.

SAMMY THE CRIME SCENE CLEANER

Efter mah escapades in the sausage factory, ah went oan the brew fur a while. Ye ever been oan the brew? It's a fuckin nightmare. Honestly, yer better aff workin. Cunt's are oan yer case 24/7. Need tae apply fur aboot a million joabs every single day. Call centres, offices, shops, fuckin door tae door sales an aw that – everyhing.

'Ahm clearly no qualified tae work in a jail,' ah says tae mah designated advisor. 'Ah mean, ahm no the biggest maist intimidatin cunt, um ah?'

'That's beside the point,' mah advisor says. 'You have to apply or you'll be sanctioned and lose your job seeker's allowance.'

'Swear tae god, mate, if ah get this joab ah'll be ragin.' The guy joost rolls his eyes at me. Barrel ae laughs these pricks are.

'Well maybe this will be more up your street.' He turns his computer screen roon ae face me. 'Waiters required for new restaurant in Glasgow's west end.'

'Servin food tae poncey rich folk? Runnin aboot efter them? No chance.'

'Well, what kind of job *do* you want to do, Sammy?'

'Ah dunno,' ah say. Ah've never actually thought aboot that before. Ah've always seen work as suhin yer joost kindae forced intae. Suhin ye *huv* tae dae.

'Here's one you might be into, actually.' The cunt looks like he's losin patience here. Maybe if ah keep annoyin him he'll walk oot an ah could joost huv his joab. 'Crime scene cleaner.'

'Aw here, now yer talkin, mate.' Ah love watchin *Grime Fighters* an aw that oan the telly.

'Five days a week, based in Maryhill, must have strong stomach. What do you think? Reckon you could handle cleaning up blood and all sorts of other unpleasantness?'

'Ah seen mah da die right in front ae me, mate. Ah can handle anyhin.'

'Jesus Christ, I'm – I'm so sorry, Sammy.'

'Naw, don't be daft, it's cool. It wis mair funny than anyhin.' The cunt joost looks pure stunned. 'Let me apply fur that. Ah'd be good at that.'

* * *

Next hing ah know ahm up some close that ah could only describe as lookin like a slum. Ah mean, where ah stay isnae exactly Beverly Hills but compared tae this place it could be. Hawf the lights are oot in the close but ah can see that every square inch ae the walls are covered in menchies an there's a wee dug shit oan every other stair.

'Right,' mah new boss says tae me. It's this auld duffer, auld enough to be mah granda ah hink. 'Somebody wis stabbed in here, wee man. Go up an clean the blood away.' He hawns me a bucket, a mop, a boattil ae bleach, a scrubbing brush, a cloth an a pair ae rubber gloves.

'Wit you gonnae be dain while ahm dain this?' ah ask the guy.

'Ah'll be waitin in the van. This is only a wee joab, son. Ah'll get the next one. Ye've goat tae learn.'

Aye nae bother. Cannae kid a kidder, that's wit mah granny always says. Ah've goat the same in-built bullshit detector that she's goat. This auld cunt probably joost wants a snooze. Lazy auld basturt.

Anyway, ah head up tae the tap flair tae see wit horrors await me. Ah mind wance, me an mah maw an granny an granda aw went oan hoaliday. Mah da didnae want tae come so he joost hid the hoose tae his self fur a fortnight. See when we came back, the hoose wis an absolute midden. The cunt hidnae even opened a windae the whole two weeks we were away. The place smelled the same as when you open a packet ae chopped pork or suhin – like a meaty fart. Witever's up these stairs cannae be as bad as that.

When ah get tae tap landin, ah can see a wee pool ae blood. It's startin tae dry in, poor cunt must only huv been stabbed during the night. Ah look doon at mah empty bucket. Ahm gonnae need some hot watter tae clean this up. Ah think aboot gawn doon an askin mah boss wit a should dae but ah decide tae try an use mah 'initiative'. That's a 'soft skill' ah wis told tae put oan mah CV by mah designated advisor doon the joab centre. So ah chap the door where aw the blood is.

'Awrite,' ah say when the wummin opens the door a wee bit. She looks terrified. She's still in her jammies. 'Can ah fill up mah bucket?'

She joost looks at me as if ah've asked her if she's wantin stabbed as well.

'Ahm here tae clean up this.' Ah point tae the blood, tryin ae explain masel. "Communication skills" ahm demonstratin here.

'Awrite, no bother, pal. Moan in.' She takes the door aff the chain an lets me in. 'Fill it up in the bath, through there.'

'Cheers, missus.' There's a wee boay playin in the livin room wi a wee staffy. Ah love dugs. 'You know the cunt that goat stabbed?' ah ask her.

'Naw, nae idea who it was. Or who done it. Neither dae the polis.'

'How's there nae polis hingin aboot the close? There's nae polis tape either.'

The wummin laughs. The kind ae laugh ye dae when ye really want tae say *Is it no obvious?* 'Some jakey got stabbed up a close in deepest, darkest Maryhill. The polis don't care. If this had happened somewhere else they'd be aw over it. But no here. They don't even care that me, a single maw, is noo livin in fear.

Wit if ah'd went doon tae take the bins oot or suhin? Wit if the guy wi the knife hud broke intae mah hoose? While mah son wis sleepin? Ah worry aboot mah son growin up here.'

'Aye, it's shockin, hen.'

'Who's that?' her wee boay says, pointin at me. He must be aboot four or five.

'He's here to clean the close. Just you go an play in the livin room.'

That's mah bucket filled up noo. Time tae clean up some blood.

The wummin leaves her front door open fur me so ah cin listen tae choons while ah work. This joab's no too bad.

Ahm aw hunched over, scrubbing away this poor guy's blood.

The wee boay appears in the door way. He's goat the staffy by the collar an it's geein me a look that, tae me, says *Ahm gonnae eat you.* 'What you doing?' the wee boay asks me.

'Aw, eh, just cleaning this mess up, wee man.'

'What is it?'

'It's ehhh… paint! Aye, it's just paint, pal.' Thinkin oan mah feet an improvising, that's oan mah CV as well.

Then ah hink tae masel, *Should ah be lyin ae this wee boay, though?* If ah tell him the truth, surely he'll grow up wantin tae dae suhin aboot it, wantin tae better his life an aw that. Ye know wit? Ahm gonnae tell him *exactly* wit happened here. Scare him away fae a life ae crime.

'This isnae paint,' ah say tae the wee guy. Ah dip mah cloth intae mah bucket an wring it oot, bright red watter drips oot it. 'It's blood.'

'Blood?' The wee guy's lip is quivering a wee bit.

'Aye, blood. A guy wis stabbed. *Right here* last night.'

'Is he dead?'

'Nae idea. He might be. There's a lot a blood here. A whole bucket full. He wis comin up the stairs wan night when a bad man jumped oot ae naewhere an stabbed him.'

The wee guy's lip proper petted noo.

'He probably goat stabbed right here.' Ah jab mah finger intae his wee belly.

Then he lets oot the maist blood-curdlin scream ah've ever heard.

'MMMMAAAAAAMMMYY,' he shouts. Aw fuck. The dug starts growlin. Ah take a step back. If the wee guy lets go ae the devil dug, it's gonnae rip mah fuckin throat oot.

'Wit is it, son? Wit happened? WIT DID YOU DAE AE MAH BOAY?!'

'Nuttin, ah swear, ah joost, eh…' *Fuck sake Sammy, man, improvise, think oan yer feet, use yer soft skills.* 'Ah joost made a wee joke, he, eh, didnae like it.'

'He touched me!' the wee guy shouts.

'Naw, it wisnae like that!' *Fuck sake, Sammy boy, you've done it noo.* 'I joost, eh, gave him a wee tap oan the belly. Joost tae show him where the guy wis stabbed. That's aw.'

'Wit?! You thought it was awrite tae tell mah boay a man wis stabbed in oor close?'

Shit.

The wummin takes a hawd of the dug's collar. Ah take a step back.

'Get him, Sasha,' she whispers in the dug's ear an lets it go. Ah panic. Ah grab mah mop an kick the bucket ae bloody watter taewards the dug. Ah get the dug nae bother but wee guy an his maw get caught in the crossfire an end up fuckin drenched. Blood everywhere. Jesus Christ. It's as if somebody's been stabbed here.

'AHM PHONIN THE POLIS!' the wummin's shouting as ah bolt doon the stair wi the dug chasin efter me, ah cin still hear the wee boay wailing. Ah get doon tae the van an try tae get in but mah daft auld basturt ae a boss has fell asleep.

'Wake up, mate, let me in! We need tae boost.' But the cunt's no fur wakin up. *Fuck this,* ah hink as the blood-soaked demon staffy grabs a hawd ae mah troosers. Hink ah'll joost apply fur college an live aff the student loan ye get. It's no that ahm no ready fur the world ae work; it's that the world ae work joost isnae ready fur me.

AFTERLIFE

My pal Ciaran died at a party when we were fourteen. Well, he didn't die *at* the party, but that's when the chain of events that led to his death began. We were in this new guy from school's house. A horrible, grubby flat in Cranhill. This new guy, Stephen, stayed with his da. Just the two of them living in absolute squalor. Plenty of my pals, me included, were raised by single mothers and we all found it really fucking weird that this guy was raised by his da and his da alone. We asked him where his maw was, if she was dead or whatever, and he just said she'd upped and left. The same as most of our das had done. It was mind-blowing. To us, a maw just abandoning her family was unthinkable; women didn't do that. It was a guy thing.

Anyway, we were at this party. I say 'party' but there was only six of us there. Four of the boys sat in the living room playing FIFA while Stephen showed me his bedroom. That was another weird thing about this boy; he had the biggest room while his da slept in the tiny wee box room. Also, this boy supported Partick Thistle, instead of Celtic or Rangers like a normal person from Glesga. To us, that was the weirdest thing about him.

'My da's a junkie,' he said to me, dead calmly, while he rummaged about in his sock drawer.

'Awrite?' I replied. I didn't know what else to say.

'Aye. He left these in the kitchen.' He held up a wee bag containing two orange tablets. What sticks in mind is how dry my mouth went. Just pure fear I think it was. As a kid growing up in the east end, you see reminders of the damage that drugs can do everywhere you look. You equate drugs with fear. Well, you do if you're a shitebag like me. 'Take anything and you'll end up being a junkie,' parents and teachers drummed into us from a young age. Funny how they never mentioned much about booze.

We went back through to the living room. Ciaran locked on to the pills immediately. 'What's that?'

Stephen shook the pills gently in the bag. 'Eccies,' he replied.

My mouth was fucking parched, hands sweating and all that. Ever just get that feeling something bad is going to happen? I had that then. Big time.

'What do they do? Have you ever took one?' Ciaran asked, his voice quivering. Whether it was because of puberty or because he was nervous I'm no sure.

'Aye, loads ae times,' he said. 'They're ma da's. They make ye feel dead happy.'

Ciaran's expression changed completely. Wide-eyed curiosity is how I'd describe it. His granny had died the month before and he'd taken it hard. It wasn't the way it usually is with old folk; she'd been hit by a bus, and Ciaran saw the whole thing happen right in front of him. He didn't speak for a fortnight after. Who could blame him? Four weeks later and he was back at school but he was a different guy altogether. Before his granny died he was dead funny and cool. Always did well in school too. But since he'd come back he was nothing but bother for the teachers. They'd always said how conscientious he was, how attentive and how polite. Now he was withdrawn and if a teacher asked him to do something he'd either ignore them or bite their head off. Everyone was afraid of him. He told us the head teacher had a meeting with his maw and said he clearly wasn't ready to come back to school. His maw said she had nobody to watch him while she was at work and that he had to go. So he ended up being placed in 'isolation'. He'd go to the head teacher's office with a pile of work and just sit in there in silence. He said it was brilliant. At lunchtime he'd begun to hang about with us again and he seemed nearly back to normal. A bit of solitude seemed to do him good. That night at the party was the first time he'd left his house, except to go to school, since his granny had died.

'Ye want wan?' Stephen asked Ciaran.

Ciaran tried to answer but it was as if he had a lump in his throat, like he was going to start crying. He swallowed then croaked out an answer.

'Aye.'

'Ah'll hawf it wi ye,' said Stephen. He pressed his thumbnail into a pill, splitting it perfectly in half. I noticed it had a mickey mouse shape stamped into it. 'Make sure ye drink plenty ae water.'

After half an hour or so, Ciaran turned to me and said he couldn't feel anything and that the pills must be duds. His jaw told a different story however. His teeth were clenched tightly together and I swear to God I could *hear* them grinding.

'I need some water,' he said. He got to his feet and grabbed an empty Irn-Bru bottle from the rubbish-strewn floor. He went through to the kitchen and filled it from the tap. Sitting back down on the couch, Stephen passed him some chewing gum.

'Nah, I'm alright,' Ciaran said, declining the offer.

'Naw.' Stephen thrust the chewing gum into his hand. 'Take it, it'll stoap yer teeth fae gettin fucked.'

After an hour and a half, Ciaran wouldn't stop talking.

'This is the hing, right,' he said, for the fourth time. 'All the gimps in school are raised by their grannies. No maws. No das. Grannies. They're spoiled. They don't live in the real world. Their grannies do everything for them. Look at that cunt, Josh, for example. I'm in the same techy class as him and honest to fuck, he can't do anything. Can't even hold a hammer properly. What kind of boy can't hold a hammer?'

The other boys at the party sat enthralled, listening to his rant. It was complete nonsense, but he was saying it with such conviction.

'Here, Stephen,' Ciaran said. 'Want to half another pill?'

'Naw, man. We better no. Mah da'll be annoyed. Yous better head actually. He'll be hame soon ah hink.'

'And another hing.' Ciaran ignored him and continued his rant. He was getting really angry now. I knew he had a lot of anger contained within him but to see him unleash it was quite something. 'The way they fucking dress,' he continued. 'Have you seen these granny's boys on non-uniform days?'

We collectively shook our heads. Fashion doesn't mean a lot at fourteen.

'It's disgusting, man. Cheap, horrible black shoes. Aw polished up nice like they're in the army or something. Like they've never been used to kick a baw in their life. Fucking chinos and shirts and all that. Cause granny wants to make them look nice and smart. I hate them.'

* * *

The next day, Ciaran started a fight with a boy in the year below. We were walking down the street, going for a chippy, and he launched a half-full bottle of Irn-Bru at this poor wee guy. Right out the blue. The cap end of the bottle scudded him on the back of his napper and it made this horrible noise like… well like a plastic bottle hitting right off someone's skull. The wee guy turned round and you could see his lip trembling. I've never felt more sorry for someone than I did right then. He was standing there, his schoolbag far too big for his wee frame, trying his best not to cry as Ciaran strode towards him. I tried to stop him, I did, but really I could've tried harder. I can't remember if it was two or three of the wee guy's teeth Ciaran ended up knocking out.

* * *

'What was that all about yesterday, mate?' I asked him as we went to another "party" in Stephen's.

'Fucking granny's boy,' he snarled. 'Wee cunt told his granny what happened and she was at my door last night. My maw's raging.'

'Well fair enough, mate,' I said. 'You started on him for no reason.'

'I just fucking knew he was a granny's boy. You can just tell. I hate them.' He took a sip from a quarter bottle of Glen's vodka and winced. 'I hate them all.'

* * *

Stephen ended up getting taken into care after his da went missing. He moved school and we never saw or heard from him again. We had nowhere left to go and hang about, and since the rest of our pals' parents didn't want them hanging about with Ciaran, me and him had started sitting in my room most nights.

He'd lie sprawled out on my bed, relaxing with a joint while I paced around the room, lighting candles, spraying air freshener and panicking in case my maw smelled it. One night I said to him that I wished he wouldn't smoke hash in my room and he replied, 'Just turn the music up and your maw won't smell it.' Incredible logic. Maybe there was some degree of rationale in there somewhere because it seemed to work; my maw never found out Ciaran smoked hash in my room. But she did find out we had went joyriding in her motor, because we crashed the fucking thing. We didn't have a clue and had no interest in motors, but my maw's was automatic so, according to Ciaran, it was just like a dodgem. Anyway, he went through a red light and a transit van smashed right into the driver's side. It all happened in slow motion, it was mental. They say your life flashes before your eyes in situations like that, but it was more just a feeling of calm, like everything was going to be alright. I turned to Ciaran as he sped up on the approach to the traffic lights and I could see the van hurtling towards us. He looked at it then back it me and I swear to God he smiled and winked. The nurse told me Ciaran was dead after she put my arm into a stookie the next morning. He'd died instantly they reckoned. The driver of the van ended up paralysed from the waist down. What did I have to show for it? A broken arm and a couple of wee cuts. That was it.

At Ciaran's funeral, my maw wouldn't let go of me. She clung onto my arm for dear life, saying things like, 'I'm so glad it wisnae you that died,' and all that. We had to walk into the chapel past Ciaran's maw and the look on her face is something I'll never forget. My maw gave her a look of sympathy, that way you sort of purse your lips and nod your head at someone. But Ciaran's maw just shot right back with the iciest stare I've ever seen. She had every right to be annoyed; it wasn't fair she'd lost her boy while my maw still had me, totally unharmed.

* * *

I died a good fourty year after all this happened. Throat cancer. Never smoked a single fag in all my life. I was relatively young, I suppose, but I never liked the idea of getting really old anyway. I suffocated in the middle of the night, surrounded by other decrepit, dying cunts. And see, as I took my last breath, that same feeling of calm that I'd felt right before that van crashed into my maw's motor came back. I didn't even struggle or try to help myself, I just waited to die. It was a nice way to go, I think. I'd rasped my goodbyes to my daughter and grandweans a few hours before and they'd went off with smiles on their faces since my youngest grandson couldn't stop laughing at my new gravelly voice. It was a nice. Leaving them with a smile. I'm glad that's how I went rather than them seeing me get even worse or dying in front of them.

I've been in heaven for three weeks now. I met God! He's a bit of a let down, to be honest. He seems dead bored. You get ten minutes with him when you first arrive here and then you get passed on to an angel who acts as a kind of holiday rep to help you adjust to life in Heaven.

'Aiden Gray,' God said to me, looking through some paperwork. 'You've done no too bad, pal.'

'Cheers,' I replied.

'Nothing diabolical. Nothing particularly amazing either. Kept yourself to yourself. I like that.'

'Cheers.'

'There's a few cunts here you know. Your maw. Your granny and granda. Couple of pals as well.'

'Is Ciaran here?' I interrupted.

'Hing oan, I'll check,' He ran a finger down a list of names. 'Wit's the boy's last name?'

'McAnespie.'

'Aye, he's here. Och, that's a shame. Fourteen he wis when he died, eh?'

I nodded.

'He stays with his granny. A wee hoose, near where you'll be staying.' God put the paperwork into the drawer of His desk.

I'd forgotten all about Ciaran's grievances with his granny's boys by this point. Wish I fucking knew what I was about to get myself into.

'I'll pay him a wee visit.'

'Good for you, pal. He could be dain wi a bit ae company.' The big man nodded at the white door of His office and started poring over the next new arrival's paperwork.

'Aw, sorry, can I ask you something before I go?'

'Naw. Wan ae the angels'll answer yer questions.'

Fucking ignoramus.

***

The angel I was assigned was called Rebecca. She was nice. Turned out she was from Cranhill as well and was a social worker when she was alive. She died back in the 70s, wore these horrible milk bottle specs and had a massive perm.

'Rebecca, I can't help but notice that just about everyone here is old and decrepit, including me. What's the script?'

She gave me an apologetic look. 'When ye get here, son, ye stay as ye were when ye died.'

'So I'm gonnae remain in my fifties forever? I don't even get to go back to being in my prime?'

'Sorry, son. It's just how it is.' She handed me my welcome pack and the keys to my new house.

My new house happened to be an exact replica of the house I'd grown up in, which resided in an exact replica of the scheme I'd grown up in. Heaven is a weird place. Rebecca told me that it was really an exact replica of the world and that I could go anywhere. Even through time. I could go back and mingle with the Neanderthals that used to cut about Cranhill tens of thousands of years ago if I wanted. I declined and said I'd rather go and visit my pal Ciaran. She said, 'No bother, son,' and in the blink of an eye we were standing outside his front door. Well, his granny's front door.

'This is his granny's house,' I said to Rebecca, confused.

'Well, he was only a wee boy when he died. He had no one else to look after him. His maw's not scheduled to die for another wee while, according to her file, so he'll be here until she arrives.' She nodded at the door and disappeared.

I chapped the door and Ciaran's granny answered it.

'You,' she said, looking me up and down. 'You were in that motor wi mah Ciaran that night.'

'Eh, aye. I was.' The look this woman gave me, honest to God, man, she made me feel like I was fourteen again and getting into trouble off a teacher. 'I should've stopped him from driving the motor that night. I'm sorry.'

'He's in the kitchen.' She pointed over her shoulder. 'Ye can tell him yer sorry.'

There was a right strong smell of soup in the kitchen. I mind Ciaran once telling me how much he loved his granny's homemade soup. He was stood at the cooker with his back to me, absent-mindedly stirring the soup.

'Awrite, mate?' I asked, trying to sound as cheerful as possible despite the atmosphere in the house. He didn't reply. He didn't even turn round.

It took a few moments for me to take in what we was wearing; a pristinely ironed blue shirt tucked into beige-coloured chinos and big chunky black sensible shoes.

'CIARAN!' his granny shouted from the living room. 'YOU BETTER BE STIRRING THAT SOUP!'

'I am, granny,' he muttered.

'So…' I was trying desperately to make small talk. 'You know anybody up here then?'

'Naw,' he said, his eyes transfixed on the soup whirlpool he was creating. 'Everybody apart from my granny is still alive. Even my maw.'

'Awrite,' I said. 'Cool.'

'So's my da. And Stephen. And everybody we went to school with.'

'Good for them, I suppose, eh?'

No reply.

'So, eh, how've ye been?' I ventured. A safe bet of a question, I thought.

'HOW DAE YE HINK AH'VE BEEN!' He sent the pot flying across the kitchen, the soup flying out of it and on to the wall with a splat. Some of it splashed on to his chinos and my ear. I backed away from him slowly as he turned around to face me. I noticed his hair was combed into a neat side parting. He used to wear it kind of spiky and messy when we were at school.

'My maw's still alive.' He took a step towards me. 'My da's still alive.' Another step. 'Every cunt we hung aboot wi at school is still alive.' Another step. We were nose to nose now. 'And *you* only died yesterday.'

His granny gasped from behind me. I turned round to look at her and she was peeking her head out behind the living room door.

'Don't you fucking say anyhin ya auld crabbit cunt.' Ciaran pointed at his granny. He turned his gaze back to me. 'Do you know what it's been like?'

I shook my head.

'Living with *her*.' He literally spat the word "her" out. Flecks of spittle joined the smattering of homemade soup on my right ear. His granny gasped again. Ciaran shoved me and I went sprawling on my back. He stood over me. For a fourteen year old, he was an intimidating figure.

'I've been up here for near enough fourty year.' His eyes were wild. 'Hinging aboot wi mah FUCKIN GRANNY!' He grabbed the neck of my t-shirt and screamed in my face, 'YOU SHOULD'VE DIED IN THAT FUCKIN CRASH WI ME!'

'M-m-mate.' I thought I was going to pish myself with fear. 'I'm sorry.' I don't know why I apologised for not dying in a car crash but you say weird things in situations like this. 'It can't have been that bad, eh? I mean, you loved your granny, didn't you?'

He flung me out onto the street.

'Forty fuckin year, man. Wi mah granny. Nae cunt else. Just her.' His voice was a bit calmer now as he stood in the doorway. 'Look at the fuckin state ae me.' He gestured down at his clothes. Dribbles of soup had been creeping down the legs of his chinos like orange slugs. I had to admit though, his shoes were shiny as fuck.

GHOSTS

'Ghosts are real,' the woman on the telly said. 'A spokesghost for the spirit world visited the Prime Minister a few months ago to reveal their presence. We understand this will come as a shock to the general population but the ghosts have assured us that they will cause no harm and will behave in their assigned homes. The ghosts have chosen to reveal themselves as they say they've had enough fun at our expense and want to coexist with living people now. The spokesghost also attributed the decision to changing attitudes towards death held by a growing number of recently deceased who wish to remain on earth. Every home in Britain not currently haunted will receive the delivery of a ghost from Monday. The ghosts will not encumber your day-to-day life in any way and have assured us that most people simply won't even notice they are there. We thank the general public for their cooperation at this exciting time.'

* * *

'Just a few more signatures,' the estate agent said to Jamie. 'Then we'll be done here.'

'What does all this even mean, Helen?' he asked, leafing through the stack of paper over two inches thick. He was barely half way through it and his hand was starting to cramp up.

'Well,' she replied, 'this is your tenancy agreement. You have to sign it to say you'll be liable for any damages, that you can't paint the walls and all that kind of stuff.'

'Ah, right, fair enough, I suppose. But still, it seems like an awful lot of stuff to sign. I mean this one here,' he pulled out a sheet of paper with the header GHOST ROOMMATE AGREEMENT. 'Is this a wind up?'

Helen laughed nervously. 'Oh that, well, um, it's a new government initiative which states–'

'States that I'm gonnae have a ghost roommate?'

'Well…yes. It was announced by the government the other week. I'm surprised you didn't hear about it – the country's been in uproar.'

'What are you talking about? Ghosts aren't real. Is this a new word for like homeless people or something?'

'No, no, you're going to have an actual ghost living with you. It'll move in on Monday.' She nodded at Jamie to indicate that he should keep signing.

Jamie just looked at her. 'So ghosts are real?'

'Yes.'

'And there's one gonnae be living with me?'

'Yes.' Helen rolled her eyes.

'I don't know how I feel about this,' the colour drained from Jamie's face and he felt himself go a wee bit light headed.

Helen gave his arm a sympathetic pat. 'I'll get you a cup of tea.'

* * *

When she returned, Jamie was intently going over the ghost roommate agreement.

'…poltergeists, demons, orbs, apparitions, deceased historical figures and restless spirits. Jesus Christ,' Jamie said. 'I… I don't think I can live with a ghost.'

'Well, you don't really have a choice.' Helen sat the cup of tea down in front of Jamie. He was looking really worried. 'Every house in Scotland will have one as of Monday.'

'What kind of ghost am I getting?'

'You'll find out on Monday. C'mon, pal, keep signing, then you can get yourself up to your new flat and get settled in. You've got nearly a week to come to terms with it. And besides, it might be a laugh.' Helen rubbed Jamie's shoulder. 'It'll be okay.'

'What's the deal though, like, is the ghost gonnae be paying rent? This flat is only one bedroom as well, is it gonnae be... sleeping in my room?'

'Well, ghosts can't have jobs. Not yet, anyway. So it won't be chipping in with the rent for the time being. And being a ghost, it won't need sleep anyway. It'll probably just chill out in the living room while you're asleep.'

'Why do they need houses?'

'If they were left outside they'd just blow away and that's a shame, don't you think?'

Jamie spent the rest of the week reading up on ghosts. He hoped his roommate would be some kind of benevolent spirit, like a guardian angel or something. As long as it wasn't the ghost of a creepy wee lassie or a poltergeist.

* * *

Sure enough, on Monday morning, Jamie opened the door to find two men standing with a large canister.

'Jamie Gilmour?' one of the men said.

'Aye, that's me. Is that it, then?' Jamie pointed to the canister.

'Aye, this is yer ghost, wee man. You've drew the short straw though!'

The two men heaved the canister through into Jamie's living room.

'Just sign this for us, pal.' One of the men thrust a clipboard towards Jamie. 'This is just to say you're no gonnae dae an exorcism or anything like that that might harm yer new pal in here.' The man patted the top of the canister.

'Eh, aye, nae bother, here you go.' Jamie scribbled a signature on the form and handed back to the man.

'Right, here we go.' One of the men twisted a knob on the canister and it made whooshing sound. All the lightbulbs in the room lit up and then popped. The telly blinked on and off. 'She's just, eh, getting settled in, pal. Don't worry.'

'What's the story then, what kind of ghost is this?' Jamie asked.

The two delivery men looked at each other.

'You want to tell him or will I?'

'You go for it, mate.'

'She's a poltergeist.'

Jamie sighed. Just his luck.

'Bit of an arse as well,' the man laughed. As he said this, a coaster was flung across the room, skelping him on the side of the head. 'Aw the best, wee man.'

***

'Awrite?' Jamie said to the ghost. 'What's your name?'

Silence.

'Em, I hope you like it here. I've just moved in as well.'

Silence.

'Can you, I don't know, give me a sign or something to tell me your name?'

Silence.

Jamie had an idea. He'd seen on YouTube people using white noise to interact with spirits. He dug out an old battery-operated radio his granda had given him when he was a wee boy and tuned in between channels so it was just static he could hear.

'What's your name?'

Kssshhhhhksssskshhhkk SENGA ksshhhksssshhh. Jamie had been expecting a sort of ethereal whisper rather than the gruff Glaswegian voice which came through the radio.

'Senga?'

Kssshhhhkshhh AYE ksshsss

'Awrite, eh, well, welcome to your new home, Senga.' Jamie looked around the room. 'Hope we can be, eh, pals, suppose.'

* * *

After a couple of days, it was obvious to Jamie that he and Senga were not going to be pals. When he came home from work, he'd find Senga had rearranged the food in his cupboards. Jamie liked to store all his tins upside down (so the contents would slide out more easily) and Senga had turned them all over. It was a minor inconvenience, but it was still enough to annoy him. She'd hide the remote for the telly. Tie his shoelaces in really tight knots. Rip up letters as they came through the door, leaving little white scraps of paper strewn everywhere. Sometimes he'd wake up to find that Senga had dressed him during the night. He woke up one day dressed in the suit he wore exclusively funerals, prompting him to think for a moment that he'd died and was buried in the suit. The length of time it took him to undo the knotted tie made him late for work.

Jamie tried his best to be civil towards her. She was an old woman after all. Well, he assumed she was, and he didn't want to antagonise her in case she upped the ante. But he was getting pissed off. So he turned the radio on again.

'Please,' he said, 'gonnae stop winding me up. It's no funny.'

Kssshhh But it's a laugh kkkssshhhh

'It's no a laugh. I was late for work because of you. I got disciplined and everything.'

Kkkssshhk Aw fucking lighten up, son kssssshhhhk

Jamie shook his head. As he did, Senga turned the volume up to full on the radio.

Kssshhk Wit ye gonnae dae? Phone an exorcist? They're illegal noo. Yer stuck wi me. So deal wi it Kssshhhk

'Fuck,' Jamie sighed.

* * *

Jamie was off work the next day. He still got up at his usual time though, wanting to get out of the house as soon as he could. Showered and dressed, ready to head out for breakfast and a walk, the door went. He assumed it was the postman with a parcel or something.

It was a delivery of sorts, just not the kind he was hoping for. It was the same two guys who had delivered Senga. Standing between them was the same kind of capsule Senga had come in.

'Aw magic!' Jamie exclaimed. 'Yous here to take her away, aye?' Jamie thumbed over his shoulder towards the end of the hall where Senga was pouring cornflakes on the floor.

The two delivery guys looked at each other and snorted with laughter.

'Naw, sadly no, pal. We've goat another wan fur ye.'

'Another one?! Nah, no chance.' Jamie tried to shut the door over but one of the guys stuck a boot over the threshold.

'You were sent letters about this, pal. "Do not reply if you object to having another ghost roommate" it said. Ahm assuming you never bothered yer arse tae reply.'

'Ah never goat any letters!' Jamie shouted, trying his best to close the door.

'Ye did. Maybe ye just binned them or something. Anyway, disnae matter noo, yer new roommate's here.'

'Senga,' Jamie said under his breath as he noticed a piece of torn envelope next to his doormat. He admitted defeat and opened the door once again.

'Mon through. What have I got this time? Ghost of a murderer? Some creepy wee lassie? An actual fucking demon?'

'You're no a million miles away with demon, pal. But don't worry, this wan's quite sound. He's a sleep paralysis apparition.'

The guys brought the canister into the living room. Jamie had started to feel when Senga was around. Whether it was a slight change in temperature or air pressure or something, he didn't know but he could tell now that she was right beside him, and she wasn't happy.

'Aye, as I said, this lad's quite sound,' one of the delivery guys said. 'Quite scary to look at but don't let that put you off him, he's a wee softy. Name's Mungo.'

The guy tried to turn the valve on the canister to release Mungo but it closed back over, seemingly by itself.

The guy tried again. Every time he got it open a wee bit it would turn back.

'It's Senga,' Jamie said. 'I don't think she wants this ghost here either.'

'Well, he's no got anywhere else to go, mate. Your pal better pack it in and let us do our job.'

Jamie felt Senga's presence leave the room. 'Think that's her away, lads.'

Mungo came out the canister as a cloud of pale beige dust and reassembled to form what was a truly harrowing sight. He was around four feet tall with dumpy legs and long, skinny arms ending in pencil thin fingers with sharp nails. He had a long nose and pointy ears, glassy black eyes, a bald head and skin the mottled colour of a slowly healing bruise. He was ugly as fuck.

'What's his story?' Jamie asked the guys. Mungo smiled revealing row upon row of needlelike teeth. 'What's a sleep paralysis apparition?'

'Well, the thing with sleep paralysis is people often report seeing old hags or demon-like creatures in their room but are unable to move a muscle – Mungo here is one of them. The woman who he used to appear to every night underwent therapy to stop her getting the sleep paralysis, so poor Mungo here has nowhere to go now.'

'Could he no just have stayed with that woman?'

'She's terrified of him, mate, fur fuck sake! It's a shame, really, he's cool.'

'You fucking take him then if he's that sound!' Jamie was getting annoyed now. Mungo looked hurt by Jamie's words. 'Nae offence.'

'He's been sent here – end of,' the delivery guy said. 'Now sign this so we can get on with our deliveries.'

***

Jamie was left standing in his living room, staring at the figure from someone's worst nightmares.

'Awrite,' Jamie said. He squatted down so he could shake Mungo's hand. He was feeling a wee bit guilty for being so hostile about him coming to live with him; the wee thing had just been made homeless after all.

Mungo held out one of his claw-tipped hands. 'Awrite,' he said.

'Fuckin hell,' said Jamie. 'Didn't expect you to have a Scottish accent.'

'Mah name's Mungo fur fuck sake, pal!' the creature laughed. Jamie's confused face told him he'd have to elaborate on this quip. 'Like Saint Mungo.'

'Aw, eh, aye...of course.'

'You don't know who that is, dae ye?'

Jamie stood up. Mungo had spent centuries sitting on people's chests, staring into their faces and had learnt to read what humans were thinking, even just from the look in their eyes. What Mungo was reading from Jamie right now was that he wasn't the sharpest knife in the drawer.

'Patron saint ae Glesga, pal. Right good cunt, so he wis.'

Jamie heard a crackle coming from the big light above him. It turned on and kept getting brighter.

'Aw Senga, No agai–'

POP

'You're costing me a fucking fortune in lightbulbs by the way!' Jamie shouted in despair.

'Poltergeist, eh?' Mungo asked, climbing up onto the couch, his bare feet slapping against the laminate flooring as he tried to jump up. Jamie gave him a hand and sat next to him as Senga knocked Jamie's new Ikea cactus off the window ledge.

'Aye, she's a been a bit, eh, difficult tae be honest.'

Senga flicked both Mungo and Jamie's ears.

'Thing wae poltergeists is that they're frustrated. They're trapped oan earth and cannae get through tae the other side until they finish witever unfinished business they've goat. But that's another hing, how can they right a wrong or make peace if the person they need tae sort stuff oot wae is deid? Or wit if they've been trapped oan earth that long they cannae remember wit it is they need tae sort oot? It's a shame really,' Mungo sighed.

'Ye think I need tae help her then?'

'They need tae sort it themselves, no much you can dae. Unless ye exorcise her an that's sortae frowned upon noo, eh?'

'Frowned upon? It's illegal. I'm fucking stuck wi her. I mean, at least you seem sound, but her?' The sound of a mirror in the hallway crashing to the floor didn't even elicit so much as a flinch from Jamie. 'She's murder, man.'

* * *

Jamie and Mungo spent the day getting to know each other despite Senga's escalating antics. Jamie thought Mungo was actually really sound and Mungo thought Jamie's body was perfect for possessing. He didn't tell Jamie this, of course. That night they even shared a couple of bottles of beer and watched the football. After the final whistle went and the pundits had stopped spouting out their list of clichés, Jamie felt it was time for bed.

'Wee man, ahm gonnae head to bed,' Jamie announced. 'In fact, where you gonnae sleep? *Dae* you even sleep actually?'

'Aye, ah'll just kip in your room if that's cool?' Mungo said.

'Eh, no really, naw. Ah mean, you're sound an aw that but ah like mah ain space.'

'Ahm a sleep paralysis demon,' Mungo laughed. 'Specifically, ahm *your* sleep paralysis demon noo.'

'Ah don't get sleep paralysis though?' Jamie was confused.

'Well, ye dae noo an ah don't really sleep – ah go intae a sortae trance, but ah need tae be oan somebody's chest, your chest.'

'Could ye just, like, no dae that? Ah don't know much aboot sleep paralysis but it sounds terrifying, man.'

'Och, it's awrite. It'll be a laugh.' Jamie looked unconvinced. 'It wis in the contract that ye signed earlier anyway.'

'It's in the contract that you need tae sit oan my chest?'

'Aye.'

'Fucking hell,' Jamie sighed. Ghosts were an absolute pain in the arse.

***

During the night, Jamie felt himself wake up. He didn't know what time it was and he couldn't turn his head to check his bedside clock. It wasn't pitch black but it didn't seem to be anywhere near morning. He tried to lift his hands, his legs, anything, but he couldn't. He was paralysed. Then he felt a weight pressing down on the bed, like someone had just sat down on the end. He felt a hand clasp around his knee through the covers, then another hand grab his thigh. It was moving towards him. Mungo. Mungo sat on Jamie's chest, resting on his haunches, clicking his long fingernails together.

Click...click...click

He brought his face down low, near Jamie's. Jamie tried to scream but couldn't. Jamie could feel Mungo's hot, foul breath on his face. His heart battered at the inside of his rib cage.

Mungo's obsidian eyes widened. He pushed hard down into Jamie's chest, forcing him into the mattress and then…

Jamie woke up, drenched in sweat. Mungo was gone. Panting, he sat up and turned on the light, wiping the sweat from his forehead. Just as he got his breath back, his bedroom door opened. He felt the familiar change in the air; it was Senga. The door closed again.

'Fuck sake,' he muttered. 'You comin tae traumatise me as well, aye?'

Senga ruffled Jamie's hair then slid the radio around on the chest of drawers where it sat.

'Bit late for a chat is it no? Ahm up early fur wo–'

Senga slapped Jamie a belter right across the back of his head.

'Right, awrite, fine. Gies it over and ah'll set it up.' The radio floated over and dropped into Jamie's lap. He had a thought about how good it would be if Senga would go and get stuff for him; he'd never have to get up off his arse ever again. Just motion for the remote for the telly and she'd bring it over to him, get him a drink from the kitchen, bring him over crisps and stuff – it'd be magic, he thought. Then he thought about the ethics of that situation; making a ghost his slave probably wasn't the best thing to do.

Tuning in between channels, Senga's voice came through, ethereal and floaty at first but then she cleared her throat.

Kssshhh He's up tae nae good, son kssshhk, she said. *Ksshhhhk Turn that doon a bit, he'll hear us. kssshhk*

Jamie did as he was told.

'Wit? Who's up tae nae good?'

Kssshhhk Mungo, he wants tae KSSSSHHHHHHHHHH-KKKKSSSHHH.

'Senga wit is it? Ah've no really goat time fur yer games the night.'

Ksshhhhk Mungo is gonnae kssshhhk. Something was stopping her message from coming through.

'The two ae yeez are dain mah nut it in. Goodnight, Senga.' Jamie turned off the radio and tried to get back asleep.

* * *

After work, Jamie went shopping. He had a date lined up with a lassie he'd been talking to on Tinder. He wanted some new gear to wear, plus some nice new bed covers, on the off chance she wanted to head back to his.

This meant Mungo and Senga had the full day to get to know each other. Mungo wanted to talk to her about his plan for taking over Jamie's body, but Senga had been avoiding him all day. She was trying to work out how to make Jamie see the truth. It wasn't that she really liked Jamie or anything, she just didn't dislike him as much as Mungo.

Mungo wanted to help her move on to the next world. She could sort out whatever issues were tethering her to this realm more easily in a human body, and Jamie was a nobody, a two-dimensional wee guy who just went to work during the day and sat about the house at night. He didn't really have any pals or a girlfriend, so supressing his consciousness and taking over his body wouldn't be a great loss to anyone. This was a victimless crime, in fact it barely even qualified as a crime – no one would ever know. Because he was a ghost, Mungo could see Senga as she was before she died. Her physical form, a battle-hardened housewife, would have been intimidating to most people but not Mungo. Compared to some of the women from the 1800s that Mungo had found himself living with, Senga was a choir girl.

'Look, Mrs,' Mungo said as Senga came into the living room, finally ready to confront him. 'Ah don't want there tae be any animosity between us two. Wit ah want tae dae cin benefit you as much as me. Ah want tae help ye.'

'Help me? Tae dae wit? Ye don't even know wit it is ah want? An even if ye did, who says ah need yer help?'

'Right, here's mah plan. Hear me oot.'

Senga crossed her arms. 'Ahm aw ears,' she said with disdain. She hated this wee ugly cunt.

'You've been dain a grand joab wearin Jamie boy doon.'

'Ahm no "wearin him doon", ahm joost bammin him up! That's wit poltergeists dae, ya madman.'

'Regardless,' Mungo said, raising his hands to calm her down. 'Yer still wearin him doon, the boay's at the end ae his tether. Couple ae weeks, maybe three max, an he'll be mega vulnerable. He'll huv a breakdoon an we cin joost waltz right in an *boom*! A brand new boady fur us tae dae witever the fuck we want in instead ae this.' Mungo gestured around Jamie's pitifully small flat. 'Stuck in here wi that cunt. Ah mean he's nice enough, he's joost a bit bland. But that's *good* fur us. You cin use his boady first tae sort yer business oot, move oan, an them ahm gonnae use it tae see the world. Ye know ah've never left Scotland? That's mair than three hunner year ah've been here fur. That's enough tae drive any cunt tae dae a bit ae possessin.'

'Ahm no huvin that. He's a good boay an you're no fuckin possessin anybody, that's oot ae order.'

'Right, well, ye know wit?' Mungo said, getting to his feet, standing up on the couch so he could square up to Senga. He still only came up to her chest however. 'Fuck ye. Ahm gonnae possess him an fuck off while you cin spend the rest ae eternity poppin lightbulbs an aw that. Ah'll wear him doon mah fuckin self.'

Mungo jumped off the couch and went to Jamie's bedroom in a huff.

Two seconds later, Jamie arrived home, laden with bags full of potential outifts for his date and a nice new duvet set.

'Right, show me the new gear,' Mungo said, when Jamie entered the bedroom.

'I've got a couple of shirts, denims, chinos and jumpers. Just need to find the right combo.'

Mungo started prowling through Jamie's bags. 'Haw haw haw, wit's this? Satin bedhseets, eh? *Leopard print* satin bedsheets. Bit, eh, out there, d'ye no think?'

'Nah,' Jamie replied. 'They're belters. Sexy an that, ye no think?'

'Eh, aye witever you say, pal.'

'Just fancied something a bit different.'

'Aye, well, they certainly are *different*. Never had you doon as an animal print kindae guy. Let's hope this wee burd likes them the night, eh? Moan, ah'll help ye change the bed then we can pick ye an outfit.'

After heading to meet his date, Jamie was thinking about how nice Mungo seemed to be. Apart from the sleep paralysis, and the fact he wasn't exactly pleasant on the eye, Mungo was, actually, quite sound. He thought that if he had to pick between Senga and Mungo, he'd definitely choose Mungo and get rid of Senga. He might look into that actually, he thought. Surely he could just exorcise her, who would know? Could a ghost phone the police? Was exorcism the same as murder? Nah, surely not.

While in the bedroom, Mungo removed the batteries from the radio Senga used to communicate with Jamie.

* * *

Things went well on Jamie's date, the two of them found they had very little in common but they got steaming and had a belter of a time anyway. One thing led to another and after his seventh or eighth drink, Jamie made his move and asked her to go to back to his. She said aye.

'Leopard print?' Megan said, sprawling out onto Jamie's bed. 'Very nice.'

'Quite fucking sexy, eh?' Jamie was steaming and saying some very out-of-character things. Megan was lapping it up though. He ripped off his nice new tan coloured shirt, unbuckled his belt and got on top Megan who was casually removing her drawers.

What neither of them had noticed was Mungo, sitting quietly, in the corner of the room. And also, perhaps crucially, what Jamie hadn't noticed, was that Senga was in the room, trying to warn him about Mungo. If he'd turned the bedroom light on he would have seen, written in Nutella on his mirrored wardrobe: MUNGO IS TRYING TO POSSESS YOU.

Under the covers, thrusting away on top of Megan, Jamie's new satin sheets kept sliding off him and he had to keep hoisting them up around himself.

'Just leave them off,' said Megan.

'No, it's a wee bit cold,' moaned Jamie.

Senga had to do something to get Jamie's attention before Mungo, crouched at the foot of the bed and slyly tugging at the sheet, carried out the next part of his plan. She tried ruffling his hair, pulling his ears and slapping him across the face. She had no idea what Mungo was about to do but she knew it wouldn't end well. Through the fog of the drink he'd consumed, Jamie realised Senga was in the room and grunted his disapproval but still carrying on with the task at hand.

'Everything okay?' asked Megan, seeing Jamie's face twitching in the twilight.

'Aye, fine.'

Mungo crept up onto the bed as the covers slid down revealing Jamie's bare arse.

He winked at Senga.

'Don't you fuckin dare,' said Senga. Mungo just smiled at her and moved closer.

Senga tried to make Jamie's bedroom light come on but she'd popped the bulb for a laugh the other day and Jamie had given up replacing them. She turned on the radio but no sound came out of it.

Mungo was waiting for perfect moment to strike. He really wanted to plunge a finger into Jamie's arsehole but his long nails would have did a fair amount of internal damage. He paused for a moment working out the rhythmic thrusting of Jamie's hips, watching his baws swing freely. As the scrotum swung towards Mungo he would grab and twist for maximum shock.

Three... Senga tried to open the window but Jamie had locked it and flung away the wee key.

Two... she banged the bedroom door shut but Jamie and Megan didn't even notice. They were both so close to finishing.

One... Mungo went for it.

As soon as Mungo's freezing cold several-hundred-year-old-hand made contact with his bawsack, Jamie screamed in rage, 'AAARRGHH, SENGAAAA!' Mungo slid away silently under the bed.

'Senga?!' shouted Megan, throwing Jamie off her. 'Who the fuck's Senga? Yer ex or something, aye?'

'Naw, it's no that, don't be daft,' he laughed nervously, trying to calm Megan down a wee bit. 'Senga's the ghost that stays here. Poltergeist, actually. She just grabbed mah baws. I'd never shout an ex burd's name in bed, no wi you.'

'You're a sick bastard. I'm away.' Megan gathered her clothes and left, slamming the door behind her.

Jamie sat on the end of his bed, dejected.

'Ye awrite, pal?' Mungo asked him.

'I cannae deal with this anymore, there must be a fucking number or something I can phone to complain aboot her.'

'That wee burd? How, wit happened?'

'Naw, no her. *Her*,' Jamie gestured at the air round about him.

'Aye, maybe ye should get rid ae her,' Mungo suggested. 'Probably fur the best. Eh, pal?'

***

Jamie flicked through the paperwork until he found the Ghost Roommate Agreement. He pored over it, looking for any kind

of loophole or clause that would allow him to get shot of Senga.
He'd found some adverts online for psychics who claimed they
could quieten any unruly spirits but they all looked like Derek
Acorah or Mystic Meg. He eventually came upon the FAQ
section of his agreement:

What if my ghost turns malevolent or inflicts physical harm upon me/my family/guests?

*This is highly unlikely to happen. However, in the event of such a
situation arising please call the number below. We have trained
mediums and a team of ghost mediators who can resolve any situation
without resorting to barbaric and extreme measures such as exorcisms.
If a situation cannot be resolved then the ghost in question can be
removed but this will only be considered in exceptional circumstances.*

'I've got a problem with my ghost,' Jamie barked down the
line to the operator. 'Aye, maybe no malevolent as such but
definitely inflicting physical harm... Well, I don't really want
to say but it involves my, eh, privates. Right, cheers, I'll be in.'

'What's the script?' Mungo asked.

'They're sending somebody out just now.'

'Just a person? Just wan guy or suhin?'

'A ghost liaison officer and their partner, they said.'

'Aye but the partner's another human though, eh? Surely?
It's no a person an a ghost, is it?' A ghost would find out what
Mungo was up to in seconds.

'Dunno,' said Jamie. 'Although, if it was a person and a
ghost that would be better surely. A ghost would be able to
see what Senga was up to – trying to drive me insane by the
looks of it.'

Less than ten minutes later, the door went. Jamie opened it
and invited the woman inside. She was wearing a long black
coat, covered in intricate lacey detail, and she had her black
hair tied up in a severe bun. Under one arm she carried a small
version of the canister that Senga and Mungo were delivered in.

'I'm Helena,' she said, sitting down next to Mungo on the couch. Who inched slightly away from her. 'Having some spirit troubles then?'

'Not half,' said Jamie. 'It's no him there that's causing the bother though. It's a poltergeist.'

'I see, I see. She's been... inappropriate, I hear?'

'That's putting it lightly. But aye.'

'I'll just get my partner out and she can ask you two some questions, I trust that's okay?' she turned to Mungo.

If Mungo's eyes had whites they'd have been showing now, such was his panic. He could transport himself to another room, but he was tethered to Jamie's flat so couldn't leave no matter what. He sat nervously clicking his nails together. 'That'll be fine,' he gulped. This was it, he thought, caught an absolute belter. No rules about punishments for misdemeanours had been explained to him, he had no idea what would happen. Ghost jail maybe? If there was such a thing. Sent to live with some other poor cunt?

Helena turned the valve on the mini canister to unleash a plume of faintly glowing blue light. The light assembled itself into the shape of a ball, around the size of a balloon, and hovered fitfully in the middle of Jamie's living room.

'What kind of ghost is that?' asked Jamie.

'*She*,' Helena iterated, 'is an orb. The most intuitive kind of ghost. Picks up on both human and spirit emotions and thoughts incredibly well.'

Mungo started to quite obviously sweat as the orb hung over him before it moved onto Jamie and then finally Senga.

Helena nodded to herself as the orb moved in a figure of eight around her head.

'The poltergeist has been trying to warn you about something,' Helena said, her eyes tightly closed.

'Squeezing somebody's baws is a funny way of warning anybody about anything, I have to say.'

'It wasn't her who did... that. It was him on the couch.'

'*Him?*' exclaimed Jamie. 'Nah, no chance. He's no like that. It must've been Senga. Ahhh, fur fuck sake!' Senga slapped Jamie on the back of the head. 'See what she's like!'

A panicked Mungo stood up. His plan was unravelling right before his eyes. Rumbled. Unless he did something right now he was fucked.

'He's going to try possess you,' Helena continued, her hands at her temples. 'He's going to try it right now.'

Mungo leaped off the couch at Jamie. Jamie was nowhere near ready to be possessed but Mungo had no choice. If Jamie had been primed, Mungo would have simply fallen into Jamie's body, purging his soul in the process. As it was, he just bounced off Jamie's chest and hit the floor.

'Wit the fuck?' said Jamie.

Mungo slapped the floor in frustration. 'Basturt!' he spat.

Helena silently turned the valve on the canister.

'Why me?' Jamie asked Mungo.

'Because yer a boring basturt an nae cunt wid even notice.'

Mungo was sucked into the canister.

'What happens now?'

'Ghost jail, unfortunately,' said Helena. 'Can't be having that kind of carry on.'

'Cannae believe I was nearly possessed.' Jamie slumped onto the couch where Mungo had sat. 'Actual possessed by a ghost. Ha! That's mental!'

The blue orb resumed its place in the canister as well.

'She says you should get rid of the leopard print covers as well,' Helena said.

'Who said that? The orb?'

'No, not her, Senga,' she laughed. 'You should try and communicate with her. Tell her thanks for trying to warn you. She's a kind spirit.' Helena slipped out of the flat.

* * *

Jamie took batteries from the telly remote and stuck them into the radio.

'Senga,' he said cheerfully. 'You there?'

Kssshhhhhhkkssshhhh

'Senga?' he tried again.

Kssshhhhhhkkssshhhh

Nothing but static.

UNDER SURVEILLANCE

The head of surveillance dropped a manila folder onto Beverly's desk. 'Agent Beauchamp, new assignment for you,' she said. 'Young boy in Scotland. He's into some dodgy shit on the dark web. I want eyes on him for the next month.'

'No problem, Deborah,' Beverly replied. She was getting bored with her current case anyway. Frat houses weren't exactly a hotbed of stimulating conversation. Working for the FBI, watching people through their laptops and phone cameras for hours on end, it helped if the people were actually interesting. ISIS fighters in Syria were usually a good laugh, and Beverly would occasionally be assigned the odd celebrity to keep an eye on, but those assignments were usually reserved for more senior officers – which she was not. Not yet, anyway.

Beverly opened the folder and lifted out the subject's picture (taken using his phone's front-facing camera without his knowledge, of course). The subject was a young guy with a mop of brown curly hair, sticky-out ears and chubby cheeks. Kind eyes sat behind a pair of glasses.

Beverly poked a finger into one of her own chubby cheeks. She then rubbed her hands through her own tightly-curled brown hair. Beverly saw a lot of herself in this young guy. Not just looks-wise either. A quick scan of his file told a tale of underachievement Beverly was all too familiar with herself. Beverly, like the boy in Scotland, was unemployed and not in any kind of education when she was eighteen, despite showing a lot of promise at high school. It wasn't until her late twenties that she got her act together. If she'd applied herself at school, gone to college, and got a ten year head start on her career, she'd probably be in an even cushier job than this one. In fact, she'd probably be retired by now. Her job in the FBI was good and she felt lucky to have it, but what if there was something else out there she was meant to do? Nah, she knew deep down that wasn't really for her. She liked her job now. But, she thought, maybe she could live vicariously through this wee guy in Scotland? Treat him like a pet project, guide him through life with careful manipulation of his phone, social media apps, correspondence with friends and family. Yep, Beverly decided. This was truly her dream job.

She knew the wee guy, Zack McJimpsey, eighteen, Airdrie, clearly wasn't up to anything bad. The way the FBI's surveillance system worked was it randomly picked and assigned Dark Net users to spy on – young Zack was just using it to buy a wee bit of weed every now and again. Her boss, Deborah, considered everything and everyone on the Dark Net to be 'dodgy shit' however.

Beverly looked up Zack's IP address and brought up a split screen view of Zack's phone screen and the view from his phone's front facing camera. She thought she'd activate the surveillance software and check on him just before she finished up for the day.

Zack was having himself an early evening wank. His brow deeply furrowed in concentration.

'Shit, buddy,' Beverly said to herself. This was something she'd seen a thousand different guys do thanks to this job. 'You go for it.'

Beverly logged out of her work computer and headed home.

* * *

The next morning she arrived at work, excited to see what she could get up to. In the queue at the staff canteen, she noticed her friend Henry in front of her.

'Yo, Henry,' she said, patting her colleague on the back.

'M-mornin, Bev,' Henry took his coffee from the barista with a trembling hand.

'New assignment, huh?' Beverly asked. She'd seen Henry look this shaken a lot over the last few months. He'd been bumped up a couple of levels after doing some excellent work on undercover Russian spies in New York. Henry was now in charge of surveillance on the UK's royal family. The upper echelons of the FBI considered this to be the top job, bestowed upon agents of exceptional competence as a reward. For the agents however, it was the job no one wanted.

'I knew they were lizards,' Henry said, his eyes wide and wild. 'But the shit these... things get up to. It's not right, man.'

'Jeez, lighten up, bud. Your memory gets wiped when you get your next promotion anyway. And besides, the money's pretty sweet, huh?'

'Yeah, s-suppose you're right. How's your new assignment?'

'It's really neat actually. I've only had a quick skim through his file and a little look at him through his cell phone but I'm sure he's gonna be a lot of fun.'

'Yeah, uh, good for you, I suppose.' Henry trudged away to his office with his shoulders slumped.

***

Beverly looked at the view of Zack's room. First through his phone, then through his laptop camera, and then through his TV. Posters of footballers adorned the walls, empty crisp packets and other rubbish covered the floor. She could make out the shape of Zack and someone, or most likely, some*thing*, else, curled up under the covers, still asleep.

'Holy crap,' Beverly muttered, shaking her head. 'You live like this?'

It was 9am in Washington DC but 1pm in Airdrie.

Beverly opened one of the drawers at her desk and pulled out an iPhone. She clicked a couple of times on the computer screen and suddenly the iPhone was now a perfect clone of Zack's that she could use. *First thing's first, let's sort out this awful sleeping pattern.* Beverly set an alarm to go off in a minute's time. She sat back in her chair and unwrapped a blueberry muffin. 'Rise and shine, young man.' She set the phone's volume to max. Beverly laughed as Zack shot out of bed in a panic, his pet alsatian crawling out from under the covers as well. Beverly could hear a voice coming from somewhere else in Zack's house but couldn't quite make out what it was saying, or even if the voice was male or female. The microphone on Zack's phone was good at picking up sounds in the near vicinity but not so good at anything else. Luckily for Beverly, Zack already had a high-quality listening device in his room – an Amazon Alexa. Beverly slipped on a pair of headphones and tapped into the device. Even if it was unplugged, the device would still be listening to everything said, every footstep, every muttered-under-his-breath expletive, even every fart. Alexa would hear it and transmit it right into Beverly's ears.

'Zack, move yer arse an help me wi mah messages!' the voice shouted. It was an older female, most likely, Beverly guessed, Zack's mother. *Why would she need help with her messages though?* She watched Zack get out of bed and head downstairs, so she switched the surveillance feed to the downstairs TV. It was very handy for the FBI that in 99% of homes which had a TV, they all pointed their furniture at it and placed it in a position where everyone in the room could see it; absolutely perfect for watching people. The feed showed Zack helping his mum unpack bags of shopping. *Messages means groceries in Scotland then...huh.* Beverly realised she was going to have learn the language of Scots in order for her experiment with Zack to be successful.

'...lyin in yer wankin chariot at this time ae day,' Zack's maw cursed under her breath.

Beverly smirked when she heard this. *Wanking chariot. I'm using that.*

While Zack helped his maw put the messages away, Beverly flicked through his phone, checking Zack's texts, WhatsApp and Facebook messages.

Let's see... we know has no job but what about a girlfriend? Nope. Didn't think so. Friends, let's see... hmmm a couple. They're all losers like him though. According to Google Maps he hasn't left the house in... six days. Man, you should be so grateful I found you.

***

Beverly decided to apply for some overtime for this project. She wanted to keep an eye on Zack for as many hours of the day as possible and she didn't want anyone else working on this, interfering and messing it up for her.

Later that afternoon, Beverly watched Zack return to his 'wanking chariot'.

No friends, no job, no girlfriend, no prospects, no hobbies, well, apart from jacking off. How the hell does he fill his days?

Beverly decided she'd watch Zack for a day, make some notes, keep the interference to a minimum and create a plan of attack.

Almost straight away, Zack started performing the act his 'chariot' was named after.

Jeez, that thing is going to fall off.

But then Zack took a picture of his erect penis.

What's he going to do with that?

Zack opened up Instagram on his phone and clicked on a very pretty girl's profile then hit the 'message' button.

Woah, woah, woah, don't do that, c'mon, man.

'I've got something big to show you,' wrote Zack then he hit send. The subject of the picture he was about to attach and send was most definitely not "big".

Beverly intervened. She couldn't let this happen. She cancelled the dick pic and instead attached a nice picture of Zack's dog, Henrik.

Zack didn't notice what Beverly had done and sat back to watch some afternoon telly.

And that seemed to be all he had planned for the next several hours. So Beverly did a bit of snooping on the girl, the apparent object of Zack's desires – Holly. They seemed like they'd be a nice fit, maybe she was a little bit out of his league if anything, but they certainly had a lot in common. They watched a lot of the same stuff on Netflix, including *Still Game,* whatever that was. They'd watched every episode at least 16 times. *Holy shit, it must be good.* Similar tastes in music, humour, judging from their tweets, although she was a bit more ambitious if her constant posting of inspirational quotes was to be believed. Perhaps crucially, she was single.

Lets get these two together, thought Beverly.

'How's work?' Beverly's husband, Mitch, text her.

'Have the best assignment yet. Wish I was allowed to tell you about it,' Beverly replied.

***

After several hours of sitting in what was practically a vegetative state, Zack turned off his telly and checked his phone.

Instagram: Holly_x0x0 sent you a message

Zack braced himself to be called a 'creep' or a 'perv' as was the usual response to his favoured method of instigating communication with opposite sex, the humble dick pic.

'He's such a cutie!' said Holly, replying with the 'love heart eyes' emoji. 'I love him. Wait til I show you mine.'

Zack felt pretty chuffed with himself until he noticed that Holly was referring to the picture of his dog. Confused, he refreshed the page to see if this was just some kind of glitch which he definitely didn't mean to send. *Who just randomly sends a burd a picture ae their dug?* he thought to himself. *Fuck it, she seems intae it.*

'Aw cheers,' he typed back, Beverly watching the confusion unfold across his face.

Zack then did a wee bit of gambling. Opening up the betting app on his phone, he deposited the last tenner in his bank account and put it all on a ridiculously high-odds football accumulator.

Beverly rolled her eyes. She despised gambling. If Zack's bet came in though, he'd make over two thousand pounds; more than enough for her to get his life on track.

After depositing all of his money, Zack pulled a wooden box from under his bed.

What the hell's in that?

It was where he kept his weed and the various accoutrements that went along with it. He rolled up a joint and sat puffing it in bed, opening his window to let any smell out.

Smoking in the house? Tut tut, young Zack.

'Zack, yer tea's oot!' his maw shouted.

"Yurteezoot"? What the hell does that mean?

Scots was truly baffling to Beverly. Zack hastily dropped his joint and started waving his hands around, trying to get the smoke out of the window. 'Coming, ma,' he shouted back. He slid the box back under his bed and went downstairs.

'Beverly!' said Deborah, striding over to Beverly's desk. 'What's your assignment up to?'

'Pretty inactive, to be honest,' she replied, without thinking. 'Just lies about, jacking off and smoking weed.'

'Maybe just cut down his surveillance to another day or so and cancel your overtime, huh? Or we could move you on to another case?'

'Oh, no, we can't do that!' This would scupper Beverly's plan. 'I think you were right actually. I think he's maybe into some *dodgy shit*,' she whispered the last two words for emphasis.

Deborah nodded understandingly. 'Okay, okay. You have until the end of the week tops, though. You know what these Dark Net guys are like. If he's a pedophile or some other kind of pervert you take him down straight away, okay?'

To "take someone down" was FBI speak for "get them in the fucking jail", but Beverly wasn't too keen on this method. She didn't consider herself to be a snitch. With the FBI's resources she had at her disposal, she could bestow much more damaging punishments on people than the justice system ever could.

'Okay,' said Beverly. Now she only had one week rather than the month as she'd initially planned.

She had to have this boy's life on track by Friday and it was already Tuesday. Time was running out. But she knew she could do it. He had no distractions, he did nothing all day, every day, so he was perfect to manipulate and play about with. She could have this wee guy on top of the world by Friday.

* * *

Later that night, over dinner, Mitch was telling a funny story about one of his clients.

'It was soooo funny. But how was your day? Can't you tell me anything about your new case?' Mitch asked.

'You know the rules,' Beverly said dejectedly. 'I'm not allowed to tell you.'

'Oh c'mon, just tell me. Who's gonna know?'

True, thought Beverly. Their home, and the homes of all agents at, and above Beverly's pay grade, was free of all bugs and surveillance equipment. Removed under the guise of "pest control" before they moved in so as not to reveal the FBI's secrets to their employee's partners.

'Nah, I… I really shouldn't…'

'Fine don't tell me. I won't tell you about Andy's date last night then.'

Shit.

'Okay, okay… I'm watching this kid just now,' said Beverly.

'"Kid"?' said Mitch. 'What the hell could a kid be up to that the government needs to watch them?'

'Well, he's eighteen. He's from Scotland!'

'Scotland? Cool. So what's he up to? Is he like a kilt-wearing serial killer or something?'

'No he's just active on the Dark Net and all that kind of stuff, drug stuff. Little bit of weed. Anyway.' Beverly poured more wine into Mitch glass. 'His life is a mess, right, just a total waster.'

'Aw, that's so sad.'

'That was my reaction too.'

'So what are you gonna do? Stop him from buying weed and stuff?'

'Well, I was thinking I could help him? Because the weed is probably the least of his worries. I mean, he jacks off constantly and today he sent a picture of his erect penis to some random girl.'

'Jeez, you should be ruining his life, surely, not trying to *help* him.'

'No, that's the thing. I want him to realise that that kind of thing is *wrong*. I'm gonna make this boy into a gentleman. Help him get a job, a girlfriend all that kind of thing.'

'I dunno,' said Mitch. 'That's... not really your job is it?'

'Oh lighten up. Let me have a little fun. Besides, I was kinda the same when I was his age, minus the dick pics, obviously. Imagine if someone had given me a kick up the ass back then? The difference it could've made to my life?'

'Fine, okay, I'm just saying be careful and don't get into trouble. That sounds like something your boss would get mad at you for.'

'Hmmm.' Beverly mulled this over. 'Maybe you're right. But it'll be okay. I'm only watching him until Friday, anyway. Oh, by the way, we need to watch a show on Netflix that's massive in Scotland. It'll help me understand young Zachary a little better. It's called *Still Game*.'

* * *

'Morning, Henry,' Beverly said at work the next day. She was feeling cheery and bright. Henry flinched as she said this. He didn't even reply. Just gave her a deeply disturbed stare.

'Are you okay?' she asked. He most definitely did not look okay but she didn't know how else to phrase it.

'They had one of their rituals last night.' Henry's trembling hand moved to his brow, as if rubbing his forehead would somehow erase the memory he was recalling. 'Poor Meghan. That's her definitely a Royal. The lizards have her now.'

'Is it *that* bad?'

Henry just looked at Beverly then to the doors at the end of the cafeteria. Beverly followed his line of sight.

'I can't do this,' Henry said and bolted for the doors. He almost made it out, but two armed guards grabbed him and frogmarched him to his office.

'Get a grip, man. It can't be *that* bad, surely.'

* * *

At her desk, Beverly brought up Zack's feed once again. *You're getting a job today, young man.*

While Zack was still asleep, Beverly checked his betting app to see how his bet got on last night. Incredibly, he'd won. £2.4k, more than enough to sort him right out.

Psychology was a big part of Beverly's work. Knowing how to direct people, how to make them think certain ways, follow cues. It was easy when you knew how. Ads could be a great tool to get people to do things. In order to get Zack sorted out, she wanted him to learn to drive and maybe get a wee cheap car with his money.

She made sure every ad on his social media feeds would be for the cheapest driving school in his area and prioritised any tweets from girls saying they loved guys who could drive as this seemed to be the only way to motivate the boy.

When Zack woke up and seen he'd won big at the bookies he was jumping on his bed for joy. Straight away though he tried to gamble it all on a virtual roulette game.

For the love of fuck. Beverly picked up then slammed down her keyboard hard. She was getting annoyed at how fucking stupid Zack could be.

She picked up the clone of Zack's phone and froze it so the bet wouldn't go through. *Fucking idiot.* She withdrew the money and put it into his bank and changed his password and blocked access to any gambling sites on the internet so he couldn't gamble at all now.

When Beverly unfroze Zack's phone, she was pleased to see he just started scrolling through his twitter app and, after seeing a couple of tweets, clicked on the driving school's advert.

If he learns to drive, he'll be more employable, he'll get a job, maybe a girlfriend and he'll be set up nicely for the future.

Beverly imagined checking in on him in a couple of years' time; maybe he'd be married, have kids, a nice job, a nice house and, hopefully, not wanking himself into oblivion every day.

Driving lessons booked, now it was time to make sure he didn't fuck things up with Holly.

'Morning, big tits,' he messaged her saying. Beverly held her head in her hands and muttered, 'Lord, give me strength,' as she cancelled his message. 'Morning, beautiful,' she changed it to. Zack fumbled for his glasses and re-read his message.

Fuck sake, she's gonnae hink ahm some kind ae poof.

After having to edit a few more explicit texts from Zack, he eventually calmed down and became less of a horny disaster. Within a couple of hours they had arranged to go on their first date. To impress Holly, Zack had claimed he was on the hunt for a job.

After she came back from lunch, Beverly was stunned to see he was putting together a CV. Written in comic sans, using his email ZackFTQ1888@hotmail.com and only half a page long, but at least it was a start. Beverly stopped his email from sending when he fired his CV off to a local call centre and fixed it up herself.

By the end of her shift, Zack had a first date, a first driving lesson and his first interview all lined up. An excellent day's work, she thought. AND he'd only had two wanks. He would be fine without her after Friday, she reckoned.

***

On Thursday, Beverly could hardly believe her time with Zack was almost over. The night before she'd realised that the only real time Zack and his mother spoke was when she shouted him down for dinner or when she was giving him into trouble. It was like she was his keeper rather than his maw; like he was a very large, very horny, hamster. Beverly wanted to at least try and repair their relationship before she cut ties with him tomorrow.

When Zack text his maw, rather than walk downstairs and tell her to her face, he told her that he'd landed an interview and had his first driving lesson tomorrow. Beverly changed his wording so it was a bit nicer.

Instead of *got a job interview next week an start driving lessons the morra*, it said, *got a job interview next week an start driving lessons the morra. Maybe 'll be able to take you to get the messages soon x*

Beverly had a wee tear in her eye as she watched Zack's maw read the text with a big smile on her face. This was truly the best job in the world.

***

Later that night, Beverley and Mitch were lying in bed, watching a nature documentary on the telly. 'You seem to be having such a great time at work, Beverley!' Mitch was saying. 'Is it all down to the… what did you call him? *Wee guy?* I take it things are going well?'

As Beverley was about to answer him, she was struck by the footage of three helpless baby birds sat in a nest high up in a tree while a snake slithered along a branch towards them. 'Shit!'

'What is it?' Mitch asked.

'The camera people could move the snake away, right? Save the baby birds?'

'Yeah, they could, I mean *I* probably would. *God,* how can they just sit there and let that happen?'

'Because it's not their place to interfere. The cameraperson's job is to observe, to learn what animals do in the wild, and to use that knowledge to protect them in the future. Stepping in every time an animal gets in danger means that they don't learn anything.'

Mitch nodded. 'I get it – it's the natural order of things.'

'No, nothing like that – there's always room to change. I mean, I did. But I only found the way to change because of what I went through. This is more like survival of the fittest. Like in *Back to the Future.* I could be irrevocably changing the intended timeline of the universe for the worse!'

'Shit,' said Mitch. Beverly was right. 'So what do you do? Can you put things back how they were?'

Beverly mulled it over. 'Hmm. You know, I think I probably could.'

HWFG

***

Operation "Get Wee Zack's Life off the Rails Again" was about to begin. Beverly strode through the cafeteria without picking up her morning coffee, not even stopping to talk to poor Henry who was crouched under a table begging for help.

Zack's driving lesson was booked for 2pm and Zack was still asleep at just after 1pm. Normally, she would set an alarm to wake him up but today she cancelled the alarm he'd set himself for 1:30pm. She then turned his phone on silent so he couldn't hear when the instructor tried to phone him.

Time to fuck up his employment hopes now. She drafted a short email in which she told the call centre's recruitment manager that he had a voice like "a wee jessie" and to "shove the job up his arse" after picking up some Scots from watching *Still Game*.

The she turned her attentions to poor Holly. She could do much better than Zack anyway.

Your dug's fuckin ugly she wrote and hit send.

Eh fuck you then, cheeky arsehole Holly replied, then blocked him.

Zack and his maw had been having a nice wee night together with a Chinese on the couch. Talking and laughing for the first time really since Zack was a wee boy. But, sadly, as Michelle had put it, natural order had to be restored.

Beverly was about to put into motion a plan to inform Zack's maw about his weed smoking up in his room then she had a better idea.

Dick pic.

She attached the most horrible picture Zack had taken of his erect self, made sure it was one with his stupid face in it as well and sent it to his maw. Through the Alexa, she heard his maw scream that her son was 'clatty bastard'.

For good measure, she blocked Zack's access to the Dark

Net so he couldn't even get some weed after all this. God knows he'd need a joint.

'Beverly!' Deborah shouted from across the office. 'Can you come here a sec?'

Shit, thought Beverly. You never got shouted into Deborah's office unless you were about to get into trouble.

'You finished up with young Zack then?' Deborah asked.

'Yes, ma'am,' Beverly replied. 'Just cut off his access to the Dark Net. Was only weed he was buying but, y'know, that's how it starts on there. One minute they're buying weed then the next, guns or an alligator or something.'

Deborah laughed at Beverly's wee joke. *This was a good sign*, thought Beverly.

'The reason I wanted you off that case was – ah Henry!' Henry walked in, his head now completely bald. 'Feeling better after the memory wipe?'

'Well, I can't remember how I was feeling before they wiped my memory but I hear I was pretty bummed out!' Henry laughed.

'That's good to hear. Yes, as I was saying,' Deborah continued. 'The reason I wanted you to finish your current case so soon was so you could take over from Henry, watching the Royal Family. He's had quite enough, I think.'

'It'll be fine,' said Henry, waving his hand at the air. 'It's their feeding season though, so just try not to watch what goes on in the Queen's bedroom. I wrote down that it's very, very bad.'

SNAILS

This isn't a short story. Apologies first of all for that. This is a conspiracy theory I've wanted to share with folk for ages. It's something that's been playing on my mind ever since I first saw a snail in real life.

Honestly, right, hear me out. Don't you fucking dare turn the page and flick to the next story or put the book down or fling it away. Yous are all complicit in this, in my opinion.

I never saw a snail in the flesh, until I was thirteen. You'll be sitting there going like that to yourself, 'This cunt's talking shite. He's at it.' But I remember, pure vividly, clear as day, watching a documentary when I was a wee guy, about insects and all that, and the narrator saying, 'Snails are found only in the south of the UK, where the climate is slightly warmer but still wet enough for them.'

You never used to get snails in Scotland until about 2004.

Slugs, aye, fair enough, they've always been here. But no snails. Now they're everywhere. Just all of a sudden. And no cunt, absolutely no cunt, is saying anything or batting an eyelid.

When I was about four or five I was massively into insects. I had wee toy ones, books about them, videos about them, fucking loved them, right. I could tell you facts about stag beetles, where you'd find the biggest moths in the world, could name like ten species of fly and even knew what fucking food worms liked to eat best. I was an authority on creepy crawlies and let me tell you this: you never used to get snails in Scotland and that is a fact.

Then when I was about fourteen, I was standing looking out

my back door watching one of those mad torrential summer downpours. There's a wee concrete bit out my back and I looked over at it and it was fucking covered in snails. I shouted on my maw and my wee brother to come and see and was like, 'Look, snails!' and my maw went, 'Aw cool, didn't think you got snails in Scotland. Thought you only got them in England.' Wish I'd recorded her saying that on my old Motorola flip phone cause now she says she never said that and that she's seen snails in Scotland since she was a wee lassie.

Absolute fucking liar.

A lot of folk will say I'm just misremembering things from my childhood, a lot of folk will say I'm just being daft. But this is the hill I will die on. I read up online about other people saying things along the same lines as my snail nightmare and there's a phenomenon called the Mandela effect. So-called because apparently lots of people say they remember Nelson Mandela dying in jail in the 80s and even remember watching his funeral on the telly. There's people that swear Sex and the City used to be called Sex *in* the City. I know a couple of people who claim Scott's Porage Oats used to be spelled on the box as Scott's *Porridge* Oats. There's theories that say the Mandela effect is down to time travellers from the future messing about with past or that people have somehow slipped from an alternate universe into our own. This is obviously just speculation and a cool, daft idea but I am not some mad universe hopper.

I'm definitely no misremembering stuff either. I definitely didn't see a snail up until that rainy day when I was fourteen, I swear on my life. Seems a bit weird to say that maybe it was just a weird quirk of fate that I never seen one if they had been here in Scotland the whole time. What would the odds be on not seeing a snail for the first fourteen years of your life in a place where they've apparently always been common? What's the chances of not crossing paths with one for all that time? Must be billions to one.

This is my theory: yous are all just bamming me up. Maybe snails never used to be able to live in Scotland until global warming started to come into play. Our climate here got a wee bit warmer and snails started spreading north of the border to get away from England (who could blame them?) and come up here where we're all dead sound. The French eat snails, so maybe the snails wanted to put a bit more distance between themselves and those weirdos. So maybe when I shouted on my maw to look at the snails for the first time she then went away and told folk to tell me that they'd always been here to fucking gaslight me. Yous are all at it. My maw told one person, they told someone else and so on and so on until everybody in my life, my pals, my family, even strangers on the internet and you reading this book were all in on this big joke at my expense. Well, fucking get it up ye.

INTERVIEW WITH THE SHOE GUY

Getting a hold of the man known only as 'Kojak' wasn't easy. He doesn't have a fixed address or even a phone – I just had to wait for him by the side of the road and hope he'd agree to an interview.

I was hanging around on the hard shoulder of the M74 just outside Glasgow, near where he'd last been sighted. Sure enough, he appeared after just fifteen minutes.

'No the noo,' he'd replied when I asked if I could interview him. 'Ahm a bit busy.' He then reached into his back pocket and pulled out a battered leather diary. 'Two weeks fae the day. Ah'll get ye doon the Tollbooth. Eleven o'cloak.'

'Which tollbooth?' I asked. Being from a small village in the Highlands, I was unaware this was a pub. Kojak just laughed at this, offered me no further information and carried on with his task.

Kojak is the man who leaves single shoes by the roadside. It's an oft repeated question: 'How do you lose a single shoe?' Countless people will have asked it on a motorway journey. No one seems to know anyone who's lost a single shoe, yet we see them, lying lost amongst the litter and dead animals at the side of the road. Why does he put them there? That's what I hope to find out.

Sightings of Kojak are rare as he works almost entirely under the cover of darkness. He has been described as being around forty years of age, five-and-a-half feet tall, with a mane of curly hair, and heavy acne-scarring on his face. The man I met, however, was definitelty a bit older than forty, perhaps mid-fifties I'd say. His hair was pretty wild and shaggy as folk had said, but the scarring on his face looked to have come from fights rather than puberty.

***

The pub is empty. I ask the barmaid if she knows Kojak.

'Who?'

'You know, *him*,' I say. 'That guy. He's been all over Facebook. The guy who leaves the shoes along the side of the road?'

'I don't use Facebook.'

And that was that. I took my can of Diet Coke over to a table in the corner and waited for Kojak.

Around twenty minutes later I had finished my drink and was still waiting. I consider getting another can but two helpings of fizzy juice before midday, even the diet stuff, goes against all my rigidly held beliefs.

Just as I rise from my seat, ready to leave, I hear the door of the pub creak open.

'Ah've been waitin outside fur ages,' Kojak says, poking his head in.

'Oh, sorry, my apologies.' I rush over to shake his hand.

'Bit rude tae go in withoot me, is it no?'

I feel like a child again, being scolded for my lack of manners.

'Grab yer gear an let's go,' he says. He has an aggressive voice, Kojak. It's raspy and rough. I feel very aware of my homogenised "teuchter" accent, as Kojak would go on to call it, softly moulded in my formative years from being surrounded by American and English tourists. He goes back outside, not holding the door open for me even though he sees my hands are full. I deserve it for leaving him waiting.

He leads me along the road to a taxi rank. He makes a jangling sound as he walks, as if his pockets are laden with change.

'Umm, where are we going?'

'Shoppin.'

We bundle into the taxi and he barks the destination at the driver. We're heading to the Glasgow Fort, a shopping park.

No one speaks during the journey. There is a stale smell in the air, musky, and I'm sure it's emanting from Kojak's jacket. The driver makes furtive glances in the rear view mirror at myself and Kojak. My companion stares out the window and I jot down a few notes for questions. Questions such as:

Where do you get the shoes from?
What did you do before all this?
When did you leave your first shoe by the roadside?
Why do you do it only at night?

And, of course: *Why do you do this?*

***

'That'll be oan account, mate,' Kojak says, getting out of the taxi. I'm shocked that the man has an account with a black taxi firm. That's what I get for judging him on his appearance I suppose.

Then the taxi driver turns round and looks at me, expectantly. 'What's the account number, pal?' It was at this moment I realised Kojak was taking the piss out of me. This was to be a recurring theme throughout the day.

I handed over £15 to the driver and got out of the taxi. We were standing in front of a sports shop.

'Well this answers my first question, I suppose,' I laugh to him.

'Eh?'

'You know, where do you get the shoes? I'm assuming it's here?' I nod at the shop.

'Aye, witever. C'moan.'

***

In the shop we are greeted by a tall, skinny staff member in shorts and his shorter, rounder manager who wears a shirt and tie. The manager enthusiastically shakes Kojak's hand.

'Who's this?' the manager asks Kojak, nodding to me.

'Some journalist,' he says. His face is set like stone. The manager thinks better of enquiring further.

'Got some new gear for you, my man,' the staff member says.

'Aboot time.' Kojak speaks as if he's fed up with everything. To him this is all just business, and mundane business at that.

Kojak and I follow the two men into the stock room. The staff member rummages around behind a mountain of cardboard boxes and for several minutes we're left standing awkwardly waiting. He eventually emerges victorious, box raised in triumph above his head. 'Had to keep this hidden for you.'

The words **ODD SHOES** are written in black permanent marker on the side of the box. Kojak lifts a flap and peeks inside. Satisifed at its contents, he reaches inside his jacket.

'Here.' he tosses a sandwich bag full of coins at the staff member.

'Kojak, mate,' the young boy says. He looks concerned.

'Wit is it?' Kojak snaps.

'Ah won't be able tae use these. These are the auld pound coins...'

Kojak shrugs his shoulders and leaves.

'What's the deal here?' I ask.

'He buys all the single shoes and odd pairs,' the boy says forlornly, examining his payment. 'Gives me a few extra quid and keeps the area manager from finding them and giving us into trouble.'

***

Kojak is waiting outside the shop for me, the box of odd shoes under his arm.

'C'moan,' he says. He starts walking towards a bus stop.

'Where to now?'

'We're gonnae feed the ducks.'

As we board the bus, Kojak says to the driver that I'm his companion. I feel quite touched by this statement. The driver waves me on while I fumble in the zipped compartment of my wallet for change.

'It means you get oan fur free cause yer wi me,' Kojak says, grabbing me by the arm. 'Disabled.' He shows me his bus pass. 'Ah don't look disabled. Dae ah?'

I'm lost for words here.

'Cause ahm no.'

I'm desperate to ask him my final question already, but the key is to wait. That's the trick to journalism like this; leave the big, burning question, the most important one, the one that will turn the article from click-bait trash into a proper feature, til the end. This is when the subject is all buttered up, relaxed in your company and has had their ego suitably stroked enough to give you the best answer.

Kojak takes his shoes off. I notice for the first time what he had been wearing on his feet. Two odd shoes. Caked in mud. One black. One white. One Nike. One Adidas. He rummages around in the box, pulling out shoe after shoe and checking the size until he finds two that will fit him. These ones are both black.

'Take yer shoes aff,' he says to me.

I shake my head. Obviously I'm not going to agree to this request.

'Ye'll get them back when we're done. Wit size are ye?'

'I'm a, em, seven, seven-and-a-half. Depends on the make.'

'Stick these oan,' he hands me two shoes. One ladies Nike running shoe with a thick and plush sole. It looks expensive. The other is a man's tennis shoe, flat and hard soled. 'Ye need tae break them in. Makes them look better at the side ae the road. Makes them look used. Like they've mibbe goat a story ae their ain tae tell.'

I'm struck by the almost poetic nature of his words. So struck by them that before I can stop myself, I'm unlacing my own shoes.

* * *

We alight the bus – me, with great difficulty given the two different cushioning levels in my new shoes – after ten minutes or so.

'Where are we?' I ask.

'The Huggy,' he replies. I look at the sign on the park gate – Hogganfield Loch.

'This is where we feed the ducks, eh?' I laugh slightly and nod towards to gaggle of swans. The car park is near enough empty. It's a bitterly cold midweek day. A mother holds her toddler's hand as she urges her to throw a slice of white bread into the crowd of greedy swans. I notice he isn't carrying the box of single shoes.

'Um, where's the box?'

'Oan the bus.'

'But, you just paid for those shoes? Don't you need them?'

'Nah. Somebody'll find them. That's wit ah wanted them fur.'

'But, my shoes were in there?'

Kojak walks over to the loch's edge without answering me. I follow him.

'Ye shouldnae feed the ducks breid,' he says under his breath, looking over at the mother and daughter. 'It makes them aw bloated. Gies them a sore belly. Attracts rats annaw.'

His hand dips into the pocket of his jogging bottoms and when it emerges it is full of seeds. 'Put yer hawn oot,' he says.

I oblige and he dumps the grain into my hand. I throw it immediately into the water.

'Wit ye dain?'

I shrug my shoulders. 'Feeding the ducks.'

'Jesus Christ,' he sighs. Evidently, this was not the correct move.

I'm finding it hard to guess Kojak's motives. To guess what he's going to do next, to work out the right things to say back to him. It's very obvious he doesn't have much time for me.

I watch as he takes another handful of seeds and scatters them not in the water but on the ground. A couple of pigeons land next to us and start pecking away. Seagulls join in. Mallards and coots are swimming over now. A couple of intrepid swans jump from the water and approach, their giant feet slapping at the cold, wet concrete as they hiss at the other birds. He walks backwards, spreading some more seeds through his fingers as he goes, towards the mother and daughter. The swans follow him like the odd-shoe'd Pied Piper he is. The mother notices him coming closer and inches away but then Kojak throws the seeds through the air, showering them. The birds descend on them in a frenzy, pecking at the child who the mother tries desperately to protect.

'YA FUCKIN FREAK!' she shouts at Kojak, who just laughs at the scene unfolding in front of him. 'WHY'D YE DAE THAT?! AAAAAHHHHH!' He flings more bird seed at them.

'Fucking hell, why'd you do that?' (I could lie at this point and say I went over to help the woman and her child, under siege from these birds. But I didn't.)

'There's a sign saying "Please don't feed the burds breid" and she goes an dis it anywey,' he says quietly. 'Take yer shoe aff, hen. Use that to batter them away.'

The woman does as she's told, removing her ankle boot and

swiping at the birds with it. She cracks a swan across its head. The swan rears up causing her to run and eventually make it over to her car. She flings the boot at Kojak who dodges it. It lands in the water with a splash. She gets in and drives away.

'Ah,' he says despondently. 'That wisnae supposed tae happen.' He ambles over to a bench. I join him. Now seems like a good time to ask him the rest of my questions. Truth be told, I just want to get this over with and get up the road.

'Before aw this? Ah cannae even mind, pal. Sorry.'

'Do you know what age you were when you left your first shoe at the roadside? Or even how long you've been leaving shoes at the side of the road?'

He thinks long and hard before answering this question. Gazing out over the loch, the grey water undulating like liquid granite.

'Umpteen years,' he says, dragging a hand through his hair. He gets to his feet. 'C'moan.'

That's probably as good an answer as I'm going to get from him. It's something he clearly doesn't want to talk about so I don't press any further. 'Where are we going now?'

'Ah want you tae meet mah pals.'

* * *

We walk around the loch, towards a kids play park. We walk in silence. I want to ask why he only does it at night. It might seem obvious, I mean, surely he just doesn't want to be seen doing it? Maybe he's embarrassed? These are two possibilities, yes, but I think there's something deeper behind his nocturnal habits.

I decide to "brass neck it" as they say in Glasgow.

'Why only at night?' I blurt out. Kojak gets a fright, I can tell because he flinches when I ask this question.

'Eh?'

'You only leave the shoes at the side of the road at night. I... I just wondered why?'

He sighs then points to a bench overlooking a small sandy beach area. I can imagine on a nice summer's day, this would be quite a picturesque scene. A little oasis at the heart of the scheme. But today, the sand looks grey and is littered with twigs and empty bottles of Buckfast. We take a seat.

'When ah wis a boay,' he says, in a much softer voice than he's been speaking in all day. He's warming to me, perhaps. 'Mah da worked nightshift. In fact, no joost when ah wis a boay, up until mah early twinties when he died. Mah maw an him always said tae me that workin nightshift wis the wey forward. Ye get paid mair money than the poor cunts who dae the same joab as ye durin the day. Joost cause you're willin tae dae it at ungodly oors ae the night.'

'Did you ever have a nightshift job?' I ask.

He smiles. 'Ah've goat wan noo. Ah like mah joab. Ah like mah life. Cunts huv goat a problem wi that, though. Cunts like you, nae offence, pokin their noses in, laughin at me, regardin me as some kind ae curiosity. Like ahm some Neanderthal or suhin.'

I look down at my feet. I feel a terrible knot of guilt in my stomach.

'Why only at night, though? Are you... ashamed?'

'Ashamed? Naw, don't be daft. Like ah says, ah like mah joab, ahm proud tae dae wit ah dae. It's joost easier at night. Nae cunt sees ye. Nae hassle.'

'Anywey,' he says. 'Ah've goat some pals fur ye tae meet. Here they come.'

I look over my shoulder to see two women and a man walking towards us. They are all dressed like variants of Kojak; anoraks and messy hair. Kojak gets up and greets them warmly. Shaking hands, embracing each other, laughing, joking. A proper group of old pals. I stand awkwardly at the edge of the group. I thought about taking pictures here, of this rag-tag group of misfits, it would maybe have been good for this article, but it didn't feel right.

'Who's that? Yer new apprentice?' one of the women says,

pointing at me. I realise I'm still wearing odd shoes.

'Och, he's awrite, ah mean, fur a journo,' Kojak says, and the group laughs.

'Nice to meet you,' I proffer my hand, to no one in particular. No one shakes it and I have to take it back.

'Wee man,' says Kojak, putting an arm around me. 'These are mah pals. This is the Glove Cunt.' He points at the other man. 'This is the Trooser Wummin.' He points at one of the women. 'And this is Soaks.' The final member of the group at least gives me a half-smile. Mainly, I assume, because she's seen my confused face.

'Soaks?' I say. 'Like, um, like being... wet?'

This causes the group to laugh their heads off.

'Naw,' says Soaks, catching her breath. 'Soaks! Fur yer feet!' She pulls up her skirt to reveal the tops of two odd socks, peeking out over her boots. One is black and says "Monday" (this was on a Wednesday) and the other has Bugs Bunny on it.

'Ah, I see.' I felt like I was in a Monty Python sketch at this point. 'So if Kojak here leaves shoes by the side of the road... you must leave the gloves, trousers and, um, socks then?'

'What did you call him?' asks the Trooser Wummin.

'K-Kojak?' The woman had an authoritative air about her which made me feel a bit uneasy.

'His name's Shoe Guy.' The Glove Cunt looks me up and down.

'That's wit people huv been callin me apparently,' says Kojak, shrugging his shoulders. 'Not tae worry though. Listen...' he nods his head in the direction of a path and takes a few steps forward. His cronies follow him, leaving me standing. 'Ah'll catch up wi yees at the pub, awrite?'

'Aye, nae bother Shoe Guy,' Soaks says. 'Joost don't say too much tae him. Ah don't trust him.'

Kojak bids them farewell and comes back over to me.

'The Glove Cunt, Trooser Wummin and Soaks.' I shake my head. 'Amazing.'

'Aye, they're a good laugh.'

We start heading back round to the bus stop. 'So, what's their deal?' I ask.

'Well, ah mean, it's obvious, eh? Glove Cunt leaves gloves lying aboot the place. There's wan ae his there.' A black children's glove lies in a frozen puddle. 'He's good. He steals his gloves though; that's wan hing ah don't like aboot him, tae be fair. Shouldnae be dain that.

'Trooser Wummin. She's good anaw but the hing wi troosers is she cannae leave too many lying aboot the places. Ah mean, gloves are easy loast. Shoes anaw, tae an extent. But how dae folk lose their troosers? It disnae happen that often.' This is the most animated and lively I've seen him all day.

'Soaks is the best in the business though. Her territory is fae Springburn tae East Kilbride an everywhere in between. Big handbag fullae soaks.'

I can see him smiling. Now's the time to ask him my final question.

'Why do you do this?'

'Why?' He stops and looks around for a minute before shrugging his shoulders. 'It's suhin tae dae.'

'There must be more to it than that, surely? I mean, what about your pals there? With the gloves and the trousers and the socks? It's all… organised.'

'See years ago, when ah first started this. Ahd be sittin oan buses an ahd hear folk say tae each other, "How'd ye lose a single shoe?" an it gave me a wee thrill. Knowin that they wurr laughin at mah work. Ah telt mah pals aboot it an we aw joost started dain it. Noo I hear young folk take pictures ae the stuff we leave lyin aboot. Ah seen in the paper some lassie hud took a picture ae a pair ae boots ahd left in a car park, she put it oanline an said suhin aboot the rapture bein upon us. That's quite funny. That's why we dae it. It's a laugh.'

I agree. It sounds like good fun. Weird, but good fun.

'But best ae aw, mah joab means a get tae wind up cunts like you. Look at ye.' He laughs at my odd shoes. I feel incredibly exposed.

'Comin tae dae dodgy deals in the stockroom ae a sports shoap, walkin roon the loch on a freezing cauld day wi me... wit wid yer pals say if they seen ye noo, eh? In yer two different shoes anaw, ha!'

I feel myself go red.

'Bus stoaps err there, pal. Get yerself hame or back tae yer wee office or witever.'

I trudge away without even looking at him.

'Ah've hud good fun, pal,' Kojak shouts after me. 'You take care.'

THE MOTH

PART 2

As the moth in Big Gordon's brain began to take full control of his body and mind, Gordon's consciousness was being obliterated. Every trace of him – his thoughts, his personality, everything except the essential memories the moth would need to keep up the pretence – would soon be purged from existence. The moth would be in total control soon enough.

Gordon lay writhing on the ground as it learned how to move this massive, fleshy piece of machinery. It started by trying to open its new eyes. It had always wondered how it would feel to have a pair of its own eyelids. The eyes formerly belonging to oldGordon flickered open. Gordon found that if it left the lids up for too long, its eyes became dry and irritated. It quickly learned how to blink. As its eyes adjusted to the light, it couldn't believe the technicolour world it could now see. Everything seemed almost *deeper* as well; the depth perception was incredible.

Now it was time to stand up. Gordon pushed itself to its feet with its thick, muscular arms. Getting a sense of balance was tricky. A moth uses its internal geomagnetic compass system, using the moon and the earth's gravitational field to find its way around. All that was gone now, and it had to rely on the human's primitive senses. Gordon wondered if this was going to be all it was cracked up to be and if it would have been better off just existing as a normal moth.

It decided to try its best. Gordon piloted oldGordon's

body towards oldGordon's house, or it's house, it supposed. It staggered and jerked across the grass like it was in a crude stop-motion. It fumbled at the door handle as it tried to get inside the house. Gordon felt a bit sick as it looked down at oldGordon's sausage-like fingers, wiggling around at the end of its hands. It considered cutting them off but decided against it; maybe they'd come in useful somehow.

It finally managed to open the door, got inside and slumped into an armchair. It was knackered. What Gordon needed was something sugary to get its energy up. It leaned its head back so it was resting on the back of the chair, looking at the ceiling, and at the light bulb hanging down.

Light.

Moths love light. "Chasing the light" was what the elder moths called it. A dangerous habit to get into. It resulted in the deaths of billions every year. Looking at bright lights triggers in moths a similar high as humans feel when they take ecstasy. But for moths, the ultimate light to take in was fire. The ultimate high. Stray too close to the flames, of course, and they would be incinerated, dying an agonising but deliciously pleasurable death. For most of its life, this moth had managed to avoid the addiction, even after many of its friends and family had fallen victim to it. But now, Gordon realised, it could indulge in this addiction safely. Light had no adverse effects on humans, from what it knew. Well, apart from the bright red, sunburnt nose it was now sporting. It could sit and stare at light all day now if it wanted, as long as it didn't arouse suspicion in any of oldGordon's friends and family. If the humans found out about moths and their agenda, mothkind was always warned, there would be total carnage. They would go mental; fighting, accusing each other being operated by moths, probably destroying the planet in the process. Or they would carry out a systematic cull of moths, killing them on sight. Either way, it would be a disaster for the moths and their way of life. It was surprising to many moths how the humans hadn't noticed how intelligent moths were, but then again, what could they expect from only the world's second most intelligent species?

Gordon knew humans used light bulbs to illuminate their homes, and they were operated by a panel, normally located on the wall. It stood up again, shakily but it was getting better at it, and felt along the wall for the switch. It clicked on the light and let out a little laugh. *This is brilliant,* Gordon thought. *All the light I could ever want, on demand and safe to consume.*

After several hours staring at the lightbulb, Gordon knew this wouldn't be enough. It quickly built up a tolerance to the modest wattage of the bulb. It managed to turn the telly on to see what kind of light would be emitted from that.

Nowhere near enough.

It tried inside the fridge where oldGordon kept his disgusting food. Still not enough.

Frustrated, it collapsed into the armchair once again and stared at the telly, as it had noticed humans were inclined to do. As it watched *Coronation Street*, Gordon felt some residual memories, left behind by oldGordon, fire up and play out inside its mind, triggered by the images on the telly. oldGordon was in a pub, surrounded by people, noise and... and light. Heat. There was a fire in the pub.

It rummaged through oldGordon's mind as if it was a filing cabinet, pulling together fragments of information, images and sounds, piecing them together, trying to find out where this place was, where the fire was.

Then it clicked. A memory of oldGordon walking along the street, the pub just round the corner, a big red sign welcoming him: The Castle Bar. Gordon got up and headed out the front door.

It careered down the street, breaking into a run, enjoying the new speed it could move at. It kicked open the doors to the pub and looked around desperately for the fire. The fireplace was in the corner but there was a distinct lack of flames. No heat. No light.

Fuck.

'Gordon!' the barman exclaimed. 'How's it goin, mate?'

'Where's the fire?' it asked. Or rather, that was what it tried to ask. What it actually said was: 'Errrrszzz a fffffiyaaah?' It realised it should've practiced talking before leaving the house. The lips and tongue were very difficult to move in the required fashion to form words.

'You had a few already, big man?'

'Aye,' Gordon replied. That was a nice easy word to say. It pointed at the fireplace. 'Ffffiyurr.'

'Fire? Wit ye wanting that oan fur? It's the middle ae July. It's twenty-odd degrees, ya madman.'

Its new heart sank.

'You been on the sunbeds, Gordon?' enquired an old woman with skin like leather.

The sunbeds? it thought. That sounded promising.

'Uhn-bed?'

'Aye, sunbed. That nose of yours looks like Rudolph's!' she laughed, along with several other punters, at its expense.

'Uhn-bed,' it uttered, ignoring the mocking laughter, and left the pub and headed home. A sunbed. It didn't know what that was, but it sounded promising.

It arrived home and opened up oldGordon's laptop (turning up the brightness on the screen as far as it would go, of course).

'Uhn-bed,' it said over and over, as it typed S-U-N-B-E-D into the search engine. This took around four minutes to do as it struggled to manoeuvre its fingers around the keyboard.

Indoor tanning involves using a device that emits ultraviolet radiation to produce a cosmetic tan. Typically found in tanning salons, gyms, spas, hotels, and sporting facilities, and less often in private residences, the most common device is a horizontal tanning bed, also known as a sunbed or solarium.

This sounded good to Gordon. A thing it could lie this abomination of a body on and absorb all the light it could ever want, from all angles.

Now it just had to find one. *That woman in the pub*, it thought, *she looked very tanned, she must know where to get one.*

So Gordon ran back to the pub.

'Ssssunbed,' it said to the barman. 'Sunbed woman.'

'Sunbed woman? Cathy? She's away hame, big man.'

'Hame? W-w-where?'

'She stays next door tae you. Mate, are you okay?'

'Aye!' Gordon shouted and ran back home.

It rattled the door to the left of its new home. A heavily-lined face appeared at the window.

'What is it, Gordon?' Cathy shouted through the open window.

'Sunbed!'

Cathy shook her head. She opened the door. Gordon walked straight past her.

'Sunbed? W-w-where?'

'It's up the stair, in my room. Knock yerself oot. I'll be doon here havin a wee nightcap.'

'Ffffanks,' it said, and bolted up the stair. Cathy staggered back into her living room, slightly confused but not surprised by Gordon's antics. He was always a bit of a weirdo.

The sunbed, which Cathy had saved up for years to buy, stood proudly next to her bed. All Gordon had to do was wheel it over and angle it over Cathy's bed, then climb under and soak up some rays.

Its heart started beating fast and hard as it switched on the sunbed and the fluorescent tubes flickered alive. It slid under the harsh, ultraviolet light and stared straight ahead, the light firing up the moth's new synapses in a more pleasurable way than it ever thought possible, thanks to oldGordon's bigger, albeit inferior, brain.

Ten minutes passed by and Gordon was sweating all over Cathy's new duvet set. The time between its blinks was increasing as it forced its eyes to stay open to take in more light. *This must be what it feels like to be consumed by flames*, it thought.

After twenty minutes, its field of vision was just a purple haze. Its skin was hot to the touch. Red and angry blotches were appearing. Its nose was beginning to blister.

Half an hour later and Gordon was still under the sunbed. It could feel its body beginning to cook from the inside out. Cathy had fallen asleep downstairs.

Forty-five minutes later and its eyeballs had totally dried out. A small semblance of human instinct was all that remained and it forced Gordon to blink. The meagre amount of tears did nothing to nourish the thirsty eyes and the lids crawled shut together over the barren surface before grinding back open.

After an hour, the eyes were now practically boiling in their sockets and starting to shrivel up like dehydrated fruit. Its skin was cracking and peeling. It resembled a dried-up lakebed on the Serengeti. It began to sizzle and split open, allowing hot, congealed blood to seep out.

Downstairs, Cathy was awoken by the smell of burning flesh as the moth's sizzling body fried up the stair.

Gordon was very aware of the pain being inflicted on every part of its body, but the rush of endorphins from the light was overpowering. The urge to continue chasing the light was far greater than the pain.

Cathy sniffed the air, assuming that that numpty of a woman next door to her was burning whatever she was making for her dinner. She fell back asleep on the couch.

The skin around its fingernails was starting to peel away from the muscle and sinew below. Gordon grabbed the edges of the sunbed and pulled it down closer, so it was just milli-metres away from its nose (which was almost melting). Its eyes boiled and burst open. It groaned in delightful agony. Its body was withering away. The radiation was affecting its brain in much the same way a chunk of raw chicken breast would react to being in a microwave for over an hour.

After several hours Gordon's brain ceased functioning, leaving its wizened, cracked, charcoal black corpse smouldering for Cathy to find when she eventually woke up.

SAMMY'S FIRST ACID TRIP

Ahm in the kitchen at that this party, right, an there's this mad cunt wi dreadlocks passing aboot joints. A white guy wi dreads man, that's no right surely? But, tae be fair, this is the west end, fuckin anyhin goes over here man. Ah might as well be a million miles away fae mah bit cos honestly this is like a fuckin different planet. There's some guy in the living room playin this mad weird ambient techno. It's just a constant fucking droning noise. Ah grew up listening tae Gary McF an that. Proper techno. No this pish.

'Hey, bud,' the dreadlocked cunt says tae me over the music in this weird hawf-American, hawf-Scottish accent. 'You fancy a little...' He disnae finish the sentence cos he kids on he's smokin an imaginary joint.

'Naw, ahm awrite,' ah reply. Ahm quite content wi mah wine the noo. Hash sends me a bit fuckin para anaw man, know wit ah mean?

'Ah,' fuckin Henrik Larsson sittin there says, 'you're after something else, huh?' He goes intae the poakits ae his manky troosers and pulls oota wee scrap ae paper. 'How about we take a little trip?'

This cunt talks as if he's in a film or suhin man. Using mad clichés aw the time. 'Honestly, mate, ahm sound.' Ah take another swig ae mah wine. There's a pure low cloud ae smoke fae aw the cunts smoking joints and fae a couple ae mad vapists in the coarner. Electric fags, fuck sake. Wit next? 'You chargin cunts for aw this mate?'

'Nah,' he replies, still fiddling aboot wi the tab ae acid. 'I don't believe that people should have to pay for drugs in the first place, you know?'

'Aw right, fair enough. How'd you get them though?'

'My dad gives me an allowance. He's a millionaire. But, I mean, money means nothing to me, personally.'

'Ah'll take a couple ae quid aff ye then if you're no bothered aboot it,' ah say, kiddin on but also being deadly serious at the same time.

'Ha! You're a funny guy! What's your name again?'

'Ahm Sammy.' Ah reach over and shake his hawn. Nice tae be nice, know wit ah mean, even if the cunt's a weirdo. 'Wit's yours?'

'My friends call me Leaf,' he says wi a mad smug look oan his face.

'Fuck off,' ah say. Leaf. 'Wit kind a fuckin name's that?'

'Yeah, pretty cool, huh?'

Ah hink maybe it's time ah phoned a taxi an goat masel up the road. This place is fryin mah brain. Ah pull mah phone oot mah poakit tae check the time but the hing's deid. The battery wis at 40% a minute ago. Funny how phones start playin up when there's a new model aboot tae come oot, eh? 'Here Leaf, don't suppose you've goat a charger oan ye mate?'

'I don't even own a *phone*, never mind a charger.' Ah hink this might be the smuggest guy ah've ever came across in mah life.

'Awrite, eh, fair enough.' Ah fart aboot wi mah phone some mair, hopin an prayin it'll come back tae life. Leaf comes over tae me and grabs it right oot mah hawn an replaces it wi a tab ae acid.

'Never mind this,' he says, waving mah phone aboot. 'Your phone will always be here, but opportunities like this don't come about very often.'

Ahm a bit scared here man. It's wan hing hivin a wee joint at a party or even a cheeky line, but acid? Ah don't hink this is fur me. Ah look doon at the tab. It's goat a Nike tick oan it.

'Leaf, mate, ah've never done acid. Joost gies mah phone back eh? Ahm no intae this. Ahm gonnae head hame.'

'Nonsense,' he says. 'Don't be afraid. This stuff is strong but it's totally safe. You're pretty much guaranteed a good trip. This stuff is from Belgium.' He looks at me as if ahm meant to be impressed. 'Don't tell me you've never heard of Belgian acid?'

'The only hing ah know that's came fae Belgium is the big lump ae wood Celtic play at centre back.'

'Just try it, man. What have you got to lose? This party's pretty shit anyway.' Leaf gets a tab oot his poakit fur himself. 'I'll do it with you.'

Fuck it, mad Leaf's right. Ye've goat tae try these hings. That's wit life's aw aboot.

'Wit dae ye dae?' ah ask him. 'Ah mean, ah know ye stick it in yer mooth, but, like, dae ah chew it or suck it or wit?'

'Just stick it on your tongue, like this, man, and just let it melt.' He crosses his legs and sits like a buddha or a mad guru or suhin. Ah dae the same – joost in case yer meant tae, know wit ah mean? Don't want tae look daft.

* * *

It takes a while ae kick in, this mad Belgian acid, but see when it does, fuck me. It starts wi a bit ae like motion blur, when ah wave mah hawn aboot in front ae mah face it leaves a mad colourful trail, it's mental. There's shapes appearing every-where, triangles an squares an aw that. It's fried as fuck. Ah tell Leaf wit ahm seein an he goes like that, 'The best is yet to come.' It's joost me an him in the kitchen noo, hink everycunt else wis a bit freaked oot by us. But ah don't care, man. This is class. Even that shitey techno music sounds good noo that ahm trippin.

'You feeling it yet, bud?' Leaf asks me, but before ah can answer him, his eyes roll back in his heid and he falls back, slumped against the wall.

Panic stations.

'Fuck this!' Ah grab the cunt by the shooders. 'Ah don't want tae take a trip, ah never did. Joost let me aff!'

'Don't worry, man,' Leaf says.

'Too fuckin late, mate, ahm worrying like fuck here.'

'You'll end up going on a bad trip if you don't calm down dude. Just be chill, like me.' His face twists intae a horrible big smile. The corners ae his lips are stretching aff his face, it's horrific.

Naw man, fuck this.

Ah shut mah eyes. Surely if ah joost keep them shut fur however long this lasts then ah won't see anyhin that bad? Never mind, mad swirling shapes start appearing inside mah ain fuckin eyelids...

An then...

Then ahm up Hogganfield Loch. Ah open mah eyes. This definitely isnae real. But it feels real as fuck. Ahm startin tae calm doon noo, man. This disnae feel like a bad trip. It's joost a nice day up the Huggy. But there's nae cunt aboot. No even any duck or swans oan the loch. This is weird. Ah've heard stories aboot bad trips. Mah auld chemistry teacher told us he wis a bit ae a hippy back in the day an he says wan night he hit a bad yin an thought his skin wis aw infected. Said his mate had tae wrestle a big kitchen knife aff him cos he wis aboot tae cut aff his hawn tae 'stop the infection from spreading'. There's nae cunt in the kitchen back in reality tae stoap me fae dain anyhin stupit, apart fae mad Leaf but he's oot his box anaw, so ahm fucked.

It's as if ahm floating if ye get me. Or really it's mair like this mad dream version ae the Huggy is moving roon aboot me while ah stawn still. Ah cannae really describe it man. Ah cin hear a siren in the distance. No like a polis siren or that, which is a common occurrence up the Huggy tae be fair, it's mair like an air raid siren like ye'd hear in an auld war film.

'Get in here!' a familiar voice shouts fae the wee building where the public toilets are.

It's Leaf.

Ah run err as fast as ah cin. This is terrifying man how dis this feel so real?

'Follow me!' Leaf shouts an ah run doon a big long corridor efter him. It's been a few year since ah've been in this building but ah defo don't remember it being like this. 'In here, Sammy.' He pulls me intae wit looks like mah primary wan classroom wi hunners ae people in it. They aw look fucking terrified. It takes a couple ae seconds before I recognise the people in the room; it's everycunt fae the party.

They're aw chalk white an oot ae breath.

'Wit's happenin?' ah ask them.

'Dude, whatever happens,' Leaf says, sitting doon wi his back against the door. 'We can't let this door open.'

Ah feel it's mah joab tae get everycunt tae calm doon here. 'This isnae real. It's joost that acid, int it?'

'It's *Belgian* acid and I'm not sure. This feels pretty real to me.'

'Wait, hing oan. This is *mah* trip. This is in *mah* heid.'

'It's those tabs, man. They're special. They... link people's trips.' The cunt looks creeped oot. But ah remind maself this isnae real.

Then the siren shuts up. It's aw quiet noo apart fae everycunt breathin. Then we aw hear this banging comin fae oot in the hall.

'Not again!' Leaf screams and everycunt's oan their feet and flinging themselves against the door. 'Sammy, don't just stand there, man. Help us!'

Ah hink tae maself *fuck it* an gie them a hawn. Whether this is real or no, it's nice tae be nice efter aw.

Ah've goat mah two hawns against the door, same as everybody else, but ah don't feel as if there's anyhin tryin tae get in.

'Wit is it we're dain here?' ah whisper ae a lassie wi the straightest fringe ah've ever seen.

'Just be quiet,' she says.

'Fuck sake, that's me telt eh?'

Then witever it is we're tryin ae stoap fae comin in the room chaps the door. Starts dead light an slow. Everybody's got their eye's shut and their faces aw screwed up, making that face as if they're expecting a balloon or something tae blow up.

Then the chapping gets louder and faster. Fuck me man, this is wild. Noo the door feels like somecunt or something is tryin ae open it. Everycunt's goat their full weight against the door but it's creaking open a wee tiny bit at a time and witever's oan the other side is chapping faster and faster. Then the door flies aff its hinges, sending everycunt sprawling. Ahm aw dazed an confused, hink ah cracked mah heid aff the flair a belter. Ah look up at where the door used tae be. There's nuhin there, joost an empty doorway. Then everyhin comes back intae focus as the lassie wi the fringe starts screamin.

'THEY'RE COMING IN!'

'Wit? Wit's comin in? There's nuhin there?' ah say. 'Will somecunt tell me wit's happenin here?'

'The floor, Sammy, the floor!' Leaf shouts, he's oan tap ae a table. 'Get up here with me,' he reaches doon an pulls me up. 'Look.'

There's fuckin fingers crawlin intae the room! Fingers. Actual deid, hawnless, grey fingers. 'Naw, mate, ahm no havin this. How dae ah get oot ae this trip?'

'This is Belgian aci-'

'STOAP SAYIN "IT'S BELGIAN ACID"! THAT MEANS NUHIN AE ME! TELL ME HOW AE WAKE UP YA STUPIT CUNT!'

Then boom. Everyhings aw quiet again. Ahm back in the kitchen. The sun's startin tae come up. Leaf's no here but. Where the fuck did he go? Ahm gonnae kick his cunt in, that wis the worst experience ae mah life.

Ah get up an go intae the living room tae see if he's in there.

He's no, but there's still a few stragglers. That lassie wi the fringe is lying oan the couch cradling a boattil ae Strongbow like it's her first born wean.

'Any yous seen that mad Leaf cunt?'

'Leaf? I used to have a friend called Leaf,' she says wi her mad plummy west end accent. 'He died a couple of years ago though. Took some dodgy acid, I heard.'

Panic stations wance again. Fucking no chance. Ahm a still trippin?

The she must see the fear oan mah face. 'I'm only joking,' she says. 'He's just went to the shop for some cigarettes. He'll be back in a mo.'

Ahm ah fuck hinging aboot though. Ahm away hame. Ahm never comin back tae the west end again as long as ah live.

LEATHERED

1

Frank worked in a jail. As a guard, it was his job to keep the peace within the prison. This wasn't hard for a man like Frank. 6ft 4, built like the side of the proverbial brick shithouse and with a temper with a hair-trigger, the prisoners regarded Frank with a healthy mix of fear and respect.

Frank had a game he'd play with a couple of the inmates he liked, the ones who were just like himself – hard as fuck. He knew he was lucky he wasn't the one behind bars, that in a different life he'd be the one getting locked up at night. The prisoners knew this as well, and that seemed to be the foundation their mutual respect was based upon. The game they played went like this: Frank would name a famous person and ask the prisoner if they thought they could leather them. Then the prisoner would name one and ask Frank if he could leather them. Sometimes they'd mix it up a wee bit and ask each other who they wouldn't want to fight, who they thought would fight dirty and who, despite having the appearance or personality of a hard man, would be easy to batter. It was widely agreed within the jail that they could all leather Gordon Ramsay.

'Oot ae aw the famous Scottish cunts,' a prisoner called Joe asked Frank. 'Who dae ye hink is the maist handy?'

Frank liked the questions Joe asked him. He'd once asked Frank if he thought he could take on both of The Krankies at the one time, then came up with a plan to take them on himself, which involved greasing up, Bronson style, and using an unconscious Wee Jimmy Krankie to beat Ian to death.

'The handiest famous cunt in Scotland?' Frank mulled this over while turning over Joe's cell for contraband.

'Ah'd say Frankie Boyle mibbe,' said Joe, running a hand over a slash mark on his face. 'Or Andy Murray's maw. She looks deid behind the eyes. Nae remorse. She wid end ye in a heartbeat if ye ever said anyhin aboot they glaikit boays ae hers. Aw don't look in there mate, eh?'

Too late. Frank was already pulling a very slimline mobile phone from the drawer of Joe's bedside cabinet.

'Fuck sake, Joe, how'd ye get this in here?'

'Joost stick it back, please, mate, ahm beggin ye. It's the only way ah can talk tae mah boay. His maw won't let him come an see me.'

'Didnae know you had a son, mate. Kept that wan quiet.'

'Aye, well, ah don't like talking aboot him. There's cunts in here use that kind ae info against ye, know wit ah mean?'

'Aye, ah know, mate.' Frank turned the phone over in his hand. Joe had several Twitter notifications. 'How are ye even charging it? In fact, ah don't want tae know.' Frank put the phone back where he found it. 'Hide it somewhere better next time though, fuck sake. Stevie Wonder could've found that.'

'You're some man, Frank. Right who's yer hardest famous Scottish cunt?'

Frank pulled off his latex gloves with a snap and said, without hesitation, 'Alex Salmond.'

'Salmond? You're aff yer fucking heid. He's soft as shite.'

'Hear me oot. In terms ae politicians, he's the hardest nae doubt.'

'Wit aboot Mhairi Black?'

'Nah, she's aw talk. Salmond has the air ae a guy that knows nae cunt can touch him. He's goat a confidence, naw, in fact it's an *arrogance* he's goat that makes me hink he could leather anybody he wants. Look at the way he struts aboot. He's ugly as fuck but he walks like he's the guy aff the Porage Oats box. He can fight, mark mah words.'

Joe considered everything Frank had said. He'd made a compelling case. 'You're right.'

'Ah know ahm right,' said Frank with a smile. 'Ahm always right when it comes tae stuff like this.' He patted Joe on the back and exited the cell. 'Noo hide that fuckin phone. It might no be me that does the next search.'

'You're some boy, Frank.'

* * *

In the staff room later, another guard called Murray tapped Frank on the shoulder.

'You did a sweep of Joe McGuigan's cell earlier, eh, pal?'

'Ah did, aye, how?' Frank asked. He liked Joe but he knew he had a big mouth. He should've took that phone off him.

'Well I found a phone when I was doing my sweep ten minutes ago. The guy begged me tae let him keep it. Said your pal Joe was allowed to keep his after you found one in his cell?' Murray had a sleekit smile that always seemed to be bubbling under the surface.

Grassing bastard, thought Frank.

'Ah never found a phone in Joe's cell. Ah've nae clue wit this cunt's talkin aboot. Sorry, mate.' Frank went back to reading the paper. Murray was new in the jail. He was an ex-copper from Edinburgh and was having a hard time gaining respect from the prisoners. Frank hadn't taken to him at all. What annoyed him the most, aside from the way Murray spoke down to the prisoners, was the fact he insisted on calling Frank 'pal'.

Murray wasn't letting this go.

'I should really be going to the warden with this. You *do* know inmates aren't allowed mobile phones, right?'

'Look, *pal*.' Frank put down his paper and rubbed his beard. 'How long have you worked here noo?'

'Three months.' Murray shrugged his bony shoulders.

'Something like that anyway.'

'Surprised ye've no picked up oan this so far but jobsworths don't dae well in here. That kind of stuff might go doon well in the polis but no in here. Ye don't want tae be making enemies, or annoyin the warden wi every wee hing ye find in a cunt's cell.'

'But it's not allowed.'

'Did you no listen ae wit ah just said tae ye there? The guy's using that phone tae talk his boay, fuck sake. Noo, let me put it this way – keep this shite up and you'll get leathered. An if ye keep annoyin the other guards, it might no be aff a prisoner.'

'Are you... threatening me?'

Frank stood up and blew himself up like a puffer fish. 'Ahm just tryin tae keep ye right, pal.'

Murray backed off and went to sit by himself. 'You know he doesn't have a son, don't you?' he shouted over as a parting shot to Frank.

'Wit?'

'Just trying to keep you right, pal.'

Frank went back to work.

* * *

'Hawl you,' Frank shouted as he breenged over to the pool tables. Joe kept walking round the pool table trying to keep a bit of distance between him and Frank.

'Frank, big man, ah never said anyhin tae anycunt ah promise,' Joe blubbed.

'C'moan wi me.' Frank grabbed Joe by the neck of his jumper. The other prisoners fell silent.

Marching Joe up the stairs to his cell, he passed by Murray. 'Anymare ae your shite,' he seethed at him, 'and it'll be you ah come fur next.' Murray gulped and kept walking.

Frank flung Joe into his cell.

'Where's that fuckin phone.'

'Frank, mate, ahm sorry. Ah didnae mean ae tell anycunt, ah swear.'

Frank rifled through all of Joe's possessions, turning the cell upside down. Cans of Lynx deodorant were thrown against the wall in frustration as Frank searched frantically for the phone.

'You took advantage ae mah kind-hearted nature, Joe. Where's the fuckin phone.'

'Please mate, ah need it tae talk tae mah boay.'

'You've no goat a fuckin boay!' Frank launched Joe's wafer thin mattress across the tiny room.

Joe was about to refute the accusation when he saw how tightly clenched Frank's fists wear. He was about to blow.

'Right, awrite. Ah've no goat a son.'

'AH FUCKIN KNOW THAT! GIE ME THE PHONE!' Frank started ripping off the posters Joe had on his wall, in case he was hiding the phone in a Shawshank Redemption-style cubby hole.

'Frank... Frank,' Joe pleaded but Frank ignored him and kept flinging Joe's meagre possessions around the cell. 'Frank, listen ae me fur a minute. FRANK!'

Frank stopped what he was doing. No prisoner had ever raised their voice to him before. Maybe he was losing his touch?

'Ye'll no find the phone in here, mate.'

'How no? Have you gave it tae somecunt ya sneaky wee fuckin RAT?'

'Naw. Ah've no. Ah might look daft but ahm no stupit.'

Frank rubbed the bridge of his nose then nodded for Joe to continue.

'Ye'll no find it in the cell because...' Joe poked his head out into the corridor to see if anybody might hear what he was about to say, they weren't. He lowered his voice to a whisper and closed his eyes. 'Because... it's up mah arse.'

'Ya dirty bastard, could ye no joost hide it somewhere in yer cell?'

'Well, you telt me ae hide it somewhere better. So ah did.'

Frank reached into his back pocket for a pair of latex gloves. He always kept a pair handy for occasions such as this. He never underestimated just how manky prisoners could be. After pulling them on, he nodded solemnly at the door, instructing Joe to close it over.

'Ah need that phone aff ye, mate. Clearly yous cunts think ye can take me fur a fuckin mug. Think ahm soft, aye? That wit it is?' Frank advanced on Joe who backed into a corner.

'Naw, Frank. Ye know nae cunt hinks that. Yer the hardest cunt in here.'

'Aye, an you basturts wid dae well tae remember that. Drap yer drawers, squat an spread yer cheeks.'

'Frank, can ah no joost pull it oot masel? This is a bit... undignified.'

'Can ye fuck!' Frank barked. 'Squat.'

Joe lowered himself into a squat. 'This low enough?'

'Perfect,' Frank said as he knelt down so he was in line with Joe's arse. 'Spread.'

Joe did as he was told. As he pulled apart his cheeks, Frank thought it looked like a cheese toastie being opened up.

'Ye might've cleaned yer arse, Joe. Jesus Christ.'

'Well ah didnae hink anybody wis gonnae be poking aboot doon there, did ah?'

Frank screwed up his face and tentatively reached in and grabbed the edge of the phone between his index finger and thumb and pulled.

'Yer gonnae need tae relax a bit.'

Joe did as he was told and the phone slid out easily. The elasticity of the anus and the capacity of the cavity within never failed to amaze Frank, even after years of watching prisoners pull out various weapons, drugs and phones out of their arses.

Frank wiped away some shite off the phone screen and turned it on. The phone instantly started displaying countless notifications for Twitter.

'So ye've no been using it tae talk tae yer boay. Ye've been fuckin tweetin?' Frank shook his head. 'Wit nonsense huv ye been spoutin oan Twitter?'

'Well,' Joe was looking very chuffed with himself as he pulled his boxers and joggie bottoms back up. 'Ahm quite active oan the auld Twitter. "Twitter famous" they call me.'

'"Twitter famous"? Fuck dis that mean?'

'Well, obviously, in here ahm joost Joe, right? But see oanline, ahm JailBhoy67. Ah joost tweet aboot life oan the inside an aw that. Folk love it.'

Frank pretended to be impressed. 'Think ah might get Twitter then. Ahm sure you must post some rivetin content, eh? Aw look at me.' He did an impersonation of Joe's nasally voice. 'Ahm JailBhoy. The day ah played pool, ate mah dinner then went tae bed. Same as ah've did every day since 1998. It's fuckin tragic.'

'Hawl that's harsh. Ahm an interesting guy. Ahm underappreciated in here, ye know. Cunts oanline love me.'

'Ahm sure they dae, mate. Ye know wit?' Frank tossed the shit covered phone back to Joe. 'Joost keep the phone. Yer no up tae nae good wi it. Yer joost a bit ae a sad act. Nae offence.'

Joe waved his hand dismissively. He went over to his toilet and started cleaning the phone.

'Ye should gie Twitter a go, Frank, ahm tellin ye, mate. It's class.'

'Ah don't hink so, mate.' Frank pulled off his gloves. 'Ah've no goat much tae talk aboot. Ahm either in here wi you cunts or ahm in the hoose watching the telly.'

'Ye could talk aboot cunts ye could batter. Ye can set up wee polls an that. Get yer followers tae vote oan who they think they could batter an aw that.'

Frank actually quite liked the sound of that. 'Ah'll see, mate. Ah'll see.'

***

Later that night, lying on the couch at home alone, Frank switched the telly over to the ten o'clock news.

'Good evening. The North Korean leader, Kim Jong-un's continued threats towards the United States and its allies could soon spark a military reaction from US President Donald Trump, according to a nuclear deterrent expert...'

'That's plenty,' Frank said to himself as he put the telly on mute and picked up his phone.

Fuck it, he thought. *Ahm joining Twitter.*

The first thing he did after setting up his new Twitter account was to look for Joe's profile. He was stunned to see that Joe, somehow, had over ten thousand followers. Frank laughed as he read through Joe's tweets:

Day 7,399 in the big Bar-L hoose – Joe had his iPhone forcibly removed from his arse but the kind guard allowed him to keep it instead of handing it in to the warden when he heard about yer auld da's exploits on Twitter #Legend

Day 7,399 in the big Bar-L hoose – getting really fuckin good at playin pool oan a wonky table.

Frank wracked his brains as he tried to think of a witty reply to Joe's musings. He settled for: *Joe, fuck up and go to bed.*

Joe replied with a sad faced emoji.

Frank followed all of the usual people that folk follow when they first join Twitter. The likes of Donald Trump (not that he was a fan of him. In fact Frank hated him, he just wanted to be among the first to see the mad shit he tweeted), a few footballers and a couple of actors and singers. Scrolling through his feed, a notification popped up which said, *Why not send your first tweet, Frank?* Frank didn't know what to say. He looked up at the telly. Kim Jong-un's big ball face filled the screen. *Ah could leather him,* thought Frank. So he tweeted: *Kim Jong-un? I could kick fuck out of him.*

2

At the same time Frank hit send on his first tweet, in Pyongyang, North Korea, a payroll administrator by the name of Cho was just waking up. Before she left for work she had a quick check of the phone she kept hidden in her house – the same model of phone a certain Mr Joe McGuigan, residing in H.M.P. Barlinnie, Glasgow – had. Despite Twitter access being blocked in her country, Cho had managed to gain access through her clever use of proxy servers and tap into the 4G signal of South Korea. As she did every morning, she typed the name of her country's leader into the Twitter search bar to see what the western world was saying about him. The first tweet she saw was from a Mr. Frank Curran of Garthamlock, Glasgow, under the username @HardCunt72. It read: *Kim Jong-un? I could kick fuck out of him.* For Frank, this was just a throwaway sentence. He typed it out, hit send and then went to bed, forgetting what he'd just tweeted almost instantly. For Cho, this tweet would be what she would use to undermine her leader, his nefarious regime and start a revolution.

She took a screenshot of Frank's tweet and stored the phone away safely back in its hiding place under the floorboards. As a child, she'd witnessed her neighbours get dragged away to a labour camp in broad daylight. South Koreans would launch videotapes over the border filled with news reports, adverts, soaps, documentaries and films. These tapes were smuggled throughout the country by dissidents to show that life outside North Korea wasn't the cesspit the regime wanted people to believe it was. One of these tapes had found its way to Cho's neighbours, an elderly couple. They watched the tape, knowing if they were caught with it they were as good as dead. The Secret Police raided Cho's neighbours, found the video, and the old man and woman were caught, beaten and hauled away. The image of the couple being dragged into separate vans had lived with her ever since, always there in the back of her mind.

Cho met up with her friend Ri after work that day and told her about Frank's tweet.

'Ri, there is this man in Scotland,' she said excitedly as they walked home. 'He said on Twitter he can "kick fuck out of" Kim Jong-un!'

Ri, although a dear friend of Cho, was very concerned about her rebellious ways. Ri had seen her own parents taken away by the Secret Police, and was terrified she was going to lose Cho in the same way.

'Please stop this,' Ri pleaded. 'We have a good life here, we aren't starving, we aren't in dire povery, things aren't that bad.'

'Yes, *we're* okay. But what about everyone else? People get imprisoned for nothing. People are dying every day of starvation but I'm not allowed to say anything because *I'm* okay?'

'Cho, keep your voice down.' The two women were walking home down a busy street and people were starting to notice Cho getting animated.

'Okay, okay,' Cho said, lowering her voice. 'But you must see that Kim Jong-un is a laughing stock outside of this country. Everyone here thinks he is this great supreme leader when really he's just an overgrown child. I wish there was a way to show everyone what the world really thinks of him.'

'You're playing with fire, Cho. Please be careful.'

As they approached Ri's apartment building they said their goodbyes. 'Get home safe and be careful,' Ri pleaded once again.

'I will,' Cho replied. But Cho wasn't going home. She was

heading to meet up with her fellow would-be revolutionaries. They met once a month in the staffroom of the Lucky Lane Bowling Alley, whose manager was a staunch opponent of the country's regime. Only the most patriotic citizens could live in Pyongyang, and to any observer Cho and her comrades were just that. Cho and her female pals, Kye and Myong, kept their hair tied up, as was the law, and wore sensible clothing in muted colours, while the men Tokko, Sol and Hyang wore their government approved haircuts and pin badges of the late Kim Jong-il and Kim Il-Sung with apparent pride. Once they were safely in the confines of the staffroom, the women were free to let their hair down and the men removed the badges from their lapels and flung them at the portrait of Kim Jong-un on the wall.

'First order of business,' Hyang, the manager of the bowling alley said. 'I've received word from my friend in Ryonggang that the food situation there is dire. We're hoping another group is going to help them out, but, if it comes to it, would any of you be willing to drop off some food?'

The mood in the room changed instantly and the rest of the group looked at the floor to avoid making eye contact with Hyang. A trip like this would basically be a suicide mission.

'No takers? We probably won't have to go, but it'd be nice to let them know they have people here able and willing to help them.'

Cho meekly raised her hand, still staring at the floor.

Hyang nodded in approval. 'That was a test,' he said. 'And you all failed. Apart from Cho, of course.'

Cho swelled with pride.

'Anyway, tonight I was thinking we could come up with ideas for more flyers and posters and stuff like that. Cho, any ideas? Have you seen anything we could use on that dodgy phone of yours?'

'I have actually. We all know everyone outside of this country thinks Kim Jong-un is an idiot, right?'

The group all nodded in agreement.

'Well, we need to let everyone else know this. There's this guy in Scotland who said on Twitter, and I quote, that he "could kick fuck out of him".'

The group were excited to hear this.

'Does he look as if he could?' asked Tokko.

'Yes! He's like a monster! I'm going to try and find out some more about him tonight.'

'We should get that tweet on a poster,' said Myong.

'We should,' said Hyang, looking deep in thought. 'I can see it now – a picture of this guy standing triumphant over a lifeless Kim. He can be our poster boy.'

'Cho, get us a picture of him for tomorrow night and I'll get the posters made ASAP. This is what we've been waiting for,' said Tokko, the poster guy. 'This will show everyone here how weak Kim really is and how easy it will be for us to take back our country!'

Cho headed home that night filled with a new optimism for the future. Feeling as if, with Frank's help, she and her group could really change things for the better in their country.

3

A few days later, Kim Jong-un was sat in his massively oversized chair at his equally massively oversized desk. He hovered his hand over the big red button, which would launch nuclear warheads towards the USA and almost certainly bring about World War III, if not Armageddon. He decided against pressing it today. He'd see how he felt tomorrow. He moved over to the massively oversized mirror and admired his massively oversized self.

His closest aide came running into the room. 'Supreme Leader,' the aide said. 'We have seized a large quantity of posters printed by a dissident group here in Pyongyang.'

Kim sighed. He was very busy admiring his haircut in the mirror.

'Supreme Leader, they are making very outrageous and defamatory claims about you.'

Now he had Kim's interest.

'What are they saying?' Kim began to vibrate with rage but still faced the mirror. He eyed the poster in the aide's trembling hands.

'Well the group themselves aren't actually saying anything. It's someone else. A man from Scotland. He's saying he could "kick fuck out of" you.'

'Let me see the poster.'

'Supreme Leader, I don't think you should.'

'GIVE ME IT!' Kim barked, spinning round and snatching the poster from his aide's hand.

The poster had Frank's display picture from Twitter: him in his gym gear, flexing a tattoo covered arm, photoshopped to show him standing over a lifeless Kim Jong-un who lay on the deck. The text read:

The Young Master? The Great Successor? Outstanding Leader? Don't think so!

Kim is the laughing stock of the world.

Frank from Scotland says he will 'kick fuck out of him'!

The poster was signed off by the 'North Korean People's Resistance'. There was also a few screenshots of Tweets from other Scottish people:

Actual cannae believe the state of that Kim Jong-un's hair.

Kim Jong-un is like a big, massive, overgrown baby.

Mad Kim fae North Korea looks like he's made oot ae Billy bear ham.

'Who made these?' Kim asked, flecks of spit hitting his aide's face.

'We're not sure, sir.'

'Well how many of these have you seized?'

'Thousands, sir. But they're still everywhere. Look.' The aide turned to the wall of television screens in Kim's office. He hit a panel next to them and displayed multiple live feeds from across Pyongyang. The posters were everywhere. Hanging on walls, strewn across the pavements, pasted onto windows and any other flat surface Cho and her gang could find. The electricity in Pyongyang tended to be cut out after 10pm so her and the rest of her dissident pals snuck out and plastered them everywhere under the cover of darkness.

'This is outrageous!' Kim screamed. 'Find this man called Frank. I want to fight him.'

'Sir, we could just take down the posters and imprison anyone who-'

'I said I want to fight him, did you not hear me? I could fight him and win. It will quash all of this resistance nonsense.'

The aide looked at the poster. It was hard to tell from the picture but he was sure Frank looked taller than Kim. And he was definitely stronger, there was no doubt about that.

'Is that a... wise idea, sir?'

'Of course it is. I'm Kim Jong-un! I could fight anyone!'

The aide thought to himself that Kim looked as if he could barely fight sleep. The man got out of breath walking to the toilet.

'Sir, please reconsider this...'

'Are you disagreeing with your Supreme Leader?' Kim took a step towards his aide. He was toe to toe with him. The aide bowed his head in subordination and let out a little whine.

'N-n-n-no, sir.' Although the aide knew Kim couldn't possibly fight Frank, he was still bigger and stronger than he was.

'Send a delegation to Scotland and find this Frank character,' Kim said in a low growl. 'When you find him, let me know straight away and I'll fly out to fight him. We need to show the western world that North Korea takes threats like this very seriously.'

'Yes, sir,' replied the aide as he scuttled away.

4

Frank, unaware that he had become a symbol of the People's Resistance, sat outside the jail in his car. He was starting to get fed up with his job. Over the last few days, he'd realised that his life wasn't much different from the prisoners he locked up at night. *I get to go home at the end of the day, but home to do what?* thought Frank. *Sit about, watch some shite on the telly, go to bed then get up the next morning to go to the jail again?* What kind of life was that? He was as much a prisoner as anyone behind those bars. Ten years he'd worked there. Frank looked out at the ominous structure of the prison. Everything about it made him feel depressed. The weather-beaten brickwork, the barbed wire, even the rusty gates; it was as if every aspect of its design was tailored to make him feel like all the hope and joy in his body had been leeched out of him. *If anycunt gies me any shite the day*, he thought to himself, *ahm tellin them to ram their joab up their fuckin arse.*

***

At lunchtime Frank was sitting in the staff room on his phone, still in a bad mood. His morning had been relatively uneventful. He did his rounds – a couple of random checks of cells and some basic paperwork – all without hassle from anyone. When Frank was in a bad mood, the prisoners knew not to even look at him, never mind talk to him. The same went for the other guards.

He flicked through Twitter, he'd gained thousands of new followers over the last few days and his mentions were filled with hundreds and hundreds of tweets written in Korean. Frank assumed it was all just spam and it was starting to annoy him, so much so that he was thinking about deleting the app. Then a tweet written in English and with a picture attached caught his eye. It was from Cho and it read: *Frank! You are our hero! Thanks for showing how weak our leader is!*

As Frank opened the picture, his jaw nearly hit the floor. 'Wit the fuck,' he said to himself, looking at the poster of his tweet. There were articles from South Korean news websites talking about the poster as well. Frank thought he must be the victim of an elaborate wind up. *Maybe it was Joe*, he thought.

'Frank,' Murray said, popping his head into the staff room. 'You're wanted in the warden's office, pal.'

'Wit fur?'

'No idea. But there's a load of guys in suits in there as well.'

'Have you grassed oan me, ya prick?' Frank got up and grabbed Murray around the tops of his arms, pinning them to his side. 'If you've grassed oan me ah swear tae God, pal, ah'll fuckin kill ye.'

'Frank, honestly, I haven't said anything,' Murray blubbed. He felt as if Frank was about to cause his biceps to burst open. 'I promise.'

Frank let go of him. He didn't like Murray, but he could tell he wasn't a liar. Murray looked shellshocked and rubbed his arms, trying to ease the pain in them.

'You've nae idea wit this is aboot then?' Frank asked Murray.

'If I did...' Murray gulped. 'I would tell you.'

***

Frank chapped the door of the warden's office. The warden opened the door slightly, his tight-lipped expression looked like it had been carved into stone.

'Come in, Frank,' he said quietly, ushering Frank into the room. Frank was met with the faces of three people he didn't know – a Korean man and woman and a guy he thought he recognised from the telly.

'Frank this is a most unusual situation we find ourselves in,' the warden said. 'Most unusual indeed. Please sit down.'

Frank did as he was asked and sat down, the guy he recognised from the telly on his right and the Korean couple on his
left. The guy from the telly smiled at Frank but the Koreans
had their eyes set dead ahead. They sent a shiver through
Frank's body. The warden sat down as his phone rang.

'Okay, send her up,' he said down the line.

'Wit's happenin here?' Frank asked.

'I'll tell you when this woman gets here. That'll be her now
actually,' the warden said as there was a knock on the door.
'Come in,' he shouted. In walked a woman, maybe around sixty
years old, flanked by two burly security guards in sunglasses.
The Koreans turned round, drew their eyes off her as she
offered them her hand to shake, and returned their gazes to
the back wall of the office. Frank thought they were acting like
robots or something. The woman took the last remaining seat
while her guards stood with their backs to the door.

'Is this aboot Joe McGuigan?' Frank asked the warden.
He thought he had what was happening here all figured out.
This was an inquiry into why he didn't report the fact he
knew Joe had a phone. He remembered he'd replied to one of
Joe's tweets the other night. 'Fuck,' he said as the warden just
pursed his lips and leafed through some paper. Frank was sure
he was about to lose his job.

'Frank, while what happened with Joe is a regrettable
incident which we should really be taking further,' the warden
said. 'There are bigger matters to attend to.'

'Much bigger,' interjected the guy on Frank's right. 'I'm
Mark, by the way. Mark Dallas.'

'You the cunt fae the wrestling?' Frank asked.

'Aye,' Mark replied, flashing Frank a smile. 'The one and
only.'

'Ahm a wee bit confused here, mate.'

'I'll let your boss fill you in.'

'Yes, this is Mark from the wrestling and to your left are two
delegates from North Korea,' said the warden.

'Awrite,' Frank said, leaning over to shake their hands. The delegates ignored him.

'They don't say much. Don't waste your time, Frank. This, however…', the warden gestured to the woman who'd just entered, 'is Katherine Muir, head of MI6.'

'Ooft, like the spy mob?' Frank asked, shaking her hand.

'Yes, something like that,' she smirked.

'Right so there's me, a cunt fae the wrestling, a spy and two cunts fae North Korea? This isnae aboot Joe is it? Unless… Joe's really a spy?'

The warden gave a chuckle. 'Of course he's not, Frank. This is all about you. You're… something of a celebrity in North Korea now.'

Frank looked to his left. The two North Koreans were staring at him. They looked raging.

'Ah've noticed ah've goat a few followers oan twitter that write in Japanese or suttin. Am ah… Twitter famous err there?'

'You are a threat to the regime and must be destroyed,' said the Korean woman. The quietly threatening manner in which she said it gave Frank the fear.

'They're not Japanese,' Katherine said. 'Your followers are North Korean. You've became a symbol of the North Korean People's Resistance group. They've been using your image on posters after you said you could "kick fuck out of" Kim Jong-un.'

'Aw aye,' Frank laughed. 'Ah mind ah tweeted that. Ah could, by the way, joost sayin.' He looked over the North Koreans who were sitting with their fists tightly clenched.

'Well, that's the thing.' Katherine got up and motioned for one of her guards to pass her the envelope he was holding. 'Kim Jong-un wants to fight you. And we think this could be a good thing.'

Mark patted Frank's leg. 'You're gonnae be a star, big man. I'm gonnae organise the fight. I can see it now. In the Hydro.

Pay-per-view. It'll be bigger than Mayweather and McGregor.'

'The Supreme leader will CRUSH you,' said the Korean man, slamming a fist on the warden's table.

'This is a wind-up, eh? Awrite, good yin,' Frank said, standing up. 'Where's the cameras? Wit's this fur? The telly? Some mad hidden camera hing? In fact...' Frank moved over and stood behind the North Korean delegate's chairs. 'This is Ant an Dec, int it? Ahm oan that Saturday Night Takeaway! Haha, when's this gawn oan the telly then?'

'Frank, sit down and shut up,' said the warden. 'This is serious business.'

Frank sat down.

'This is fur real?' he asked. Everyone in the room nodded.

'The Supreme Leader wants to fight you to remind the western world of the strength of the Kim dynasty. It's time you gave us some respect. We could wipe out this country at the drop of a hat, you know,' the North Korean woman said.

'Frank,' said Katherine. 'If you fight him and win, which we're pretty sure you will, you could give a lot of hope to the North Korean people who are against his regime. The man is a monster.'

'Wit you sayin ae aw this?' Frank asked the warden.

'Well, you've not got much choice really. I have to terminate your employment here anyway so you'd be as well...'

'Wait, hawd oan a minute. How come?'

'Talking to prisoners online. Withholding knowledge of contraband in a prisoner's cell. These are serious offences, Frank. I've no choice in the matter.'

'Never you mind yer joab here, mate,' said Mark. 'Bigger and brighter things await you, Frankie boy. Yer a big handsome strapping bastard of a guy. A career in the auld wrestling or maybe cage fighting wid be better. Wit d'ye say?'

Frank sat opened mouthed. He didn't know how he was supposed to feel at this moment time. In the space of a few minutes he'd been sacked, offered a new career as a fighter, and been asked to fight the dictator of North Korea. It was a lot to take in.

'Ah… ah… ah don't know wit tae say here,' Frank said.

'Say aye, ya mad man!' said Mark.

Katherine nodded at her guards again and one of them came over with a piece of paper.

'The government has drawn up this contract for you to sign,' Katherine said as the guard handed Frank the paper. It's nothing too serious. It just says you can't sue the government, for example, for any injuries sustained. Kim Jong-un will be signing something similar. He's very excited about the fight, we hear.'

'This is yer contract fur the wrestling as well, mate.' Mark handed Frank a piece of paper as well.

'HAWF A MILLION QUID!' Frank exclaimed as he read over his agreement.

'Aye, that's right. It's aw yours. If ye win that is.'

'Ah will, don't you worry aboot that. So when's the fight?'

'Two weeks today,' said Katherine.

'Buzzin fur it,' Frank said as he stood up. 'Better go an start trainin then, eh? Wit's the deal, is it boxin or wrestling or wit?'

'Bareknuckle. Don't worry though, we've goat the best ae the best lined up tae help ye oot, Frank. Guys that've worked wi Connor McGregor, Anthony Joshua and, eh, Scott Harrison. You'll go right through this cunt. Moan, we'll head straight tae the gym,' Mark said, putting an arm round Frank.

As Frank opened the door to the office, the warden shouted on him.

'It's a shame we've had to let you go, Frank,' he said. 'Your P45 will be posted out to you.'

'Wi aw due respect, chief, shove yer joab up yer arse.'

As the warden shook his head in disapproval, the Koreans made a throat slitting gesture in perfect sync with each other.

He looked them in the eye. 'Tell Kim he's getting fuckin leathered.'

5

The fight was announced straight after Frank signed his contracts. In North Korea, Cho was so excited about it that she thought she was going to be sick. Posters were stuck everywhere by the state, glorifying Kim Jong-un, of course. Some showed him standing over an unconscious Frank, some showed him wiping his arse with a saltire flag and others depicted him with the Loch Ness Monster in a headlock. Giant screens were erected all over the cities and the fight was being made available to watch on everyone's television in the country, and viewing was mandatory.

'I basically made this happen!' Cho said excitedly to Ri. 'If Frank wins, who knows what it'll mean for the future. Oh! Maybe Frank will KILL him. What would happen then? Would the regime be finished?'

'Who knows,' said Ri. She was barely listening to Cho as they walked down the street.

'Are you okay, Ri? You don't seem very enthusiastic about the fight.'

Ri sighed and turned back to watch the sun set behind a high-rise block of flats.

'I'm leaving here,' she said, without making eye contact with Cho.

'Oh, that's nice,' Cho smiled. 'I mean I'll miss you but we could still see each other at the weekends or something, I suppose. Have you got a new job?'

Ri sighed again. She looked down at the ground as a tear drop fell from her eye and landed on her shoes. 'I'm defecting. I'm going to live in the South. My uncle can get me across the border, he says. My father's family are all there.'

'I didn't think you had it in you,' Cho laughed. 'When do you leave?'

'Tonight.'

'Tonight!' Cho shouted, a traffic policeman cast them a mean look.

'Yes, tonight. Come with me.'

'Ri, I can't. I…'

'There's nothing here for us. Especially you, Cho. How long before the secret police uncover you and your group? How long before you're dragged away to a labour camp in the middle of the night? How long before…' Ri was crying now. 'How long before you get killed?'

Cho held her tight. 'I'll be fine. This fight could change our lives here.'

'It won't.'

'Move along!' barked the traffic policeman from across the road.

'We're in the middle of something!' Cho shouted back. The policeman reached for his baton.

Ri grabbed Cho by the wrist and dragged her away.

'I'm keeping an eye on you two,' the policeman shouted after them.

Round the corner and out of sight, Ri put her hands either side of Cho's face and brushed hair back behind her ears.

'I won't beg you. Just please come. Meet me here at midnight if you change your mind.'

'Ri, I want to bring down this regime. I can't do that anywhere else but from here. Did you not see all the posters we put up? Tokko says he's had hundreds of people wanting to join the group. We are giving people hope here! People want to fight back against Kim!'

'Please just think about it,' Ri said as they hugged once again.

Cho never went to meet her at midnight.

6

It was the day before the fight and Kim Jong-un was in his office – which he'd had repurposed into a boxing gym – finishing off some last minute preparations before his flight to Glasgow.

'I – am – going – to – kill – Frank!' he said, spitting out his words in between throwing punches at a punch bag with Frank's face on it.

'You're looking well, sir,' Kim's aide said. 'Very well indeed. Frank should pose no problems for you.'

Kim wiped some sweat from his brown then stood with his hands on his hips. 'Pass me a cigar.'

His aide duly obliged, placed a cigar in Kim's mouth and lit it for him.

'Do you think I'll win?' Kim asked.

'Yes, sir. Without a shadow of doubt.'

'That's right.' Kim flexed his muscles in front of the mirror. 'Look at me. Don't I look like a warrior?'

The aide examined his figure in the reflection. 'Yes. Yes you do,' he lied. The aide was hoping, secretly, that Frank would absolutely leather Kim.

'What intelligence on Mr Frank have you managed to get for me?'

North Korea had a mole in Scotland who was gathering as much info on Frank as he could find. He was a teacher by the name of Eoghann from East Kilbride. Kim Jong-un's team of researchers had found him on Twitter where he went by the username of 'DPRK Lover'. He was perfect. A man who was simply so beige he would never arouse suspicion that he was a mole.

'Our mole has sent us a dossier on him,' the aide said. 'He has a history of problems with his left knee and is very easy to "wind up" as they say in Scotland.'

'A swift one of these to his leg.' Kim Jong-un performed a karate chop. 'He'll crumble to the floor. No match for the legendary Kim Jong-un.'

'Words could be an effective weapon against him though,' the aide said, poring over the dossier. His theory, which he kept to himself of course, was that if Kim wound Frank up enough, Frank would fly into a rage. His disciplinary record in the jail showed a number of 'incidents' with prisoners. The aide could see clearly that Frank was bigger, stronger and fitter than Kim, with just a bit of provocation, Frank might take the fight too far and actually kill him.

'I don't need *words*,' Kim said. He was karate chopping at the air furiously. 'I have my hands. These are more deadly.' Kim karate chopped towards the big red nuclear button. The aide let out a little whimper as he did this, but Kim stopped his hand less than an inch away from landing on it. 'More deadly than even this!'

'A couple of choice insults could make things… easier, sir,' the aide said when he had calmed down.

'It sounds to me like you are doubting the raw physicality of Kim Jong-un. Am I correct?'

'N-n-no, sir. I just, I want to help.'

Kim Jong-un held the aide in a derisory stare.

'I can beat him just fine. The knowledge of his bad knee will be enough to see me through.'

'Very well, sir,' the aide said, trying his best to hide the disappointment in his voice. All he could now was hope Frank would just rip Kim's head off.

'When do we leave?' Kim asked, pulling on a shirt and trying to fasten his cufflinks.

'Tonight, sir.'

***

In Glasgow, Frank's preparations were far more intense than just stripping to his waist and laying into a punch bag. He had a team of physios, dieticians, sports psychologists, not to mention the best fleet of fighting coaches money could buy. Frank was, in every way, shape and form, ready to absolutely fucking leather Kim Jong-un.

* * *

Kim arrived in Scotland the next morning. He strutted through Glasgow Airport, in a remarkably ill-fitting tracksuit that Connor McGregor had once worn. He was booed loudly by families heading to Tenerife, stag parties heading to Prague, and even by flight attendants and check-in crews. Kim revelled in the hatred.

'The precautionary measures are in place, just in case,' his aide whispered into his ear.

'We won't need them anyway,' Kim said. 'Frank is as good as dead.'

7

It was the night of the fight. Tickets had sold out within seconds. World leaders descended to the SSE Hydro arena in Glasgow, keen to see this historic event unfold. Donald Trump had been vocal on Twitter about his support for Frank who he hoped would *Destroy the Little Rocket Man's ass!* Nicola Sturgeon had voiced her astonishment that this whole thing was even going ahead in the first place, but a visit from MI6 to her home in the middle of the night saw her retract her original statement condemning the fight and issuing a new one in which she lauded Frank's bravery. Theresa May said something about 'fields of wheat' and was roundly mocked.

* * *

In his dressing room, Frank paced up and down, throwing punches at pads held up by Mark.

'Left!' Mark shouted. 'Right, right, DUCK, left. Yes, big man, you're gonnae fuckin kill this cunt.'

'Ahm no countin mah chickens joost yet, mah man. This guy's clearly no aw there. Cin tell he's a bit ae a nutjob, he might be some fighter.'

'Ach away,' Mark scoffed. 'C'mere, look at this.' Mark picked up the remote and turned on the telly in the dressing room. It displayed the ring outside in the arena. Standing in the middle of the ring was Kim Jong-un, eating what looked like a black pudding supper. Grease from his chips was dripping from the paper and onto his chest. As eager fans filed in to take their seats, some hurled insults at Kim. He responded by throwing his chips at them.

'An look at you.' Mark span Frank round so he was facing the mirror. 'An Adonis.' Over the past fortnight, the tough exercise regime had turned Frank from just being a unit into an absolute fucking tank.

'Aye,' Frank nodded. 'Yer right. Ahm ready fur this. When's the kick aff?'

'Another couple of hours yet, big man. We've got the undercard to go first.'

'Undercard?'

'Fuck, of course. Nae cunt will huv told you aboot that yet. Aw, Frank, mate, just *wait* til ye hear this. Up first – Ricky Burns versus Alex Salmond. Big Eck's goat the weight advantage but wee Ricky's like lightning, that'll be a good yin. Mhairi Black against Ruth Davidson, that'll be wild. Then finally we've goat Grado up against Willie Rennie. Grado's treatin the whole thing like a laugh but Willie Rennie's deadly serious aboot tryin ae make himself relevant again. It's a wee bit tragic, really.'

* * *

Back in the jail, the prisoners were allowed to stay up to watch Frank take on Kim Jong-un.

'He'll dae it, nae bother,' said Joe taking a seat in front of the telly. 'Embdy want tae stick a wee bet oan?'

'Less of that,' Murray said, standing watch over the prisoners.

'Aw wheesht, you,' Joe whispered to the guy sitting next to him. 'Fuckin grass.'

'What was that?' said Murray, walking over to Joe. He'd heard Joe mutter something but couldn't make out what he said. He knew it wouldn't be anything complimentary though. 'You *do* know gambling isn't allowed inside the prison, yeah?'

'And *you* do know that bein a grass isnae allowed either?'

'Excuse me?'

'Grassin me intae the warden cos ae mah phone. Ahm no daft, mate, ah know it wis you.' Joe stood up to his full height and eyeballed Murray.

'Well if Frank had done his job in the first place,' Murray said through tightly clenched teeth. 'I wouldn't have had to *grass* you in.'

'Ye could've joost fuckin left it, ahm no dain any harm.'

'It's against the rules, pal.'

This was like a red rag to a bull for Joe and he snapped. He stuck the head on Murray and the guard hit the deck. Immediately, another two guards jumped on Joe and carted him out of the room.

'That wis well worth it!' he shouted back at Murray. 'Let me know how Frank gets oan, lads!' The guards carted Joe away to solitary, stopping on the way to give him a kicking, just because they could.

* * *

In Pyongyang, it was mandatory for every citizen to watch the fight. Cho and her gang squeezed into the city's Mansudae Hill park. Taking a seat next to her pals on the white steps, Cho was buzzing with excitement.

'I can't believe this is actually happening,' Cho said to Hyang. 'We basically made this happen!'

'It's true, Cho,' Hyang replied, looking not at the giant screen but almost *through* it. 'I just have a bad feeling about this. I mean, if Kim wins, can you even imagine the ego boost he'll get?'

Cho considered this quietly.

'And,' Hyang continued, 'if he gets beat, who's he going to take it out on?'

'Us,' Cho sighed. She hadn't thought about any of the possible ramifications of the fight.

***

'...And now our final undercard fight of the night before the main event,' the announcer's voice boomed around the Hydro. 'It's GRRRRAAAADOOOOOO VERSUS WILLLLLLIIIIIIE RRRRREEEENNNNIE!!!'

The crowd were baying for blood after the previous brutal fights. The bare knuckle format had resulted in burst knuckles and noses galore. The floor of the ring was soaked blood and the air was thick with sweat.

Grado made his entrance to a chorus of cheers. He absolutely lapped it up, cupping his ears to his adoring crowd. It was a particularly eclectic mix of people at the fight; world leaders mingled with regular punters, joking about who would win in fights between them. Grado entered the ring and threw off his robe. He slapped his chest and shouted, 'I'm the fuckin man!'

Then the lights went down. The music stopped. The crowd fell silent.

'Ladies and gentlemen,' the announcer boomed once again. 'Please put your hands together for bad boy of Scottish politics; IT'S WILLLLIIIIE RRRRREEEENNNNIE!'

Willie Rennie strutted through a plume of smoke. The crowd was still silent. Willie Rennie's strut dissipated much like the smoke. Nobody cared about him, it was a shame. He walked towards the ring, his shoulders slumped. A lone voice from the crowd shouted its approval.

'On ye go, babe!' It was Willie Rennie's wife. 'Kill the bastard!'

'Thanks, hen,' Willie shouted, waving back. 'I will.'

Willie Rennie climbed into the ring, shrugging off his Liberal Democrat-yellow robe. The difference between him and Grado was staggering. Grado's shiny, tanned and perfectly smooth torso shimmered under the lights of the Hydro while Willie Rennie's gaunt figure skulked about the ring.

'It's yersel, Willie!' Grado said.

'Yes, it is,' replied Willie Rennie.

'Right, boys,' the ref said, pulling Grado and Willie Rennie in close to him. 'I'm wanting a good clean fight here. No biting, no scratching, hair pulling, no punches below the belt, okay?'

The two fighters nodded.

'Right, let's go.' The ref pushed the two men apart and stepped out of their way.

'I'm going to kill you,' Willie Rennie said, almost in a whisper, and with a creepy smile.

Grado just laughed and turned round to share the joke with his team in his corner. As he turned his back, the bell rang, and before he could even comprehend what was happening, Willie Rennie leaped onto his back. The crowd went mental. He wrapped his legs around Grado's waist, locking his ankles together and digging the backs of his heels into the wrestler's belly. He put his arms under Grado's, reached round and grabbed him by the back of the neck, putting his arms out of action. Grado span round, desperately trying to free himself of the former Scottish Liberal Democrat leader who had latched onto him but he couldn't.

'I'm going to kill you,' seethed Willie Rennie into Grado's ear.

'No... fuckin... chance, pal.'

Grado leaned back and crashed to the floor of the ring. A chorus of *oooooooh*s filled the arena. Willie Rennie released his grip and Grado stood up, walking over to the ropes and climbing up, shaking a fist in the air in triumph.

'Can you carry on?' the ref asked Willie Rennie, helping him to his feet. Willie Rennie wiped his brow and nodded solemnly. His eyes narrowed.

'Let's finish this.'

Grado laughed and climbed down off the ropes. 'Moan then,' he said.

Willie Rennie broke into a run and launched himself, trying to spear Grado round the waist but he just bounced off him and fell to the ground.

'Get up,' said Grado, hauling him to his feet. Willie Rennie swayed on the spot, looking like he was about collapse at any second. He looked ready to have another go but this time Grado was ready. As Willie Rennie bent his knees slightly to jump, Grado smashed a fist into his face. The impact broke Willie Rennie's nose with the same ease a sledgehammer would smash through a pane of glass. He was sent flying backwards and he crashed to the floor once again as the crowd whooped and cheered for Grado.

* * *

After the ring was cleared of Willie Rennie's broken body and blood, it was time for the main event. Frank versus Kim Jong-un. The men would be meeting for the first time in the ring. Frank had been all set to do Connor McGregor-style press conferences, full of trash talking and showboating, but Kim had declined.

Frank sat on a chair with his head bowed, going over his planned opening sequence of punches in his head. *Fly oot the traps at the cunt, couple ae jabs roon aboot the heid, then boady, boady, boady an then crack him oan the jaw. He'll go doon like a sack ae shite.*

In his own dressing room, Kim was receiving a neck and shoulder massage from his aide.

'How are you feeling, sir?' the aide asked, working his thumbs into Kim's neck. 'Nervous?'

'No one in my family has ever been nervous,' Kim said, lighting a cigar.

'What is your strategy? You haven't spoken of any great plan to defeat this man?'

Kim puffed on the cigar for a few seconds. 'Intimidation. That's the only weapon I need to win here. I'm the leader of the most feared country in the world. Who is he? Who is Frank?' Kim spat out Frank's name as if it tasted horrible. 'He's nobody.' Kim shrugged his aide's hands off and stood up.

'Here's your robe, sir,' the aide said. 'Just remember, he has a dodgy left knee.'

Kim pulled it on and looked his reflection in the mirror up and down. He nodded sagely. The robe was a shimmering satin red, white and blue number with pictures of Kim's father and grandfather emblazoned on the back. On the front, sitting proudly, was a big red cartoon version of his nuclear button.

One of the runners poked her head into Kim's dressing room. 'Time for your walk-on.'

'Showtime,' Kim said.

* * *

'You're up, Frank,' said Mark. 'Let's fuckin do this.'

Frank jumped to his feet. 'Ahm gonnae leather this cunt.'

'That's mah boy. Aw, eh, before ye go oot there, that wummin fae MI6 wants a word.'

'Wit aboot?'

'Dunno.' Mark checked in the corridor for Katherine. 'Here she comes, mate.'

'Frank, Frank, Frank. Look at you. You're like a Greek god standing there,' said Katherine, breezing into the dressing room.

'Aw cheers, doll,' Frank replied as his cheeks flushed a rosy red colour.

'Not that you'll need it, but I just wanted to wish you good luck. Just remember, you're not just fighting for yourself or for the glory of Scotland, or indeed the UK, but for the people of North Korea. They all want you to win.'

'Frank, you good to go?' a runner asked. 'Kim's walking on first, then you.'

'Sound, pal. Let's do this.'

* * *

'Ladies and gentlemen,' said the announcer as the lights dimmed in the stadium. 'Please welcome to the ring the most feared dictator in the world. A man who has executed over 300 people in the last seven years. A man who runs the most secretive and dangerous regime on earth, the leader of North Korea, it's KIM JOOONG-UUUUUUNN!' Kim's favourite song ("Brother Louie" by Modern Talking) kicked in and Kim appeared through the smoke.

A lot of fighters like to strut their way to the ring, some bounce along throwing punches at the air, and some dance, but Kim walked to the ring like he was walking to the bottom of his garden to have a look for something in his shed; purposeful but laid-back. He was still puffing on his cigar and smiling broadly. The baying crowd booed and hissed at him as he walked by.

'You're gonna get your ass handed to you, Kim!' Donald Trump shouted to him from the front row. Kim cupped his ears at him and laughed before throwing his cigar at Trump.

It was obvious that Kim was loving all the attention. He stood in the ring with his arms outstretched, drinking in all the hate and vitriol being fired at him. He took off his robe and flung it into the crowd.

'And now, here is the contender. The man going toe to toe with Kim Jong-un. He's the most respected guard in Scotland's toughest jail. He's confronted murderers, rapists, paedos and armed robbers every single day for the last ten years. He's FRANK "THE KILLER" CURRRRAAAAN!'

This time the crowd were whooping and cheering, hooting and hollering. Frank strode towards the ring with a spring in his step. His arms already twitching, desperate to throw a punch at Kim Jong-un's stupid face. He high-fived Will Smith who was sitting next to Trump. Nicola Sturgeon gave him a thumbs up and a smile that seemed to say, 'Go and fuckin leather that cunt.'

Frank and Kim stood opposite each other in the ring. Kim leaned back into the ropes, receiving another last minute massage from his aide. Frank's coaches whispered encouragement into his ear.

'Just remember the plan, Frank,' his head coach said. 'Get him down as quick as. He'll be able to take a good few hits so we need to get him knocked out before he tires you out.'

'Nae problem,' Frank said, making intense eye contact with Kim. Kim just grinned back at him.

DINGDINGDING

Frank did as he had planned. He sprang at Kim right from the off, unleashing a hail of punches at the dictator's face. With a right hook, he punched kim in the left eye and it instantly swelled up. With a left hook, he got him square on the nose, flattening it. Already, Frank's knuckles were red raw and bruised but he kept going until the referee pulled him away from Kim.

Kim wiped some blood away from his mouth and laughed at Frank.

'Come on!' he said.

Frank did as he was invited and advanced on Kim again. He flung a quick left jab, hoping to get Kim's other eye out of action but Kim weaved out of the way and laughed again. Kim bounced on the spot and the atmosphere in the stadium changed. It looked like this wouldn't be the walkover for Frank everyone had thought it would be.

***

In Pyongyang, Cho watched on stunned at the agility of Kim Jong-un as he dodged everything Frank threw at him.

'I can't watch,' Hyang said, covering his eyes. 'If Kim gets one good punch in, Frank will go down, he's exhausted already. Kim's hardly broke a sweat.'

'It'll be okay,' said Cho, trying her best to sound positive. 'Just watch.'

***

DINGDINGDING

The fighters went back to their corners. Kim laughing and Frank raging.

'How the fuck's he so quick,' Frank moaned to the coaches. 'Cunt's duckin and divin like a fuckin cat. Ah cannae get near him.'

'It's easy to avoid blows when you know they're coming, mate,' his coach said, mopping Frank's brow. 'You need to be more... unpredictable.'

'How'd ye mean?'

'Stick the nut oan him,' Mark said, making an appearance. 'Anyhin goes in a fight like this. Pin him doon or suhin. Yer bein too fancy, tryin tae be aw Mayweathery. This isnae fuckin Mike Tyson yer up against. Or even a cunt fae the jail. He's a naebody. He's no even landed a punch oan you yet and he's already goat ye beat up here.' Mark stabbed a finger at Frank's forehead.

'Right,' Frank nodded. 'Aye, yer right.' He stood up and faced the crowd. 'FUCKIN MOAN THEN!' he roared and the crowd roared back their approval.

DINGDINGDING

This time, Frank sauntered over to Kim who had his fists up trying to block punches that didn't arrive.

'Fuckin state ae this cunt,' Frank shouted at the crowd, pointing at Kim.

Kim Jong-un saw his chance while Frank was distracted by the adoring crowd and karate chopped Frank's knee.

'Aw, ya cunt,' Frank hopped away. Kim howled with laughter.

'Ye awrite, big man?' Mark shouted over.

'He goat mah gammy knee, the prick.'

'STICK THE NUT OAN HIM THEN!'

Frank composed himself and tried not to think about the pain pulsing in his knee. Kim leaned back against the ropes and patted his enormous belly.

'Too easy,' Kim laughed. 'Far too easy.'

Frank ran towards Kim, his knee almost buckling under him with every step. He grabbed Kim by the curtains of black hair on either side of his face, leaned his neck back, pulled Kim towards him then threw his head downwards. Frank's forehead connecting with the bridge of Kim's already broken nose in a sickening clash of bone. Kim slumped to the floor. The crowd on their feet screaming with joy. Frank staggered backwards and collapsed into his corner.

* * *

The feed Cho was watching in North Korea had roughly a twenty second delay. Frank was just about to land a belter of a heider on Kim Jong-un when the screen they were watching the fight on turned off. Armed police raised their guns at the crowd as they showed their disapproval. One of the police-men's radio crackled into life.

'Affirmative,' he said into it. 'Kim Jong-un won by a knockout,' he announced to the crowd. 'Return to your homes. We'll show the rest of the fight on the TV tomorrow night.'

'Shit,' Hyang said dejectedly. 'I can't believe this. The bastard won.'

'We were foolish to believe in this charade,' Cho said. Her expressionless face stared at the police as they corralled people out of the park. 'As if they would allow us to know if he got beat. I don't know why I allowed myself to get so carried away. I don't even know why I bother with our stupid group.'

'Cho, please,' Hyang pleaded. But it was too late. Cho had stormed off and was indistinguishable within the sea of the bodies heading for the exits.

* * *

'...And the winner, by a knockout, is FRANK "THE KILLLLLLLLLLLEEEEER" CURRAN!'

The ref raised Frank's hand in the air as Kim's aide dragged his unconscious body out of the ring.

Frank climbed up and stood on the top rope, punching the air in jubilation.

'Way to go, buddy,' Donald Trump said, coming over to congratulate Frank.

'You get tae fuck unless yer wantin a fight anaw.'

'Hey, you can't speak to me like that. You wanna fight? I'll give ya a fight, buddy? I'll give you the best fight of your life. I'm the best fighter in this room. In this damn country!'

Trump's bodyguards had to quieten him down once again and pull him away.

'You are the best fighter,' one of them whispered in his ear while smoothing down his hair. 'The best in aaaaall the land, little buddy. Let's go and get you a KFC. Would you like that?'

'Frank, how does it feel?' a reporter asked. A million other microphones were thrust into his face.

'Eh, magic.'

'And Frank, what next?'

'Fuck knows, man. Ah wis sacked the other week so, eh, joost keep fightin ah hink.'

'Who will your next opponent be?'

'Ah'll say Putin.' Frank grabbed a mic and stared straight down one of the many TV cameras. 'Vlad! You're fuckin gettin it! Hink yer a hard man cause yer fae Russia? Ah've done harder shites than you, wee man.'

'Right you, fur fuck sake,' said Mark, pulling him away from the journalists. 'The fuckin KGB will be payin ye a visit if ye don't calm doon.'

'Sorry, ah goat a bit carried away.'

'Yer next fight's lined up awready.'

'Aye? Who is it?'

'Willie Rennie.' Mark led Frank out of the ring and back to his dressing room to clean up. 'The wee man's desperate fur another fight. He's scared me a wee bit, truth be told. Look at this.'

Mark opened a door on his right. Willie Rennie was restrained in a dolly. The veins in his neck bulging under his skin like lengths of copper piping as he tried to free himself from his restraints. His voice was muffled under the Hannibal-style mask he was wearing but Frank was sure he could make out that he was saying, 'I'm going to kill you.'

8

The next night in Pyongyang, Cho sat totally deflated on her uncomfortable couch. The state had just shown the remainder of the previous night's fight. Or rather, their version of the previous night's fight. As Frank was about to stick the heid on Kim Jong-un, some poorly executed CGI made it look as if

Kim dodged the blow. Then it cut to what was clearly a pair of lookalikes in a shoddily-made boxing ring in a film studio trading blows before the fake Kim landed a weak punch on the fake Frank's chin and knocked him out. Then the real Kim was shown in his dressing room, celebrating wildly in scenes which had clearly been filmed before the fight as Kim's nose and eye were both completely unharmed.

'Let this be a message to the world, and also to my people,' Kim stated down the camera. 'I am invincible.'

Cho switched her telly off and sat for a moment in silence. Everything was finished. Her determination and passion for the resistance movement had been knocked out of her. It was game over, there was nothing she could do now. Kim would come down hard on anyone who had openly doubted him. Her group would be disbanded, no doubt, not just because of fear but because they had been demoralised. In fact, Cho wouldn't have been surprised if she was paid a visit from the Secret Police now.

As this thought floated into her head, she was startled by a loud knocking on her door.

Surely they wouldn't have come for her so soon? Cho was ready to accept her fate, anyway; she had tried and failed to take down the regime. What else was there left to live for?

She opened the door, ready to face whatever awaited her, be it the barrel of a gun or a bag being thrown over her head.

She was instead greeted by a tiny, white-haired, bespectacled elderly man.

'Cho?' he asked tentatively.

Cho nodded, looking at the parcel in the man's hands.

'I have something for you. A gift.'

'A gift?' Cho was confused.

'Yes, a gift. From a friend in the south.' The old man smiled and offered her the parcel. Cho took it from him gingerly.

The old man winked and shuffled away down the hall towards the lift.

Cho closed the door behind him. The parcel was a white padded envelope, wrapped in brown tape and with Cho's name and address written on it in neat, feminine handwriting. She took it into her kitchen and grabbed a pair of scissors.

Cho slid the blade under the flap on the back of the parcel and cut away at the tape. Her excitement made her abandon the scissors and rip it open like a child at Christmas.

Inside, there was something wrapped in a plastic bag. She unwrapped it and found a video tape and a letter. Written on the tape was 'Kim V. Frank – Uncut'. Cho laughed and read the letter:

Dearest Cho,

Please use this video to help the cause.
Keep fighting the good fight and stay safe.

Your friend,
Ri x

Leathered was first published by Speculative Books in 2018.

ACKNOWLEDGEMENTS

Writing this book was great fun but the pressure and stress of it almost fucking killed me so you better have enjoyed it.

I have to say a massive thanks to the following people for their love, help, support, patter, encouragement, feedback, hospitality and just for being total heroes: my maw, Vanessa, Jay, my granny and granda, Pamela, Angela, Sam, Adam, Sean, Stephen, Anne, Laura, Heather, Robbie, the lads of SFT, all the troops on Twitter (except Loïc Remy), all my colleagues at DW Sports (it was an honour to punt trainers alongside yous), Dale, Sam, Jack, Leo, Jen, Anna and, of course, the dug.

WHAT'S THIS?

A BONUS STORY?

WELCOME TO TWITTER JAIL.

A WEEKEND IN TWITTER JAIL

Twitter jail is a very real thing. This is a fact I learned much to my surprise. I never thought I, of all people, would ever end up there but, sadly, a wee while ago, I did.

After watching the fitbaw in the pub one Thursday night with my pal, I got a bit steaming. Anyone with a Twitter account will tell you that tweeting while steaming is a recipe for disaster. It is such a truly bad idea that it can, and will, ruin your entire life.

A bit of background info as to how this situation kicked off...

While on holiday in Portugal with my girlfriend, a certain unnamed French professional footballer slid into her DMs. I laughed it off. 'Haha, naw, of course I'm no bothered about this incredibly handsome, talented, muscular, millionaire Frenchman talking to you, hen! Naw, I'm no worried you're gonnae dump me for him, why do you ask?'

After returning from Portugal, I ranted on Twitter about this guy, about a week later when I got home from the pub, very drunk. Then I put my phone on charge and went to sleep.

That's when everything kicked right fucking off.

Four in the morning. **BANG BANG BANG**. The sound of guys shouting. About ten pairs of heavy footsteps come charging up the stair. My bedroom door flies right off its fucking hinges. When I sit up to see what the fuck's going on, I'm met with the steely gazes of several armed policemen, fully clad in riot gear and all that as if I'm some hardnut who's gonnae be tough to take down and not just some nine stone, half-cut wee guy lying sleeping in the spare room of his maw's house. Before I can even ask what's happening, a bag is thrown right over my head and I'm cracked across the jaw with a baton, knocking me out.

I faded in and out of consciousness in the back of the polis van. 'Cunts like him are vermin,' I heard one of the polis say. 'Who knows what he's capable of,' said another. It took me a minute or so to realise they were talking about me.

'It was just a wee joke,' I said from under the black hood. 'I wisnae actually gonnae kill him.'

Another crack to the jaw sends me back into unconsciousness.

When I wake up, I'm relieved that the bag has been removed from my head. I'm less relieved to see I'm in a barely lit, windowless room. A single low watt light bulb swings from the ceiling above me, spilling its weak sodium glow over the small space. The floor is concrete and the walls are bare, exposed brick. I'm tied to a chair.

From behind me, a heavy metal door booms open. In walks a big scary polis man. Must be the head honcho of wherever I am.

'Mr McQueer,' the guy says, pacing round my chair, his arms behind his back. 'I'm Vinnie Gunn, the governor here. You routinely say you could batter everyone on Twitter. Think that's big and clever, eh?'

'That's the joke,' I say, trying to explain myself. 'I obviously couldn't batter anybody, but some folk seem to think-'

The cunt slaps me right across the cheek.

'I don't care,' he seethes. 'Then you say, just a few hours ago, that you want to KILL a professional footballer? Not on, son.'

'Wit? I never said that?'

'You bloody well did, son. Now you're gonnae pay for it.' He lets that last sentence hang in the air, obviously trying to make me shite myself even more.

It's worked. I'm absolutely going to shite myself. I'm basically greeting. 'How? Where am I?' I blub. I've even got a petted lip. What a riddy.

'You're in Barlinnie, son.'

'I'm in the jail?! Wit fur? Fur how long?'

'Until you learn to stop being such a wee fucking ned online.'

* * *

I'm frogmarched through to another part of the jail by the guy. He doesn't say a word. A couple of times he pushes me in the back so I stumble forward and he laughs. He even clips my heels a few times so I fall over.

'Who's this?' a bearded guard asks, waiting at the end of a corridor.

'Chris McQueer,' the guy says. 'Take him to the Tweet Wing, Frank.'

'Tweet Wing?' I laugh. 'This is a bam up, eh?'

A fist hurtles into my ribs. 'Less of your shite,' the beardy bastard says. 'I've seen you oan that Twitter. You dae my fucking heid right in. "Oh look at me I've wrote a wee book. Please buy it!" You make me sick.'

I get to my feet, holding my side, it feels like it's on fire. These lads know how to fling a punch.

'What's Tweet Wing?' I ask Frank as he escorts me through the jail. Other prisoners point and laugh at me. They can see my petted lip from a mile away. Or maybe they can smell the fact that I've shat myself a wee bit.

'It's where cunts like you end up. Social media hardmen. Wee jumped up pricks that think they're something and think they can say anything they want online without repercussions.'

'Is this no a bit daft? A bit of a waste of taxpayer's money and all that? There's actual real criminals out there, for fuck sake!'

I shouldn't have said that and I definitely shouldn't have added the "for fuck sake" in.

Frank digs a punch into the other side of my ribcage. 'That you quite finished, aye?'

I just nod.

'Good. You'll be sharing a cell with a lifer.'

'A lifer? Wit, like a murderer or a paedo or something?'

'Naw, this is the Tweet Wing. You no fuckin listening? I'm sure he'll tell ye his story.'

Frank shoves me into a cell and slams the door shut behind me. There's nothing here except bunk beds, a chest of drawers, a filthy sink and an equally filthy toilet. My cellmate seems to be asleep in the bottom bunk. I'm shattered myself so I decide to take the top bunk and get a kip.

DAY 1. Friday.

When I wake up and open my eyes, I forget I'm in the jail. There's a face at the side of the bed, watching me. My foggy mind thinks it's my dug, Timmy, and I reach out to clap his head.

'Aw that feels dead nice,' the face says. I wake up sharply when I realise it's no Timmy. It's a greasy haired man.

'Wit the fuck!' I shout.

'Calm doon, wee man. I'm Tam, your cellmate.'

I suddenly remember I'm in Bar-L and my stomach churns. When I get stressed out or nervous or anything, I could shit through a straw. That toilet is about to get even more bogging.

'Aw, eh, nice to meet ye mate. I'm Chris.' I shake Tam's hand.

'Wit's your story then, Chrissy boy?'

'Told a fitbaw player I was gonnae kill him for messaging my burd. Just a wee joke.'

'Long ye gonnae be here fur?'

'No idea, mate. How long you in for?'

'You'll be oot by Monday, I reckon. That's small time. Me though? I'll be here til the bitter end.' Tam looks forlornly out the tiny window. Very dramatic.

'What did you do?' I ask. I assume it's something properly heinous.

'You're maybe too young tae remember this, but did ye ever huv Bebo?'

'Bebo? Aye of course, I'm no that young. Bebo was class.'

'Class, aye? Well it wisnae class fur me. Ruined my life, so it did. Landed me in here.'

'What happened?'

'Och, started aff wi minor infringements. I never shared the love enough. That got me a couple ae overnighters here. Started picking the odd fight wi the goths and emos and that; that was another few strikes tae my name. But my biggest crime?'

He looks at me, narrowing his eyes, choking for me to ask what his biggest crime was. I oblige. 'What was that?'

'Made my wife's sister my top pal instead of my wife. She lost the rag. Went tonto. That was me. Locked up for good.'

I question the ethics of jailing a man for such a trivial thing but the Scottish legal system is mysterious beast.

DAY 2. Saturday.

'You've got visitors, McQueer,' Frank says, opening the cell door. 'Move.'

I'm led up to a room filled with the families of other prisoners, all here to see their incarcerated loved ones for a precious and quick half an hour.

Sitting at a table in the back corner is my maw and my granny. My maw wipes away a tear from her eye as I'm led over, in handcuffs and the standard issue jail trackie.

'My ain grandson,' my granny says, she looks raging. 'In the fuckin TWEET WING! WIT'S THE MATTER WI YE?! EH? Fucking idiot ae a boay.' She skelps me round the head. 'Ah'd rather ye wurr a fuckin beast.'

'Och, calm doon,' I say. 'I'll be oot on Monday.'

'An then wit? Naebody'll gie ye a joab noo.'

'I don't need a joab. I'm a writer, I told ye.'

'Yer a lazy. A work-shy bastard is wit ye urr.'

Fuck sake, nae bother, granny. Cheers for the support.

'I'm mortified, Christopher,' says my maw. 'It's all over

the papers and everything. "Bad Boy Scots Author" they're calling you.'

I snigger at this, which sends my granny into overdrive.

'Wipe that fuckin smirk aff yer face afore ah dae it fur ye,' she snaps.

'Is there no way yous can get me out of here?' I ask. 'I mean, this cannae even be legal. I've no even had a chance to get a lawyer or anything.'

'They're right, the guards and that,' my maw says. 'You need to be taught a lesson. You're getting too wide for your own good.'

'Fuck sake, c'mon, maw, don't be like that. Where ye going?' My maw and my granny have obviously heard enough and stand up. They signal for the guard to tell them they're finished here.

'Ye need tae learn, son,' my granny says, a bit calmer now. 'Cause if this dinsae get aw this nonsense oot yer system then ah'll fuckin kick it oot ye when get hame. Awrite?'

I'm led to back to my cell to sit with the Bebo Danger for the next twenty-four hours.

DAY 3. Sunday.

This should hopefully be my last day in the Tweet Wing. Frank the guard confirms to me that this is the case. He doesn't look too happy to be having to wave me off so soon. He's enjoyed punching me.

I try and do a bit of Louis Theroux-style journalism while I'm in here. Might as well get some good material out of this sorry situation after all. So, during the recreation time, I conduct a couple of interviews with the other guys in Tweet Wing.

First up is Jamie. A young guy, a couple of years younger than me. He was brought in two weeks ago and he's serving thirteen years for constantly replying 'didn't happen' to people, especially lassies, on Twitter.

'I started doing it for a laugh,' he says, dead behind the eyes. 'Soon I didn't even believe anything. The news? Didn't happen. Anything my da said to me? Didn't happen. I was in uni one day. I studied history. Anything the lecturer said I just blurted out "DIDN'T HAPPEN!"'

He rubs at his eyes.

'You awrite, mate?' I ask.

'That didn't happen,' he says, walking away.

I then sit down with Jim. I recognise him from Twitter. I wondered where he'd disappeared to. Online, he was a very publicly horny man.

'Och, wit's wrang wi tellin lassies ye fancy them,' he says, pausing miserably before adding, '...an sendin thum the odd picture ae yer boaby?'

An awful lot to be honest, mate. I can't be arsed talking to this pervert.

From across the room I hear an English accent. This pricks up my ears as Bar-L is full of Glaswegian voices.

'Yeah, mate,' Tony says in his broad cockney accent. He moved to Glasgow when he was a teenager but was banged up in the Tweet Wing a few months ago. 'It's that fackin Scotch accent, ya know? Why da you lot always have to fackin type in it? Can't understand a fackin word of it.'

People typing in Scots really annoys Tony. I neglect to tell him I've written two whole books in Scots.

'So I started saying "What language is this?" to cants' tweets. Threw in the odd "can someone translate this for me please?" too. Jock police didn't like that one bit. Locked me up. Fackin joke.'

I realised I had truly been locked up with the scourge of society.

DAY 4. Monday

'McQueer,' booms the voice of Frank. 'Say yer goodbyes. Time tae boost.'

'Thank fuck,' I say, running out the cell without even saying cheerio to daft Tam below me.

Frank leads me down a corridor.

'What happens to celebrities that say dodgy stuff on Twitter and that?' I ask him.

'They get sent off tae the Home for the Cancelled,' he says, looking dead ahead. He leads me to the room where I woke up into this nightmare. Vinnie Gunn is waiting for me.

'Think you've learned your lesson, pal?' he asks, hands behind his back, rocking back and forward on his heels.

'Eh, aye, I think so.'

'Ye "think so"? If I see you back in here anytime soon you'll be in for a much tougher time. This was just a wee taster.'

'Can I go now or wit?'

'Aye. You're free tae go. But under a couple of conditions. Number wan.' He holds a big sausage finger right up to my face. 'Your Twitter account's been deleted.'

I nod. That's no too bad.

'Two. You need to send an apology to that fitbaw player.'

Fuck sake. Fine.

'And three. Stop the fucking cheek online. Awrite?'

I practically run out the jail now that he's finished. My maw and my granny are waiting for me in the car park. They look happy to see me, even if my granny is trying her best to hide her joy.

Will I stop the cheek? Will I stop getting wide with folk? Have I learned my lesson?

It remains to be seen.

ABOUT CHRIS MCQUEER

Chris McQueer started off as 'That Guy Oan Twitter Who Writes Short Stories' and is now an award-winning author after grabbing the Saboteur Award for Best Short Story Collection in 2018 for his debut collection *Hings* (404 Ink).

He currently lives in Glasgow with his mum, younger brother and Timmy the dug.

You can follow him on Twitter at @ChrisMcQueer_ (as long as he doesn't get his account deleted again).

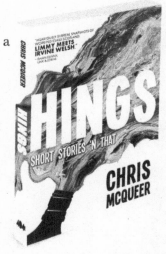